STAR DANCER

THE BOOK OF AIR

Beth Webb is a full-time writer. Her research takes her to ancient sites all over the country and she is passionate about British folklore. She lives in Somerset, England, and is currently working on the third book in the *Star Dancer* series.

Look out for

Fire Dreamer

STAR DANCER

THE BOOK OF AIR

BETH WEBB

MACMILLAN CHILDREN'S BOOKS

First published 2006 by Macmillan Children's Books

This edition published 2007 by Macmillan Children's Books
a division of Macmillan Publishers Limited
20 New Wharf Road, London N1 9RR
Basingstoke and Oxford
www.panmacmillan.com

Associated companies throughout the world

ISBN: 978-0-330-44570-2

1 3 5 7 9 8 6 4 2

A CIP catalogue record for this book is available from
the British Library.

Typeset by Intype Libra Ltd
Printed and bound in Great Britain
by Mackays of Chatham plc, Kent

To Maddy, my own Star Dancer,
and to the Kilvites, who have all
helped to write this book!
Thank you.

Acknowledgements

My thanks to Bruce Johnstone-Lowe of the British Druid Order. Also Andy, Sue and all my friends and family for their unfailing support.

Contents

1. Star Child

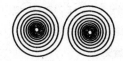

The stars danced all that night, but the midwife did not stop to watch.

The baby's wet, black head was already pushing and twisting its way into the world. At last the cord was cut, the tiny thrashing limbs bathed and wrapped in a woollen shawl. The woman took the squealing bundle to the door of the cottage and held the infant high to see the lights sparkling in the dark.

'There,' she said. 'That's for you, my dear, to welcome you to the world.'

Terrified, the exhausted mother tried to sit up. 'Get her away from there, Gilda! She hasn't been named yet. The spirits might take her!'

'Easy, Nessa, she'll be fine, we're inside the house. You know that spirits can't get past an oaken threshold.' The midwife shut the door, brought the child back and placed her in her mother's arms. 'What are you going to call her?'

Nessa sighed. 'Clesek wanted a boy – he was going to be Alwar. But now . . . well . . .' She smiled down at the tiny round face with its mop of dark hair. Huge eyes looked back at her, amazed.

'She's a pretty little thing,' Gilda said.

'She is indeed.' Nessa stroked her baby's cheek. 'I'll name her "Tegen" – *pretty thing*.' She held the child to her breast and settled back on her straw mattress.

Gilda looked down at the mother and baby. She liked moments like these. All was well. She could go to her own bed now without worrying. If the Goddess willed, they would both live. She tucked her wild curly hair behind her ears and smiled. 'Let her feed. Then you should both get some sleep. I've left a basket of dried moss and clean linen for her mess. I'll come back tomorrow. Is there anything else you need before I go?'

Nessa glanced around the tidy cottage. The fire in the centre was burning well, with a pile of spare wood in the corner. Her bed was warm, and within reach she had an earthenware pot of water and a dish of oatcakes and nuts. 'I have everything, thank you. Can Clesek be allowed back now? I am sure Tegen would like to see her Da . . . Oh, and when you go down to the village, would you ask Witton to come and bless the child for me?'

'Of course.' Gilda smiled. She knew Nessa would not be

at ease until the old druid had given his protection to the baby. 'But no talking when Clesek comes in. You two must rest.' The midwife pushed her feet into her clogs, which had been warming by the hearth, then pulled on her cloak, winding it tightly against the winter winds. 'Goodnight then, both of you. May the Goddess bless you.' She lifted the latch and pulled the wooden door back. 'Just look at that, will you?' she gasped.

Outside, the shower of sparkling lights still moved gracefully across the midnight skies.

Nessa turned her head away and concentrated on her baby. She was always nervous about the ways of stars and spirits.

Gilda called to Clesek in his forge, where he had been banished during the birthing: 'It is a girl child, but they are both well and strong. You will be blessed with a boy soon, of that I am certain.' Then she turned away briskly. She did not want to be blamed, as some men believed, for the birth of a girl.

Gilda did not need a lamp, for the brilliance of the night lit her way. The path from Clesek and Nessa's cottage down to the village where she lived was long but not steep, winding through leafless oak and hazel woods alongside a chattering stream. The sound kept her company. The wind was getting up and had a bitter edge. At a twist in the path

Gilda stood on an outcrop of rock overlooking the Winter Seas below; the black waters were roughened by the icy air and the few muddy islets were charcoal smudges in the ebony landscape. Above, the stars were being rapidly covered with a thick pall of clouds as the silvered night was plunged into darkness.

'It's almost like the stars don't want to be seen tonight,' she muttered to herself. 'I am sure the child is important, but how? Perhaps something secret is going on.'

Ahead she could faintly see the Tor, peat-black as the Goddess's breast, a lonely island rising out of the seas. Tonight there were lights on the top of the sacred hill. So the druids were watching too? Then the spirits *were* about. Nessa had been wise to be worried. Gilda guessed there would be no point trying to find Witton tonight. He would not want to be summoned from his magical doings to bless a girl child, even one born on such a night.

Icy splats of rain caught Gilda on the cheek. She tried to wrap her cloak more tightly and yawned. There was still a fair step to go before she found her own fireside and bed.

Witton was cold too. He was getting old. His bones creaked and ground painfully as he led his druid brothers along the maze-path down the Tor. But his heart was light. The stars had danced.

Just after sunset, while Nessa cried out with birthing

pains, the wise ones had gathered to celebrate Imbolg, the festival of spring. Then, as the night deepened, dancing lights appeared between the legs of the nine-pointed star pattern of the 'Watching Woman', symbol of the Mother Goddess. The spectacle grew and moved slowly on, leaving a thousand tiny sparks leaping and scattering across the sky. Below, the miracle was reflected in the dark-mirror waters.

The druids watched in awestruck silence.

For months, signs and divinations had warned of great evil to come. But there was a promise too: an untimely shower of stars would mark the birth of the one who would stem the tide. But even the wisest of the druids' sign-readers, the ovates, could not tell what the threat was, or who the child would be.

But it did not matter. The Goddess had kept her promise and given birth to the protector of the people of the Winter Seas. All would be well.

The druids watched all night, until the glory was swallowed in heavy clouds and the driving rain began. Struggling against the gale, the men processed solemnly down the muddy path to their longhouse on the shore.

Inside, by the glow of the central fire, the company shook off their damp outer cloaks and sat around wooden tables. Waiting women brought horns of warm mead and bowls of spiced porridge. The smells mingled with the aroma of juniper shavings thrown into the fire.

This was a good night.

Witton, the oldest and most honoured of the druids, rose to his feet. He wore no torques or armbands. His shirt and breeches were made from undyed wool edged with a narrow blue band. His ash-coloured beard was long and plaited, and his wide whiskers parted as he smiled warmly at his companions. When he raised his silver-bound mead horn everyone fell silent.

'Brothers, tonight is Imbolg. Spring is born. Tomorrow you will go back to your own village, knowing that, whatever may come, the evil that has been prophesied will never rule in our land. We have a long wait until the child is old enough to stand here with us, as our Generous Chief and our Hero, but until then let us celebrate! The Goddess has blessed us! Her child has been born!'

In the warm red firelight, golden rings and silver armbands glistened as the mead horns were raised. 'To the child!'

'Join me now,' Witton went on, 'in a vow to find the boy and train him.'

The men roared their approval, slapping the tables with their hands.

But seated in the shadows to Witton's left, a white-haired apprentice wearing a silver torque muttered through his teeth: 'He's gone quite mad! Can't he see a *baby* is no protection against the coming evil? We need a grown man, a strong leader . . .' Noticing Witton's eyes on him, the young man smiled and raised his mead horn in mock salute.

His master scowled. 'Hush, Gorgans, or do you think *you* can stand against what is coming?'

'And why shouldn't it be me?' Gorgans hissed. 'No one gives me the respect that I deserve!' He clutched the handle of his dagger. The firelight caught the polished blade.

'Respect has to be earned. Just because you come from the Otherworld of Tir na nÓg does not make you a god,' his master said softly. 'Perhaps you need to train for battle instead of learning the ways of wisdom?'

'You *know* why I don't!' Gorgans snapped. He longed to take a sword and be a warrior, but he dreaded the Sun God's rage against his colourless skin and weak eyes. I will find a way to take the power I deserve, he thought. Even if it means I have to work in the dark.

At the head of the table Witton was still talking loudly, exultant with mead, heat and exhaustion. 'The child's name will be "Star Dancer"!' he roared, raising his drinking horn. 'He will be robed in a chieftain's seven colours of the finest wool, honoured with silver armbands and a golden torque. When the unknown darkness comes, the boy will be ready and his triumph will make the lands around the winter waters safe for a thousand years. To Star Dancer! Long may he live!'

'To Star Dancer!' the men roared, swigging their mead and holding out their horns for the women to fill them again.

2. The Test of Fire

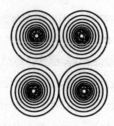

Clesek sat for a while, staring into the flames. He rubbed his callused hands together in the warmth. The child was healthy and would be of use to her mother and maybe to him in time, but he had prayed to the Goddess for a boy. His work in the forge was a man's work. The rock had to be crushed and ground to extract the silver and the lead. It took a skilled eye to tell the difference and a trained hand to know how to treat them. Then there were the bellows that had to be tended and the charcoal fires that needed watching day and night.

He rubbed his sooty fingers through his tousled hair and sighed. Why had the Goddess done this to him? Maybe he had forgotten to make the right offerings to the spirits . . . ? He would ask Witton when he came to bless and name the child.

Clesek poked at a log that had all but turned to ash. It fell, sending a shower of bright sparks up into the dark of the roof. The girl had been born at a strange time, with the stars dancing like that. Perhaps she would be a bit special. If she grew to be a beauty, she might fetch a high bride-price and bring a young man with strong arms to the forge. Clesek scratched his beard and looked at his woman.

Nessa stirred on her makeshift bed. Her long dark hair was loose and spread over her shoulders like a pool of peat water, but the birth had left her face thin and sharp. Cradled in her freckled arms, the baby was sleepily sucking milk and drooling over her shawl. Clesek smiled. As Gilda had said, at least Nessa was strong and fertile. Why shouldn't there be more children? He straightened his back and yawned. He needed sleep. He would ask Witton what sacrifices were required to ensure a boy next time.

Gilda did not have to summon the druid. He came to her. The sun was high and she had slept late. Witton called and knocked until she woke. Sleepily she pulled her heavy woollen dress over her shift and stumbled to the door, praying it wasn't another child to deliver. She was so tired she couldn't remember if any other women were due. She tried to think.

She knew Derowen, the village wise woman, was near her time, but not for another half-moon, surely?

Gilda tugged back the heavy door and was relieved to see

the old man, stooped and weary, on the threshold. She took his hand. 'Come in, Father. Can I offer you some honey cakes?'

'No, I am in a hurry,' Witton said as he sat on a stool.

Gilda knelt by the hearthstone and pushed back her sleeves as she poked the fire to life. Warm red sparks lit her plump face as she turned to smile at him. 'I was going to come and find you this morning,' she said. 'I have a message.'

'Then I am glad I came. Tell me – was a baby born last night?'

Gilda leaned back on her haunches and pushed her hair out of her eyes. 'Well, yes. That was why I was coming to see you. The mother asked whether you would give the blessing.'

Witton sighed with relief and smiled at the small patch of sky that gleamed through a gap in the thatch. 'Blessed be! He has been born. It is true!'

Gilda looked at him and frowned. 'No, Father. He is a *she*.'

Witton, still euphoric, did not hear. 'To think that I am alive to give the child his name and blessing, what an honour! There will be songs sung about this day . . .'

'Father Witton . . .' Gilda took the old man's hand once more.

'Eh?'

'It wasn't a boy child, it was a girl. She's to be called

Tegen, born last night to Nessa, woman of Clesek who works lead and silver in the hills. A healthy child.'

The old man glowered, his moustache twitching with irritation. 'Can't be a girl,' he snapped. 'Did you look properly?'

Gilda laughed and wiped her hands. 'Father, I know the difference between a boy and a girl, and Nessa's baby is most definitely a girl.'

'When was she born?' Witton leaned forward intently, his deep eyes willing Gilda to change her story. 'At dawn, did you say? Or after it started raining?'

'No. The stars were out, bright as day almost. I took her to the door to see how they danced to welcome her to the world. It was so pretty.'

Witton hauled himself to his feet, wincing as his knees creaked. 'You had no right!' he snapped. 'Now, enough about the girl. Where is the boy child born last night?'

Gilda got to her feet too. What right had this old man to tell her what she could and couldn't do, especially when it came to birthing? Hands on hips, she glared right back at him. 'I was up all night with Nessa. She gave birth to a girl. The stars were out and they gave a pretty show to welcome the babe. There was no boy – not from Nessa's belly anyhow. There was no twin waiting and there were no other calls for my help. You'll just have to go and look for yourself if you want another child from last night. But you mark my words –' she stepped forward and shook her

★ 11 ★

finger at him – 'I may not be a druid, but I know for certain that little Tegen's going to be special!'

Witton backed away towards the door and stumbled into the cold, wet morning light.

Witton was at Clesek's cottage before nightfall. He found Nessa seated in a wooden chair; her long dark hair was tied back and the shoulder pin of her dress undone so the child could feed. When the old man came in she pulled a long woollen shawl around herself and the baby.

Wheezing and exhausted, the old druid sat on a stool and sipped warm ale for a while. 'Let me see the child,' he said at last. Nessa still found walking difficult, so Clesek carried the baby to him.

Witton leaned forward and looked up at Clesek. 'Do you accept her?' he asked.

Nessa bit her lip. This was the moment when Clesek could refuse his daughter and she would be taken out on the hillside to die. It was a common fate for unwanted girls and children born with twisted limbs. She glanced at her man, but she needn't have worried.

Clesek smiled down at the precious bundle in his arms and with his work-stained fingers he touched the little one's hair, soft as down. 'I accept her gladly. She will be lucky for us. I feel it in my bones.'

Nessa's face glowed with warm colour. Her man would

never regret this moment. Tegen would be brought up to respect him and always do as he said.

Witton nodded. He stood, let his cloak fall and reached out for the child. 'I will need to examine her. If you do not wish to stay, then it does not matter. You might not like what I do, but I promise she will come to no harm.'

Clesek glanced at Nessa. 'We'll stay.'

'Then you must remain silent and not stop me, whatever happens.'

'Of course,' Clesek said.

Nessa felt her heart sink: more rituals, more inviting the spirits into human affairs. But she couldn't leave her baby, not for a moment. She stared at her hands. 'I agree.'

Witton carefully unwrapped the child and peeled the sodden mosses away from her bottom. Then he opened the door to let in light and he examined her carefully. 'She is perfect,' he announced at last.

Nessa longed to say, 'Of course she is!' but remembered her promise just in time and bit her lip hard.

The baby looked at Witton quizzically and peed over his hands and down the front of his robe. He tried not to scowl as he shook off the drips.

Then, holding the naked infant under her arms, he walked across the room and lifted Tegen high above the flames of the fire. He intoned a tuneless, wordless sound through his nose. As he did so, sparks rose to greet her, scorching the baby's back. She howled and thrashed.

Witton brushed the cinders away and peered at her skin, frowned, then handed her back to her terrified mother.

The screaming baby struggled as Nessa wrapped her in the woollen shawl and gave her a finger to suck. Then she looked up at the druid, her blue eyes bright with anger and dread. She glanced at Clesek, who was clenching and unclenching his hands, trying to control his fury. Neither of them dared to speak.

Then, hitching up the hem of his robe, Witton bent his cracking knees and lowered himself to squat on the earth floor. 'Do you have her caul?'

Clesek fetched it from a rafter, where it had been hung to dry. It was only one day old and still damp and soft. Chanting a nasal incantation, Witton laid the birth sack on the edge of the hearthstones, then he rattled a leather pouch and spilled a collection of bone shards into the bloody remains. Most of them bounced off into the ashes. The old druid stared hard for a few seconds, then bent over and with a shaking finger touched those that had stayed in place. Red lines like broken twigs were painted on each piece. He muttered as if he was talking to someone invisible.

Nessa averted her gaze lest she saw something she shouldn't. The less the spirits knew about her child, the better; there was enough bad luck in life without inviting more. She clutched her baby inside the comforting woollen wrappings, wishing she could make her disappear beneath the folds.

At last the old man looked up and stroked the plaits of his beard as he thought. His head was skull-like in the firelight. Deep black shadows hid his face, yet as he lifted his gaze his eyes gleamed. He coughed and spat.

Nessa hugged the child closer still. Why had Witton tested her baby with fire? 'O Mother Goddess, make him go away, *please*,' she prayed silently.

The old druid sucked his gums as he stooped to gather up the bones. 'Her fortune is clouded from me,' he muttered at last. He stood, pulled on his cloak and picked up his staff.

Clesek opened the door for him.

Feeling as if she could breathe again, Nessa pulled aside the shoulder of her dress once more and tucked the baby against her breast.

Witton stood on the threshold, then turned back and scowled, the white of his cloak and hair harsh against the soft evening light. For a moment he seemed to be a standing stone, cold and impassive. 'It's a shame that she's a girl,' he said. 'If she had been a boy things would have been much clearer.'

'I wanted to ask you about that,' Clesek said. 'I . . . we . . .' he added, glancing at Nessa, 'we would like . . . well . . . what do we have to do to make sure the next child is a boy?'

'I will talk to you about that,' Witton replied. 'But first, give her to me.'

The child screamed in fury at having lost her mother's milk once more.

Cradling the baby gently in his arms, the old man lifted her towards the east and chanted a welcome and a blessing.

He did not see the fear and pain in Nessa's eyes. Thank goodness she *is* a girl, she thought bitterly.

Witton finished his blessing, returned the baby and leaned on his stick. 'Gilda said you have chosen a name?'

'She's Tegen – *pretty thing*,' Nessa replied without looking up.

'Then Tegen she shall be called. Send her to me at her first bleeding; she will need a strong word of power to protect her. I will decide her true name then. Meanwhile . . .' he sighed sadly, 'give thanks to the Goddess that you are both alive.' And he turned to go.

Clesek followed him out of the door. 'Father, what were you going to say about getting a boy?'

As the two men walked away, Gilda arrived, panting from the exertions of the hill climb. Her cheery face was redder than usual, and her unruly hair almost free of its leather thong. Under her cloak she carried a small basket of dried herbs.

'Hello, my dear.' Her warm smile revealed her few remaining teeth. She closed the door behind her and pulled shutters across the wind-eyes, making the cottage comfortingly dark with just the hearth fire for light.

Nessa said nothing as the midwife gossiped and bustled about, making a tisane with boiling water from the small iron cauldron that simmered amongst the hot ashes. 'Give me Tegen,' Gilda said. 'Drink this. You look exhausted; it will help you sleep.'

Nessa sipped and sighed quietly to herself. Gilda's motherly presence made her want to spill out all her terror. But Nessa never allowed her real emotions to show. She tried to hide her loves, joys and fears under a blanket of heart-snow, scared that if she showed what she really felt, those she cared for would be in danger from the jealousy of the spirit world.

Gilda eased her bulky frame on to a low stool and unwrapped Tegen's shawl. As she turned the baby over to wipe her bottom she saw the scorch marks of a star pattern. The midwife said nothing, but touched each tiny burn in turn, her lips moving silently with long-forgotten words.

Then she took a deep breath and smiled at Nessa. 'I've been that busy since I saw you last,' she said. 'Derowen gave birth to her child this morning. It was born too early. She didn't send for me, and it died. Though what she's doing giving birth at her age I'll never know – it's far too dangerous. She's lucky to be alive, if you ask me.'

Tegen, her rage completely gone, sprawled naked and content across the midwife's plump thighs. Gilda chattered on as she rubbed the child with chamomile and oil. 'It's odd, but it was almost as if Derowen knew her baby wouldn't live. She had a funeral basket woven already. The babe was all in it and the top was closed by the time I got there. She got me to dig the grave . . .' Gilda paused. 'I don't know why she didn't call me earlier. I might have been able to help. But you know Derowen – she's so full of her being the village wise woman and all – she has to do everything *her* way!'

Despite her weariness and anger, Nessa couldn't stop herself smiling. It was so true! Although she was sad the baby had died. Becoming a mother might have softened her a little.

Suddenly Gilda stopped what she was doing and looked at Nessa. 'Do you know, between you and me I think Derowen would have liked to be a druid, given half a chance.'

'Some women are druids,' Nessa said sleepily.

Gilda was quiet for a moment and stared into the fire. Her voice was sad when she spoke again. 'There hasn't been one round these parts for years. If you ask me, Derowen is bitter. Goodness knows what about – she has everything a woman could want.' She sighed deeply. 'She's feared and respected by everyone and she's had Witton twisted around her little finger for years.'

Hastily wrapping Tegen in fresh bindings and a clean shawl, Gilda leaned over to lay her by her mother's side.

Then she heaved herself to her feet and turned away for

a moment. She stood with her head bowed, dabbing at her eyes with the edge of her sleeve.

When she turned back she was brisk and cheerful once more. 'Now, over on your side, Nessa, let's have a look at you. By the way, how did Tegen get those marks on her back? Did you lay her too near the fire?'

Nessa didn't have the energy to explain. The tisane was working and sleep was engulfing her in heavy waves. She lay quietly as she was washed.

'You'll do nicely. I expect there'll be another little one soon.'

Nessa groaned. The very thought of giving birth again filled her with dread.

At last Gilda left. Grateful for the peace, Nessa curled her arms around her baby and fell asleep.

But it was only two nights later that Clesek arrived with a squirming bundle wrapped in his cloak. He was apprehensive as he pushed open the cottage door. What would Nessa say? He was certain he had done the right thing – but would she agree?

'What have you there?' Nessa smiled as she held Tegen up for a kiss.

With his free hand, Clesek stroked his wife's long dark plaits. She looked less pale and was more like her old self. He held the bundle out for her. Nessa put Tegen into her crib, took the squirming shape and pulled back the wrappings.

'It's a baby boy!' she exclaimed. 'Whose is he?'

'I don't know.' Clesek shrugged. 'I found him . . .' he hesitated and blushed, ' . . . when I was checking the charcoal fires up by the waterfall.'

'Abandoned?' Nessa was amazed. Boys were usually kept unless they were deformed. This child seemed strong and well.

'I think he might be an idiot – a halfhead,' Clesek replied. 'Look at his eyes and hands.'

'It's difficult to tell in this light,' Nessa said, taking the baby closer to the fire as she unfolded his fingers. 'He is so cold. He must have been almost dead when you found him. Why did you bring him home? He has been left for a reason. The father must have refused him.' Nessa was confused. Part of her wanted to put the child to her breast, but she was frightened. What if they offended some spirit by snatching the child from his due fate? The child's Curse might be brought down on them all.

Clesek lead Nessa to her chair. 'Sit and listen, then decide with me what should be done. I will tell you the truth. When Witton came to bless our Tegen, I asked him what offerings I should make to ensure a boy. He told me to throw a piece of my best silver into the mouth of the River Spirit, where she flows from the cave at the head of our valley.

'I wasn't checking fires . . . I had taken my double-twisted torque and gone up to the waterfall and made my offering. You know how much we'll need a man to help us hereabouts, especially as you and I get older. No one wants to leave the comfort and safety of the summer fields to work in the hills, burning charcoal all year.

'Then, as I walked home, I heard a baby crying. I followed the sound but it stopped. Then the cry came again and I found a bundle between the trees. I picked it up and here it is. A boy child, ready born with no danger to you. It is a bitter night out, I couldn't leave him . . .'

'But what use is a halfhead?' Nessa scowled. 'He'll never be able to do anything much.'

Clesek crouched down by Nessa's side and put his arm around her shoulders. 'They work hard, and if the task is kept simple they don't complain or run away. I'll teach him to burn charcoal. Even if he's only good enough to watch it and let me know if a break appears, it'll be something. At least I can get on with smelting and casting in between times . . . It just seemed so strange to be asking for a boy child one minute and then there he was, right by my feet! Somehow it seemed wrong to just walk past and let him die . . . He may have been cast out, but perhaps the spirits had other ideas and he needed to live.' Clesek looked hopefully at Nessa. 'What do you think?'

The child was already sucking at her breast.

'Are we going to call him Alwar?' she asked, all thoughts of spirits and curses gone clean from her head.

'No. Let's save that for our own son. We'll call him Griff.' Clesek closed his eyes and bowed his head to the spirits of the East, the bringers of hope.

3. The Search

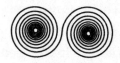

For many long years after Tegen's birth, the druids and their servants looked for a boy born on the night the stars had danced.

Dressed in their white robes of office, they walked far and wide through valleys and over hills. They followed treacherous trackways across the Winter Seas. In the dry warmth between summer's birth at Beltane and grain ripening at Lughnasadh, the flooded flatlands left the summer fields lush and fertile. Then the druids visited every remote marshy homestead that might have been missed in the darker months.

But however diligently they searched, in that whole land around the Winter Seas and Summer Lands, the quest was fruitless. There was no Star Dancer.

Witton sat in his roundhouse on its lonely little hill beyond the village palisade and watched the seasons turn the wooded hills from spring's pale green silk to autumnal fire, through winter's grey desolation and back to summer viridian again. He alone suspected the truth, but said nothing, hoping against hope that he would be wrong. A woman druid would be accepted amongst his brethren, but a female Star Dancer? That was inconceivable. The Goddess's child who would become the immovable sentinel against evil, maybe even a sacrifice for the people – could not be a *girl*. Such a thing would cause division amongst the sacred brotherhood. They would need to be more united than ever as the prophesied evil approached. There must be another child – a boy – somewhere.

As Tegen grew, she knew little of druids or sentinels, auguries or flames. Her mother's fears taught her how to avert a curse and Gilda schooled her in stories, simple charms and household spells. Tall and lithe, dark-haired and green-eyed, Tegen ran about her parents' home, chasing the geese and learning to work.

Despite Clesek's prayers and sacrifices, Nessa bore no more live children. They all came into the world with a bluish hue and no breath in their bodies. Tegen was adored and followed everywhere by Griff, the moon-faced foundling.

The boy had also grown strong and stood taller than his foster-sister. He worked hard, but he would always be a halfhead and no amount of patient teaching from Clesek and Nessa would change that.

But to Tegen, he was her foster-brother and that was all that mattered. Every morning she made sure he combed his lank fair hair and cleaned his teeth with a twig. She looked to see his face and hands were washed and she patched his tunic when it tore. They comforted each other's tears and kept each other's secrets. When her life was hard, the sight of his tongue-filled grin and the twinkle in his slanting eyes made everything better.

Together, the young Tegen and Griff learned to pile wood into cone-shaped stacks for burning charcoal. Then Clesek taught them to cut turf to seal the fires so they burned slowly. As the years passed, Clesek trusted Griff to do it on his own. The boy had a good grasp of how the wood needed to be placed. Best of all, Griff liked working the leather bellows for Clesek's smelting furnace. He laughed when the heavy blast of air made sparks fly. He loved the sweet smell of wood smoke on his clothes and hair. One day he came in triumphant with his first misshapen lump of smelted lead, which he gave to Tegen with a shy kiss on the cheek.

Clesek was pleased with Griff. Despite his clumsiness, the boy worked well. 'You'll be ready to sleep by the charcoal fires for me soon,' Clesek told him. 'It's hard to get the hill men to do it these days. I don't trust them anyway. They'll steal my charcoal as soon as burn it, even though I give them good lead for their trouble. You're a man now, so it'll be your job next time the seas flood the summer meadows.'

Griff dashed around the house yelling, 'I's a man now!' knocking Tegen's bowl of bread dough flying. 'I's gotta go and cut poles to build my own hut. I's a man and a good one too! Will yus come and see my first fire, Tegen, will yus?'

'Of course I will,' Tegen laughed and gave him a hug, 'but you're not going at this time of year. There are several moons that have to wax and wane first.'

She was sad at the prospect of losing Griff's comforting presence, but she tried not to dwell on it as she took her turn at the bellows or turned the stone quern for barley flour.

On the thirteenth anniversary of the stars dancing, the druid elders gathered. Witton was too old to travel by boat to the longhouse at the foot of the Tor, so the men met at his roundhouse at the head of the valley, near the edge of the Winter Seas.

Witton was still clear-thinking and wise and the others turned to him for advice and leadership. They needed all his insights now, for the bones and the stars both showed that the impending evil would soon be gaining strength. The ovates amongst them scried the fires, threw bones, sacrificed animals and read their intestines, but still the threat remained nameless, and the Star Dancer was beyond their sight.

In truth, the druids were not only concerned for the people whom they protected, but they were also worried for themselves. Should they fail in their duty, they would lose their positions – their livings, their homes and the respect of all who knew them. They dared not fail. The seventeen men who met in Witton's roundhouse were in a restless mood as they sat together on makeshift benches and straw bales, hot and sweaty in the choking, smoke-filled air.

It was Imbolg again. Snowdrops appearing in the woods told them the worst of the winter should soon be past, but the perpetual rain and battering winds filled the wise ones with a sense of dread.

Seated by the hearth fire, Witton was more bowed and skeletal than ever. He stayed quite still, his hands in his lap, his eyes red and watery from the smoke. Next to him sat his greatest friend, Huval, a tall, thoughtful man of forty summers, who stroked his dark brown beard and stared into the flames.

All around them the other men shuffled uncomfortably, waiting for Witton to speak. But he sat silently as the damp wood on the fire spat and spluttered. A smell of burning came from a heavy black iron pot pushed into the embers. Witton leaned forward and began to stir the contents, a stew of goat flesh and vegetables. Still he said nothing. He simply stirred and stirred as if engaged in some sacred duty.

The mood was becoming more and more restless until a tall, white-haired young man picked his way forward into the firelight. He swirled his six-coloured cloak around him to show off his rank. Once he had the light from the fire full on his pale face he leaned against one of the central roof supports and casually lifted his right hand to command attention. It was a much-practised gesture, allowing his gold and silver armbands to gleam against his well-formed arm.

Several of the men nodded in his direction and nudged one another. If their leaders weren't going to speak, they were quite willing to listen to the White One.

'You have something to say, Gorgans?' Huval asked without looking up.

'I want to know where this so-called *Star Dancer* is!' the young man sneered down at Witton. 'You've given us promises and more promises over the years, but he never comes! They say the only child born that night is a *girl*! A female Star Dancer?' He clicked his tongue and tapped his head, making the sign for madness. 'What will you think of next? My dog would do the job just as well, and he never goes on heat!'

The men laughed. They liked his style.

'Good women have served us well,' Huval said quietly.

Gorgans growled, fingering the hilt of his dagger. 'No

one knows what sort of evil is approaching. If it is Pictish raiders a thirteen-year-old *girl* won't be much use. She might be handy getting my evening meal ready . . .' The listeners laughed. He paused, made sure every eye was upon him, ' . . . but can a woman *lead* us? Heh?'

The listeners murmured in agreement. Gorgans had only recently left his long apprenticeship behind. Witton had not been happy about seeing him wearing the druid's white robe, but he was the youngest son of a powerful chieftain. More importantly, he was one of the white-skinned, white-haired beings from Tir na nÓg, a spirit from the Otherworld in human form, his red eyes always shielded from the light of the burning Sun God. It was the highest honour to have such a one in the brotherhood. Yet, despite this, the lad was an enigma. He seemed unable to do real magic, except with his tongue, which wormed his will into men's hearts.

And today he spoke the fears that were in everyone's minds.

Sensing the support he was gathering, Gorgans smiled and sauntered into the centre of the room. He would dearly like to be chosen himself. Star Dancer or Arch-Druid – the title did not matter, only the power. He lifted his chin a little to expose the dog-headed silver torque at his neck.

Huval scowled into the red and gold flames that flickered across the crumbling logs. He did not move, except to glance at Witton, who clenched the stew ladle in his fist and sucked at his gums.

Gorgans rolled his eyes in exasperation as he looked around at the gathered men. He had their attention. Now was the moment.

'Witton is scared to act!' he bellowed suddenly. 'There he sits, old and witless, with his best friend; both of them might as well be women themselves for all the good they do, stirring the stew! I say we draw lots amongst ourselves to find one who will lead us and not be afraid to make decisions. That person will also be proclaimed the Star Dancer. The Goddess has always honoured those who act with faith! Just waiting for a mere child will only end with us all being slaughtered! Who knows what the coming evil is? It may be demons, or it may be the Romans with their short swords and shorter skirts that we hear so much about. The Star Dancer was not born; he must be *made*!'

The murmurs of support swelled and there was even applause. Gorgans looked every inch a leader and he knew it.

'What do you say, Huval?' called a voice from out of the dark shadows. 'Does Gorgans speak sense or not?'

'The stars do not lie!' Huval raged as he sprang to his feet, grasping a blazing branch from the fire. 'The child was born the night the stars danced and he will be the only one to avert the evil!' Swinging the orange flames in a roaring arc, he made Gorgans jump back. Huval held his brand in front of him and jabbed it towards the White One as he spoke.

'There will be *no* vote! Witton is still the wisest amongst us and I will *not* have the Goddess mocked. We *all* know what we saw that night on the hilltop.'

Gorgans laughed nervously, one eye on the fiery branch. 'Ha! It was a good excuse for a party, nothing more. Now we need practicalities! If this child existed, he would be clearly visible to all by now. He would be thirteen years old tonight and full of magic. About as difficult to hide as a blaze in a field of stubble. I personally have looked *everywhere*. You say the stars do not lie? Well *I* do not lie either!'

The other druids grumbled and murmured in the shadows. They were taking sides. Some believed that Gorgans was truly a gift from Tir na nÓg; others saw him as a dangerous and self-centred young man.

Gorgans and Huval glowered at each other, their lips pulled back in wolf-like snarls. Gorgans as pale as a wraith and Huval brown as a chestnut, they closed in, like two deadly gaming pieces.

Sensing a fight looming, the others drew back, leaving a space for the two men to move.

Throwing back their cloaks and lowering their heads, the opponents took small, circling steps, measuring each other up. Huval gripped his burning branch tightly with both hands. Gorgans stooped quickly to snatch a torch of his own to meet the threat. The red-hot weapons clashed and locked, sending a shower of red embers on to the rush-strewn floor. There was pure hate in both their eyes.

No one else stirred, or even breathed.

Huval and Gorgans began to push against each other, the flames sparking only a hand's breadth from their faces. Jaws clenched, muscles locked, breathing hard.

Suddenly Witton raised his staff and crashed it down between the burning weapons. 'Stop it, both of you! Neither the stars, nor Gorgans, are liars. The child will appear, of that you can be sure. Beltane is coming soon, and I will invite all the boys of the right age to come to a feast. I will know the Star Dancer when I see him, on that you can depend!'

Both younger men hesitated. Witton's legs were no longer strong enough to stand for the ceremonies, but his steady, calm authority had not faded.

Huval growled and tossed his torch back on to the hearth, then sat back down.

One of the other men took Gorgans's branch from him and threw it where it belonged. The White One stepped back into the shadows, his red eyes narrowed as he silently swore vengeance on Huval. Witton would not have long to live and then Huval would quickly follow the old man to the Otherworld. There were ways. There were means . . .

Then, in the chilly silence, Witton leaned forward so the firelight fell full on his face. 'Rest assured, Brothers,' he said, 'this Star Dancer will be amongst us when the time is right. The Goddess has her own reasons for hiding him so far. Now, drink some mead with me and toast the health of the young one. All shall be well!'

Not far away, the night wind made the wooden beams of Clesek's roof creak. Tegen lay curled up on a mattress of straw, listening. It was as if the old place was talking – whispering secrets, singing quietly.

She tried to lie back and sleep. But sleep would not come, for tonight she heard another voice above the groaning of the roof timbers.

Someone was calling. The voice had come before, but never so clearly. Tegen was afraid.

Who was it? What did they want? Tegen stared up at the night sky through the wind-eye. The constellation of the Watching Woman burned brightly. It always seemed to be watching her, following her; but was it *speaking to her*?

'Come, come quickly. We need you!' the voice called.

Tegen slammed the shutters and lay down again, her heart thumping wildly.

4. Witch Child

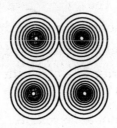

After the winter torrents, spring had been kind to the land. The shallow Winter Seas had dried, leaving the summer pastures rich and green.

True to his word, as Beltane drew near Witton ordered a feast. He invited every boy aged between eleven and fifteen years from the villages around the waters. Each family in the valley took in at least one of the visitors to eat by their hearth. They were glad to do so; the young people brought gifts and news to their hosts in exchange for the hospitality. Some of the older boys might take brides home to their villages. That was good too. New alliances were great blessings.

The boy who stayed by Clesek's hearth was a weakling, not at all the sort of lad he had in mind for Tegen, so he did not care when the lad spent most of his time with his friends in the village. There was time. Tegen was still too young to bear a child.

In the village, the feeling of excitement and anticipation throbbed everywhere. The people gossiped freely: it was said the druids were looking for a new apprentice amongst the boys. They had heard he was already a great magician who could turn a warrior to stone with a single look! But where was he staying?

Clesek knew it was not at *his* hearth.

That year the Beltane feast fell on a bright sunny day. The biggest fair ever seen in the valley was bustling almost as soon as dawn had brought enough light for the villagers to count their silver pieces.

Pottery and cloth were traded for salt and lead, dried fruits for sacks of flour. Rare spices were carefully arrayed in small wooden boxes next to skins of wine and piles of cured furs. The women congregated around a stall where a short, fat man was selling carved bone combs and needles, coloured beads, iron pins and copper brooches.

Tegen was now an almost-woman with raven-black hair twisted into a single, waist-length plait, the beginnings of breasts under her yellow dress. From first light she had stood at her parents' stall and helped to sell or barter their lead billets, silver pins, brooches and clasps. Trade was brisk, everyone's spirits were high and, for once, no one seemed to be arguing or fighting.

Several druids had come to the festival to see what sort of 'Star Dancer' Witton might find. Half a dozen white-robed men sat quietly at a table drinking and playing dice. Gorgans was their ringleader, half hidden under a broad-brimmed hat of plaited rushes to protect his eyes from the sunshine. He drank little but kept his fellows' horns full of mead and their ears filled with flattery. It would only be a matter of time before the others fell into his way of think-ing. It did not matter what Witton said or did that day. There was no Star Dancer.

Nearby, Huval leaned against a booth of hazel poles and watched Gorgans. The White One was right about one thing: Witton was getting old – but whatever was happen-ing, wherever the Star Dancer was, he must be allowed to appear in his own time. If Gorgans was going to cause a fight, Huval's sword was ready beneath his heavy brown cloak.

Halfway through the morning, a small dark-skinned boy dressed in flowing scarlet robes ran to the middle of the grass before Witton's carved oak chair. He bowed and began to beat a strange, compelling rhythm on a drum of white hide stretched over a shallow red-painted frame. The people of the lands around the Winter Seas had rarely seen these dark-faced strangers before. Many thought they were spirits from the Sun God, for they always brought exotic goods to trade and they had uncanny healing powers with herbs and salves that even the druids knew nothing of. But the most certain evidence of all was their smell – as they moved, a pungent aroma wafted with them. Only the druids used incense – so they *had* to be magical.

The first sight of the boy brought the crowds gathering in silent awe, but scarcely had he begun to strike his drum than a tall handsome man with walnut-coloured skin and wearing only flame-orange breeches somersaulted on to the grass next to him. As the drumbeat gathered pace, the man pulled wooden batons from his belt and began to juggle. The crowd drew closer as the tosses and throws became wilder. Then a great gasp of horror and wonder went up as the juggler plunged his batons into a fire pot and continued his act with whirling flames.

When the man ended his performance by opening his mouth wide and slowly swallowing the flames from each stick, the crowd screamed. 'Wizards! Demons!' they howled, but they didn't run. The show was too good.

The fire-eater moved aside, but the boy's drumbeat did not slacken: it merely changed, very subtly, as six gaudily dressed nut-brown women ran into the middle of the field and stood quite still, their arms held high above their heads. Once they were in position, the boy stopped.

Everyone froze expectantly.

The only movement was the wind fluttering the women's loose robes – wide swirls of jade, azure and purple cloth pinned at their shoulders with silver clasps and gathered at their waists.

The man picked up a tambourine and, after a few seconds of absolute silence, he nodded to the boy and they both struck a thrilling, throbbing rhythm. The women tossed their wild black hair and sang with strange throaty words as they stretched out their arms and jangled brilliantly coloured glass bangles on their wrists and ankles. This way and that they swayed and stamped, spinning faster and faster until it seemed impossible they could stay standing.

The crowds gathered closer and gawped, mouths open in disbelief.

Their world was one of water and mud, weak dyes, wooden clogs and heavy, damp-smelling wool. This show was surely a glimpse into the land of the Lady Goddess herself? Some even knelt in reverence, in case the dancers really were the Lady's emissaries.

Tegen had slipped away from her parents' stall. She watched the dance intently with wide eyes, unable to resist stamping her feet to the music and fluttering the ends of her fingers. Soon she had moved into an open space and was freely swaying her hips and wishing she could jangle thick glass bangles like the beautiful ladies. She had one silver band her father had made for her, but she needed more to make that thrilling wrist music. *Two* silver bands would sound like bells. How she longed for two, or even three . . .

She danced with her eyes closed and imagined heavily scented flowers, hot winds and midnight skies with gleaming, brilliant stars. The colours swirled into the music and the music became a part of her.

Suddenly, with a crash of instruments, the dance ended as abruptly as it had begun. The dancers held their pose for a heartbeat or two, then laughed and hugged each other as they picked up small reed baskets and moved amongst the crowd for money and gifts.

Once the baskets were full, the dancers showed their trade goods: bright enamelled jewellery and lenghs of coloured silk spread over hazel branches. The crowd gathered around excitedly and the barter and shouting began, fingers and gestures taking the place of words the foreigners did not understand.

On the grassy space where the dancers had been, an old man put out a stool and puffed air into a set of bagpipes. Once the goatskin was full, he started a drone and began to play. All around him, village children ran around giggling. At last they calmed down and took their places for a reel.

Tegen wistfully eyed the soft flowing fabrics that hung in gorgeous array from the hazel branches. Hesitantly she reached to touch purple fringes and knotted scarlet tassels as fine as spider webs. As she did so, a strong, brown hand reached for her wrist and held it fast.

'You dance good,' the woman said in a thick accent. 'Dance with silk, mine. It bring you luck, much.' She plucked at a length of fine cloth the colour of young birch leaves and held it next to Tegen's face.

The airy texture of the threads captured her with another yearning to possess. 'I have nothing to trade,' Tegen replied sadly, twining the green fringes around her fingers. Fleetingly she wondered whether to run home and fetch her silver bangle, but she knew her father would be angry and she couldn't really bear to part with it, not even for this.

'What name yours is?' the woman demanded, drawing Tegen towards her. She smelled of warm sweat and rich spices.

'Tegen.'

'That not real name yours. That come. Here. Take.' She thrust the prize into Tegen's hand. 'Your music start, soon. You dance. Yes? Send us wind, we home go. That pay me shawl for. Yes? Go!'

Hardly believing her luck, Tegen kissed the woman's hand and swept the fluttering green swathe of silk around her shoulders. The gossamer threads caught on her rough hands, but she was so lost in the joy of the moment she did not care.

Just then the piper changed to a different tune. Tegen could not help herself; she kicked her clogs aside and began to dance. As she moved, she imagined these strangers with skin like ripe chestnuts and eyes like polished sloes, dressed in the wings of butterflies as they loaded their boats and hoisted the sails.

She danced and danced without any regard for what patterns the younger children were already following or what melody the piper was playing.

Tegen closed her eyes and dreamed of the coming autumn floods, windy and treacherous, whipped into anger and threatening to drown these beautiful dancing folk as they journeyed home. As she moved, she instinctively used her feet and hands to tell the waves to subside and the wind to be calm. Then she swung her arms wide so the boat could spread its wing-like sails and fly straight home. She felt a thrill of excitement, for these people needed *her* to get them safely back. Suddenly she *knew* she could do it. She had the power to keep them safe!

Lost in her imaginings, she did not notice that the music had stopped. The children had gone and she was alone on the grass, surrounded by a crowd of silent watchers.

Suddenly old Witton stepped forward, snatched the shawl and flung the green silk back at the woman. 'Enough!' he roared as he slapped Tegen around the face. Leaning on his stick, he hobbled back to his chair under the spread of a gold-stippled oak.

Tegen stood open-mouthed, staring at Witton, her hand over her stinging cheek. Her heart raced and her eyes were wet. Everyone gawped at her. Why had he done that? She stared around, desperate for someone to come and help her, or even to explain . . .

But slowly, one by one, the crowd turned their backs and walked away. Under his tree, Witton was ignoring her as he smiled and clapped for a group of little children who had begun their show of tumbling for him. Only moon-faced Griff came and stood next to her, holding on to her hand with grimy, sticky fingers.

He looked at her wide-eyed in admiration, his thick tongue protruding slightly between his lips. Then he kissed her on the cheek. 'You was beautiful, Tegen! Witton wasn't listening to your dancin' proper. You go home. I'll come an' make you better later.'

Irritated, Tegen rubbed the wet kiss away from her cheek. 'You can't *listen* to dancing, Griff,' she snapped, as she pushed her feet back into her clogs. But she knew she was being unkind. Griff always wanted to look after her, even though he sometimes found it hard to get his own breeches on straight. 'I'm staying,' she replied more gently. 'I can't just run away.'

Griff wiped his nose on his sleeve. 'All right. I wants a honey cake, Tegen. Buy me one?'

Tegen led him across to a stall, talking as she walked. She often told things to Griff. She knew he didn't always under-stand, but he did always care, and that made her feel better. What was more, Griff loved it when she talked to him.

'I wish I knew what I did that was so wrong. Everyone

was dancing . . .' She sighed and closed her eyes. 'But *my* dance felt strange . . . as if . . . as if I could really *do* something for those people as they sail home . . .'

She stood still and rummaged in her pouch, then pushed a copper piece into Griff's palm. 'Go and buy your cake yourself. I am going to talk to Witton. I've got to know what I did wrong!'

Tegen's face burned and her mouth went dry as she ran across the grass. The old man was busy listening to three men arguing about the ownership of a goat. Tegen hung back to wait for a moment. Behind Witton there stood a taller, chestnut-haired druid with kind eyes. For a heartbeat he turned to look at her and smiled through his thick brown beard. She thought he was about to beckon her forward, but something Witton said distracted him and he turned away again.

Suddenly, spiteful bony fingers dug into Tegen's arm. It was Derowen, the village wise woman, who often stood by Witton's side. The witch took great delight in jamming her nails into Tegen's skin as hard as she could. With a malicious twist she jerked the girl backwards. 'Master Witton is busy!' she snapped. 'Go home and be glad you weren't punished worse, like you deserve!'

'But what did I *do*?' Tegen asked, trying not to cry out at the pain.

'Stop pretending!' Derowen tightened her grip. 'You . . .' she spat, 'are not the Star Dancer. Witton examined you with fire and with signs when you were newborn, and you *failed*.' She pulled back her thin lips, showing long, yellowed teeth. 'Witton has to listen to the voices of the spirits. He doesn't want to be distracted by little witch girls like you, trying to show off! Now go, before I beat you!' The old woman hissed stale breath into Tegen's face, then pushed her away.

Tegen turned and tried to run towards the woods. Her legs were heavy and slow, she could *not* make them move . . . The world was spinning . . . What was a Star Dancer? Was it the great magician people had been talking about? What fire and what signs had she failed? If she wasn't allowed near Witton to ask, how could she be expected to know? It wasn't fair!

At last she slipped between the first trees and flung her arms around a white hawthorn heavy with creamy, musty-smelling blossom. The Goddess's own flower. Her chest hurt, but slowly she forced herself to breathe. She was alone. She told herself she was safe, but she couldn't shake off the feeling that someone was close behind her. She turned and looked, but there was only a wren swooping low between the branches of the sunlight-dappled shade.

Suddenly a footstep disturbed the stillness. Her heart missed a beat.

'Tegen,' a voice called out, 'are you all right?'

It was Gilda the midwife, plump and gentle, her wild grey hair pulled back under a brown scarf. She posed no threat, but she was a gossip for all her kindness. Tegen did not want all her thoughts and fears broadcast throughout the village, so she pretended she had not heard. Turning away, she darted through the undergrowth and made for home.

She hoped her parents had not seen what had happened at the fair. She did not want them to come looking for her. She needed to be alone to nurse her confusion as well as her throbbing arm and face.

The old druid sat gripping his staff as he watched the assembling crowd of hopeful boys. He could sense the Star Dancer was – or had been – present. He looked anxiously this way and that, searching the faces for a boy who stood out from the rest. He may not be particularly tall or handsome; he might even be awkward or unable to use his legs or eyes. Boys like this often made better Wise Ones, because they listened to the way of the winds and watched the birds rather than relying on their speed or strength to get results. But amongst the crowd of hopeful, dirt-smudged faces, not one caught Witton's eye.

For a moment he remembered a newborn child screaming as tiny red embers scorched her back. 'No,' he said firmly. 'It couldn't work. I was wrong.'

He nodded to Griff, who was standing amongst the crowd of hopefuls beaming widely. He was a good lad.

Witton reminded himself to buy him a piece of honeycomb later.

That night, the other druids went to their beds drunk. Gorgans was well pleased. He had gained friends that day. The 'Star Dancer' had not come and the silly witch girl's dancing spells had made Witton and Huval look as if they were losing their grasp. Her magic was fresh and untaught . . . and a threat.

This was good.

Before going to his own bed, Gorgans went to the home of Derowen the wise woman. He had use for her. She may be foul and old, but her magic was very strong, and that was what he would need if he was to gain power. Persuasive words alone would not be enough to win his battle.

The stench of burning fur made him cough and retch, but he pushed the door wide and went in. The old woman was crouched over a dish of liquid that glistened darkly in the firelight. Her grey dress and long plaits were spattered with red stains. In the edge of the fire lay a half-burned hare with its throat cut. As Gorgans entered, he put three silver pieces into the woman's outstretched hand. She dropped the coins into the blood, looking to see which side they fell.

After a few moments she sat back on her heels and smiled

up at her visitor. 'Well, Gorgans, your chance for power is near,' she said. 'Witton is dying.'

Gorgans smiled and gave the old hag a piece of gold. She bit it and nodded. Then she poured him ale and watched as he drank.

Fool, she thought. He thinks I am going to help him become the Star Dancer. He can call himself whatever he likes, but the power will be all mine.

5. Dancing Magic

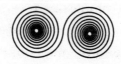

Tegen perched on the barn roof and felt angry and empty in turns. Her arm was sore, but not enough to matter. Her head ached and her cheek still stung where Witton had slapped her. When her perch became uncomfortable she climbed down and wandered around aimlessly.

Compared to most of the village roundhouses, the silver-worker's home was a palace. It was a rectangular stone-built house with a little chamber at one end for her parents and a ladder to a crook loft where Tegen slept on a wooden platform under the thatch. Three large shuttered wind-eyes made it bright and full of clean air. Clesek's forge was in the stone barn nearby, with a lean-to for the animals. Griff shared their straw and warmth at night.

In the cool shade of the stable, Tegen put her arms around the neck of the fat little pony and rubbed her face against his musty pelt. 'What is it all about? I was only doing a step or two for the lady, thanking her for the shawl and wishing them a safe journey home, like she asked. I'm not a bad dancer. Is it because I was doing it like the strangers did it? Is that forbidden for us? Oh, I don't know! I wish I had someone to talk to. Whom can I trust apart from Griff? I can tell him, but he won't understand.'

Far away, Tegen could hear the faint sounds of music and people laughing. The warm afternoon had long worn away and the evening chill brought heavy dew. She felt weary and went inside to stir up the glowing logs in the hearth.

It was beginning to dawn on her that she had more on her mind than Witton's anger. For when he had slapped her she suddenly knew it was *his* voice she had heard calling in the night. But what did he want? Why didn't he just send for her?

There was too much to think about and it was getting dark. Tegen swept the hearth and left a bowl of clear water for the house spirits. Next she kneaded the bread and baked it on the hot stones around the fire. Just as she was turning the loaves, Griff stumbled in drunk. He belched, helped himself to a small bannock, still hot, and tossed it between his fingers. 'Ouch!' he bellowed. 'Hurts!' and without even saying goodnight, he staggered out to his sleeping place with the pony.

'Come back!' Tegen called. 'Come and sit with me!' She needed company, even if he wouldn't really know what she was talking about. She waited for a short while, trying to convince herself she didn't mind being alone, but she *did* mind.

The aloneness hurt.

She ran out to call Griff again, but by the time she reached the shed, he was already contentedly snoring in the hay, clutching the half-eaten bannock and stinking of mead. He wouldn't stir until morning.

Tegen made sure she was in bed before her parents came home. She didn't want to face any questions about what had happened. She didn't want her father's sympathy and she didn't want to know what her mother thought. Not tonight.

Hearing her parents' voices, she lay still with her eyes closed. Perhaps they would just go to bed. She had done all the chores; that would please them. Steps on the ladder brought Nessa up to the loft. Tegen felt something soft as a dream pressed into her hands.

It was the green silk shawl!

'Gilda sent this for you. It's a gift from her. She said you must keep it,' her mother whispered. 'But please, no more showing off in public. It scares me. No good will come of it.'

Nothing more was said about Tegen's dancing and Witton's slap, although many of the village people made the sign against the evil eye whenever she passed. Griff just squeezed her fingers tightly. 'Give 'em no mind!' he said.

She still danced with her lovely shawl, but in secret: for she discovered that she could make strange things happen. She could make the geese lay. But she did not want her mother to notice a big increase in eggs, so Tegen was careful to dance for only one bird at a time.

The days lengthened and began to shorten again. Samhain was approaching, leaves were falling from the trees and the summer fields were flooding. Most of the charcoal was burned in the winter months, but until frost-fall, when Griff would go to his first charcoal fires alone, he crushed lead and silver-carrying rocks for Clesek to smelt. It was hot work. Even hotter was Tegen's job of pumping bellows for the furnace.

'I's thirsty!' Griff called one day. 'Hey, Clesek, can we's stop and get a drink from the stream?'

Clesek did not raise his head from the silver he was softening in a small triangular crucible. 'Yes, but Tegen must be quick. This has to stay at just the right temperature or it's ruined. I'll need the bellows again soon.'

Within moments Tegen was standing next to Griff, ankle deep in cool water, splashing it over her head and arms.

But she had left the horn of the bellows in the furnace and soon stinking yellow flames were licking across the wooden paddles. Clesek bent low to pull the bellows out, but the crucible of melted silver was still in his other hand.

As he moved, the lively liquid metal splashed across his face.

Screaming in agony, he fell forward across the dome of the furnace.

Both Tegen and Griff ran back as if all the dark spirits of the abyss were on their heels. 'Da!' Tegen screamed, 'Da! Griff, pull him off the furnace, his belly must be on fire!' Each taking a leg, they tugged until Clesek lay on the cool floor.

As her father fell and rolled on to his back, Tegen could see boiling silver splashed across his face and beard, and weeping down his neck. Ripping a length off her wet shift, she pressed it against the livid weals that were swelling on his skin. 'Fetch Mam. Quickly!' she shouted. 'She's with the goats.'

Griff hesitated as if he hadn't understood, then sprang to life and sprinted through the vegetable garden to the enclosure at the top of the slope.

Tegen sat on the floor and with shaking hands lifted Clesek's head into her lap and stroked his forehead. 'Oh, Da, I am so sorry. It was my fault, please don't die, please don't.'

Moments later, Nessa came panting, her face wild with fear. 'What happened? Oh my, is he all right? Please say he's all right!' She bent over her man and pulled the wet cloths back to show the huge red welts with pricks and rivulets of silver like ripe boils.

'He's still alive, Mam,' Tegen managed to say between welling sobs.

Nessa turned to Griff. 'Help us get him inside!' Then

between them they half hauled, half carried Clesek into the house and laid him on his bed.

Suddenly Nessa turned on Tegen and glared. 'It's vengeance! I know it is! The spirits have seen us!' She poked Tegen with a harsh finger. 'You . . . you called this down on us with your twirling around! I *told* you something nasty would happen if you messed with magic! Do you think I haven't seen you?'

Tegen opened her mouth in disbelief. 'But I . . .'

But Nessa was not listening; she was slapping her forehead and wailing a charm to turn away the evil eye.

Griff stood staring from one foster-parent to the other with wide eyes. His tongue hung loose from his open mouth as he looked at Tegen. Her heart thumped as she realized with horror it was up to *her* to save her father's life. 'Get clean water and some linen rags,' she ordered. Griff moved with surprising speed. Still shaking, she began to gingerly pick the silver splashes away from Clesek's face. Large patches of skin and strands of black beard came with each piece. She did not know whether she was doing the right thing or not, but on each peeled area she placed a small piece of wet cloth.

'Send for Derowen!' Nessa wailed from her corner. 'We need help, quickly!'

Tegen's heart sank. 'No, Mam! Not her! Please, she hates me.'

Nessa glared at Tegen. 'This isn't a time to worry about

silly things like that. We need help to save your father's life.'

'Then let Griff go for Gilda; at least she is kind. Derowen is a witch.'

Nessa slapped her daughter's face. 'How dare you accuse her of such things? She is the wise woman. Shut your mouth, child. Don't we have enough evil spirits in the house today without you spewing more? They will curse us. Your father will die for sure! Anyway, Gilda is only a midwife. She won't know the right spells!'

Tegen did not take her eyes or her hands away from what she was doing. Her father's eyelids were fluttering. He was coming round. Sweat, blood and water streaked his cheek and neck. Was a fever starting already? She wiped his forehead with a cool, wet cloth.

'Do as you think best, Mam, but Da will need herbs and kindness to get him through this, not witchcraft.' Tegen relied on her mother's fear of magic and her gamble paid off.

Nessa sighed and wiped her eyes on her sleeve. 'Griff, run to the village and bring Gilda. Quickly! Do you understand?' He did not hesitate, but sprang through the door and down the track that led to the village.

The sun had scarcely moved a hand's breadth in the sky before Gilda, led by Griff, came red-faced and puffing up to the house.

They found Nessa on a stool, staring down at her husband. Tegen was crouched in a corner, hugging herself. All her strength and decisiveness had gone. There was nothing else she could do. She felt like a small child again, needing comforting. But there was none to be had.

Gilda looked at Clesek and sat on the edge of the bed. 'What happened? I couldn't really understand what Griff was saying.'

Nessa stared at Clesek and pointed a shaking hand at Tegen. 'Her. She did it.'

Tegen turned to the wall and stared at the whitewashed stones.

Gilda frowned. 'How do you feel, Clesek?' she asked gently. She stroked his hair; then she lifted one of the dressings and saw the reddened wounds. 'Do you feel sick? Did you get any in your eyes?' She did not stop talking for a moment as one by one she peeled back the wet cloths very gently. 'Someone has taken most of the silver away. Good.' She turned to Nessa, who was pacing the room, chewing her fingers. 'I need your help,' she said firmly and calmly, placing a hand on the woman's arm, 'Boil me a handful of sage and a handful of lavender flowers. Let it cool, then bring it to me.'

Gilda turned her attention to the trembling figure huddled in the corner. 'Tegen,' she said softly, 'close your eyes. What do you see?'

'What?' Tegen stared at the midwife.

'What do you *see*, child?' Gilda looked hard at her.

'Think!' she demanded. 'What does the Goddess show you in your mind? Can you see your father healed?'

Tegen closed her eyes. 'Yes, I see him well, but he has white scars.'

'Good. Now make it real. Imagine coolness and fresh skin on your father's face. You have to *bring* it to him.'

Without waiting for an answer Gilda called to Griff: 'Fetch me fresh cloths and a beaker of cold water.'

Tegen stood and leaned against the cool stone wall. She closed her eyes and breathed deeply. Strength surged back to her as she focused. *How* could she do what Gilda said? In her mind she went back to the festival, when she danced with the green shawl and sent the beautiful strangers home in their boats. She was dancing – dancing and *making it happen*.

She did not stop to think. She ran to her crook loft to fetch her shawl. In her head she could hear the little drummer boy striking a rhythm – different from the one he had used at Beltane, but the right one for Clesek's need. As soon as Tegen returned to her father's side, she tied the silk around her waist and started to dance.

As she moved she imagined the angry red flesh on Clesek's face cooled, and the swelling gone. The bleeding tears in his skin healed and pale scars stretched across his cheeks and neck. His grizzled beard was thick and black again.

Tegen danced and danced, watching the healing over and

over again in her mind, until she started to stumble and sway. Gilda caught her in her strong arms. 'Enough, child. He is sleeping.'

But Nessa had returned with the cooled tisane. When she saw what Tegen was doing she strode forward and grabbed her daughter by the shoulder. 'Out!' she ordered, her voice strangled with fear. 'I trusted you! You said he needed herbs not spells – and what do you do? Start your witchcraft as soon as my back is turned! Get outside!' She pushed her towards the door.

Tegen staggered, her head swimming, her body weak. She felt sick. Her knees wanted to give way.

'Do as your mother says,' Gilda said quietly. 'Go and get some air.' Then she took the bowl of sweet-smelling liquid from Nessa and began to wash Clesek's wounds.

Tegen ran into the stable and collapsed on the straw. She blamed her own carelessness for the accident, but she didn't deserve to be called a witch – she had only tried to make things right. It wasn't fair! She kicked and punched at a bale of hay until her fury subsided.

A little while later, Gilda slipped in beside her. She took Tegen's aching head into her lap, loosened her plaits and stroked her long dark hair. They sat in silence staring out into the courtyard until ghostly owls began to swoop in the chilly half-light.

'What happened? Why did I go so wobbly?' Tegen asked at last, sitting up and rubbing warmth into her arms and legs.

'You healed him. It took all your strength,' Gilda said gently.

They had not heard footsteps approaching. 'Think that if you like,' Nessa sniffed derisively. In the semi-dark Tegen could make out her mother's eyes, cold and narrow with resentment. But she did not want to move from her nest by Gilda's side. She felt safe and loved.

Nessa folded her arms and scowled. She wished she dared love her child as freely as Gilda did. But it wasn't safe. She longed to gather Tegen up and hold her, and tell her how much she loved her . . . but she dared not. The spirits would take her away for sure. And now the wretched midwife was trying to be a mother to her Tegen . . . But jealously had to be squashed as well.

'You did some quick thinking, child, I'll grant you that,' Nessa snapped, 'but healing is for Derowen and the druids. Not for the likes of us.' She nodded her head towards the open doorway. 'Gilda, you had better be on your way, it is getting dark. Thank you for your help. Here is your payment.' She thrust a twisted linen scrap into the midwife's hand. 'I would be grateful if you'd say nothing in the village. It is not good to be noticed by the spirits – or by those who deal with them. I don't want any more bad luck brought down on my roof. We've had more than enough for one day.'

Nessa stood by the stable door with her back to them. She hugged her thin frame and looked out at the night.

Gilda eased Tegen aside, stood and nodded stiffly. 'I understand,' she said. She opened the cloth and found a silver pin, prettily shaped with a flower head. 'But remember this: your girl is gifted, even more than you were. The stars danced for her the night she was born and she has magic in those steps she makes.'

Nessa pushed the stable door a little wider. 'We are too busy for magic and dancing up here. We have to work for a living. Good day.'

Angry, Gilda brushed the straw from her shift and twisted her mass of greying hair under a bone comb. Then without another word she walked down the path between the trees.

Tegen sighed as she replaited her hair. So much was her fault. Now Gilda was being sent away because of her . . . She hung her head and walked inside. She wished she could run after Gilda and apologize – or at least explain that her Mam meant no harm. She longed to go home with Gilda and talk about what had happened. But she dared not.

Instead she tried to slip back up to her loft to put her green shawl away, but as she started to climb the ladder Clesek called to her. She went to him and sat on his bed. His face was swathed in damp linen, and his black beard poked out from under the folds.

He reached out and took her hand. 'I saw what you did,' he said.

She bit her lip. 'I am sorry I was so careless, Da. How

could I leave the bellows in the fire like that?' She leaned across and hugged him, her eyes burning as she tried not to cry.

'I know, little bird, but these things happen and I will live. The pain has almost gone.' Tegen wiped her tears on her sleeve and looked up at him. His face was still livid with red around the sage- and lavender-soaked bandages, but his blue eyes were smiling and proud.

'I wasn't talking about the accident. It was what you did afterwards. I could feel the pain drifting away as you danced. But keep quiet about it. Try not to prance around weaving spells too often. You don't want to get branded a witch. You'll never get a husband like that. You dance very prettily and it might bring a good man here to help me, but take my advice and keep your magic to yourself. Please. Especially for Mam's sake. You know how these things frighten her . . .'

Tegen nodded and climbed up to her attic. There she lay on her bed thinking. She had often danced before the Beltane fair and nothing strange or magical had ever happened. Why had things been different since then? She stretched her fingers between the soft folds of the silk.

Then she gasped and sat up straight. That's it! It's the *shawl* that does the magic! Tegen chewed the ends of her plaits as she thought. Everyone gets scared by what I do – yet I only try to help! Everything has gone wrong lately! Mam's in a strop, dear old Gilda's been sent away and now

Da says I've got to keep my magic quiet . . . But that doesn't make sense! If the Lady's given me gifts it's because I'm meant to help people; not to hide.

Sadly Tegen fingered the delicate silky fringe. 'Should I destroy my lovely shawl?' she whispered to the cool darkness above her head. She tried to picture herself throwing the silk into the fire downstairs. But even in her imagination she couldn't make herself do it.

She rolled over on her bed and buried her face in her straw mattress. 'It doesn't make sense,' she sighed. 'I can heal when I dance with my shawl. How can that be wrong?'

Tegen couldn't sleep that night. She stared into the darkness and thought. Suddenly she went icy cold. If she had the 'Gift', she would have to become old Derowen's apprentice! She turned over and buried her face in her pillow. 'Never!' She thumped her mattress. 'I will destroy the shawl and stop dancing. I will never work for Derowen!'

After a few moments she loosened the shutters of the little wind-eye next to her bed. She stared at the constellation of the Watching Woman. The stars hung above her parents' home as if they were taking care of her. She loved those stars. Hadn't Gilda said they had danced the night she had been born?

But tonight as she looked up, unease gripped her . . .

The alignments between the nine glistening lights were not as they should be.

6. Witton

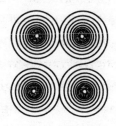

Tegen jumped out of bed, pulled on a woollen smock and pushed her feet into her clogs.

Gilda was right, she *could* see things in her mind. Right now she could see Witton's sunken eyes and toothless mouth wearing a look of forlorn despair. And there was heat – too much heat everywhere.

The old druid needed her – *now!*

She would have to hurry. It was a long walk to Witton's roundhouse and the lanes were often muddy. Rummaging in the darkness she found her magical green shawl and twisted it into a belt around her waist. Then she crept downstairs, tugged on her cloak and lifted the door latch. The loud click of the iron tongue gave her away.

'Where are you going?' Her mother called out sleepily from the back room.

'To the privy!' she lied. It was no good telling the truth.

Her mother would never let her go. Tegen was certain that Witton's life depended on her, but she would need help. After what had happened at Beltane, he might not let her near him. Perhaps if Griff came he could pretend to do the healing while she worked in the background? Halfhead or not, Witton was very fond of the boy.

She stepped out into the courtyard and ran across to the stable. 'Griff! Griff!' She hissed through the doorway. '*Wake up!*' There was no answer. Everything was silent; even the pony scarcely breathed.

Suddenly a loud snort made her jump and almost choke with fear.

Then it came again.

And again.

It was Griff. Snoring! Tegen didn't know whether to hug him with relief or kick him for scaring her. It was going to be a battle to wake him. She stepped inside and shook his shoulder, but he only moaned, scratched under his arm and turned over.

'Griff, I need you. Witton needs you. Wake up!'

'Yes,' he yawned, 'Witton needs yous, Tegen. Hurry up, jump jump!' Then he was snoring again.

Tegen sighed. This was proving to be impossible. She might as well be trying to waken the hills, but she dared not go to Witton alone. She felt around for a wooden feed bucket and filled it from the trough in the courtyard, then splashed a little water on to Griff's face.

'Oi!' he howled, springing up from his hay bed.

'Shh!' Tegen warned. 'Be quiet! Don't wake Clesek and Nessa – they'll be fitting furious and won't let us go to help Witton.'

'Whassamatter with Witton?' Griff demanded, rubbing his face dry on his sleeve. 'Witton my friend.'

Tegen sighed. Was she *ever* going to get anywhere? She spoke very slowly and clearly: 'Witton is in trouble and we have to go to him. He doesn't like me. He hit me at the fair, remember? I need you to come too. You've got to, Griff, he won't let *me* help!'

Griff yawned. 'Good idea. You go. Griff tired. Night night,' and he lay down to sleep once more.

It was hopeless. Tegen would just have to do whatever she could on her own. But she needed a disguise. In the darkness, she took off her smock and groped around for Griff's shirt and breeches, then pulled them on over her shift. Breaking a piece of twine from the end of a bale of hay, she tied her long plaits back and swapped her cloak for Griff's, pulling the hood low over her head so it partly hid her face. Satisfied, she set off down the hill to find the path by the stream. The way was dark and muddy, but she knew it well.

As she walked, clouds blew across the night sky and it started to rain. At the twist in the path she looked across the valley to the world beyond, where the blackness of the trees gave way to an expanse of lighter darkness ahead. Now that autumn was on its way the flat meadowland below was patched with pale mirrors of water.

That is a strong magic, she thought. Icy, muddy seas in the winter months put on a shawl of rich green meadows for the cows in the summer. Two worlds wrapped up in one place. It's a bit like me, I suppose. Everything looks ordinary from the outside, but when I pick up my green shawl, strange things happen!

She shivered and bent her head. She was too drenched to think about difficult things. There was not far to go now. Old Witton's roundhouse was built at the head of the valley, standing on its own, beyond the village fence, in front of the gate. That way he could meet all the spirits that swept across the skies and bar the way to those that came in anger. The path was level now and Tegen began to run, longing to get out of the battering rain. Ahead, one or two slits of welcoming light gleamed from between the thatch roof and the walls of Witton's house. She would soon be warm and dry.

In the patchy light, she saw a large black bird swoop down towards Witton's roundhouse, but it screeched and twisted away at her approach. Instinctively she knew it meant the old man would not die that night.

Tegen made sure her hood was as low as it could be and ran up the stony path to Witton's door. Out of breath at the top, she called out and knocked. Her heart sank as someone opened up and glared into the dark, her figure outlined black and ominous against the light.

Derowen!

A blast of hot, sour air caught in Tegen's nose. Suddenly she found herself shaking. What was she going to say? What was she going to *do*? She was only a child, she must have been mad coming all this way in the middle of the night. She fought the urge to run away. 'Er . . . Hello . . .' She blinked.

Derowen scowled and barred her way. 'What do you want? Go away. The druid is ill and I'm certainly too busy to deal with children. *Be off!*'

Before Tegen could open her mouth again, a weak voice came from inside the room. 'Let him in, Derowen. It is the one we have been waiting for at last. He has come to heal me, I know it.'

The wise woman sniffed and stepped backwards, making room for the visitor to pass.

Tegen tugged the cloak's hood right across her face, but she could feel Derowen's malevolence clawing at her back as she crossed the threshold. She had never been inside Witton's home before. Everything was very different from her parents' stone-built cottage.

She dared not look properly; she just squinted from under the folds of the wool. The dark interior would fit four or five men laying head to foot across the floor. All around the walls were wooden benches draped with hides. In the centre, a fire blazed within a ring of hearthstones. High above, the tarry thatch roof was supported by blackened beams. Here and there thick wooden pegs were hung with tin ladles, pans, bunches of herbs and dried fish. The rising heat made the clutter dance, casting long, umber shadows against the limed walls.

The bed-platform built against the far wall was empty. Instead, the old druid shivered on a rough mattress of straw by the fire. He was thin and pale, but his cheeks were flushed red with fever and his eyes seemed unnaturally bright. He lifted a hand towards Tegen and she came and knelt by his bed. He put his frail fingers on her head and she clutched at her cloak so he could not push it back.

'My son, I have waited a long time for you,' he panted. 'Thank the Goddess that you are here at last. Pull back your hood and let me see you. You are wet through, child. Take off your things. Let Derowen dry them for you.'

Although Tegen longed to be dry, she gripped at the cloak with white knuckles. 'No, Father,' she whispered gruffly. 'It isn't the time for you to know my face or for me to worry about wet clothes. Tonight is for healing.'

'Do you know what to do, boy? My talismans and potions are in the back room, Derowen will show you, but of course she can't help you once you cross the threshold. It is forbidden for women.'

Tegen hesitated as she tried not to panic. She hadn't anticipated this. 'No. Thank you, Father. I need nothing.' She knew Derowen was staring at her. She felt icy dread begin to creep up her spine. What could she say? She knew very little about healing and even less about how magic worked. Surreptitiously she slid her fingers inside her cloak, touching the precious shawl. Silently she prayed: 'May the Goddess let you work tonight, *please*.' She closed her eyes and tried to see what the Lady was showing her, as Gilda had taught her. All she could see was the odd alignment of the stars within the Watching Woman. If only Gilda was there. She would know . . .

Suddenly Tegen found herself speaking. 'The Watching Woman showed me what needs to be done.'

'The Goddess spoke to you?' Witton tried to sit, his breath rasping painfully. His eyes shone brighter than ever. He frowned at the tightly draped, skinny figure before him, then let himself fall back on to the bed. 'How do you know it was her?'

Tegen spoke quietly. 'She danced for me the night I was born.' She immediately regretted what she had said, for the room fell silent. Even the fire seemed to stop its crackling in the hearth.

Witton and Derowen exchanged glances.

Tegen took a deep breath. 'The stars were out of alignment tonight. That's how I know what I should do to heal you. And . . . and . . .' As another image came unbidden into her head, 'and . . . your death is near, but not yet. A crow flew near your roundhouse tonight, but it did not land.' She held her breath. How *dare* she speak like that to such a venerable druid?

'That is a true sign,' the old man whispered and closed his eyes.

Tegen put her free hand to his head. It was burning. He smelled of stale sweat and rancid straw, but there was also an aroma of stewing vegetables – beetroot and cabbage. At least the old witch wasn't trying to force meat into him. A vegetable broth was all that was needed, but not yet. 'Father, you must come outside and cool yourself in the night breezes. Mother Derowen, the straw in the bed has poison in it. Please fetch clean bedding and a fresh shirt.'

The old woman did not move. She simply stared in hate and disbelief, her shoulders hunched and her chin jutted forward between her rope-like plaits.

'Do it!' Witton barked with all his little strength. 'Do whatever the boy says.' He coughed and struggled for a few moments. 'Is there anything else? What herbs do you want? What spells will you use?'

'None, thank you, Father. The magic is this: when you come inside again, the fire must be doused so it is not so hot. Then you must bathe in water sprinkled with lavender and sage . . .' Tegen hesitated, she had no idea whether they were the right herbs, but Gilda had used them on Clesek; they were the first ones that came to her mind. She swallowed hard and continued: ' . . . and every time the candle burns a finger's depth, Derowen must moisten your face and hands with cool, fresh water and give you a beaker of water to sip. She must do this until dawn. Then the fever will leave. Now, put your arm around my shoulder and lean on me. We will go outside while Derowen works and we will give our thanks to the Goddess.'

Tegen crouched down to help Witton to his feet, her heart in her mouth. Where had all those words come from? She was terrified and exhilarated at the same time. What if she was wrong? What if she was right?

Witton was too weak to protest. He put his arm around Tegen and allowed himself to be helped to stand, his bones cracking and grinding as he moved.

Derowen crossed her arms across her long breasts and scowled. 'It's too dangerous. How do you know this boy isn't a fraud? *I've* been the wise woman in this valley since my first blood. I know all there is to know about fevers and agues. Did I not sacrifice a goose and give you the blood to drink? You're supposed to be kept hot until the fever breaks. You can't go outside. Look, it's raining! You've no cloak or amulets about you!'

Witton dismissed her grumbling with a wave of his hand. 'Get on with it! I am sick of the stench in here myself. The child's word is mine . . .' He stopped to catch his breath. 'All he has said will do no harm. It is time I greeted the Watching Woman before I die. Now shut your mouth and do as you are told!'

Derowen muttered and moaned resentfully, but she pulled her plaits back and knotted them behind her head, then kilted her skirt so she could work more easily. Tegen prayed that the old witch would never find out who she was, for her vengeance would be very swift and very sure.

Outside, the night air was sweet and clean. The shower had passed and the sky above was clearing. The few stars were brilliant in the blackness.

Tegen helped the old druid hobble outside and leaned him against the wall like a fragile child. What was she going to do? How was she going to heal him? Tegen wished that Griff were there to act out the part of the healer while she danced in the shadows. Alone she dared not dance. Not here and now. Witton would know who she was immediately. She would have to do the real healing on the way home.

The old druid was looking at her intently. She had to do or say something quickly.

'See?' Tegen opened her hand towards the sky. 'The Watching Woman is here to greet you. It is a good omen. You will live.'

Witton leaned his head very close to hers. 'Show me, boy, how did the Goddess speak to you?'

Tegen closed her eyes for a moment and tried to remember what it was in the stars that had spoken to her. She tried to see in her mind's eye what she needed to know. She relaxed, let go of her cloak and pointed to the constellation. 'There – the fourth and fifth stars are too close together. When that happens, there is too much heat around the heart, do you see? That needs to be cooled.'

Witton turned his head skywards. 'I see,' he said. Then with a small tug at the folds of Tegen's cloak he almost managed to pull it back. Terrified, she grabbed at the cloth and turned her back. 'I warn you, Father, if you ever see my face I will be powerless to help you!'

Witton peered long and hard at the cloaked figure in the starlight. The back and shoulders were thin. The height was right for a thirteen-year-old, but beneath the cloak, the clogs and feet were too small. Was this really the Star Dancer? 'Very well, child. Something about you feels familiar, but tonight I will trust you. What is your name?'

Tegen felt a stab of panic. What could she say? She dared not tell the truth, and she dared not tell a lie either. The old man would know if she did. She had not been told her real name yet: that would not be given until her woman's bleeding. What should she reply? Suddenly she had inspiration. 'My name doesn't matter. A spirit sent me.'

'Who?'

'One who cares about you.'

Witton's voice was sad. 'I am very tired. I need to lie down.'

Tegen left the old man leaning against the mud and wattle wall of his house as she looked in to see if Derowen had made everything ready. Inside, the old woman was still muttering crossly as she poured water into a wooden tub by a much-reduced fire. The cottage smelled less evil. Tegen turned back to Witton. 'Come, Father, you may go in now. How do you feel?'

'Strengthened by the night air, thank you.' Slowly he hobbled inside. Tegen helped him walk to where the bath was placed.

'Wash him well, Mother. Give him no food tonight. He can have your good vegetable broth tomorrow. For now, only plenty of clear water to drink. When I go, you must leave the door wide open. I will seal it against evil spirits.'

She bit her lip. Did she really know how to do that? O Lady Goddess help me! she thought. What if I can't seal the door? Witton will be exposed to all the creatures of the night, both good and bad.

Derowen scowled, took the pot of broth from the fire and pushed past Tegen, slopping the contents everywhere.

Tegen turned to go, ignoring the insult. As her father had said, she must keep her mouth shut.

Derowen made the sign against the evil eye at her back. Tegen felt the curse coming towards her, and with a flick of her fingers she brushed it aside.

While the wise woman helped the druid into the herb-scented water, Tegen went outside and closed her eyes. She would not let herself think about being scared. She concentrated on thoughts of keeping evil spirits at bay so Witton could recover. Soon the rhythms she needed for her dancing magic came into her head. She untied her green silk shawl and began to move in a patterned circle all around the roundhouse. The ground was sticky with mud. She wished she could kick her clogs off to move more easily, but if Derowen came out after her, she would have to run.

At last the circle was complete, so Tegen blessed the doorway and made herself scarce. A glance at the sky showed her that the stars were beginning to fade.

7. Derowen's Trap

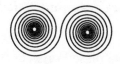

Tegen ran until she was gasping for breath. Just as she came to the top of the hill and within sight of her home, she slipped in a puddle and fell face down. She wanted to cry as the blood trickled down her chin from a cut lip. Her eyes were full of gritty dirt and she was wet through to her skin. There was no time to feel sorry for herself. Dawn was coming fast and she had to get back before Griff missed his clothes.

As quietly as she could, Tegen slipped into the barn and pulled off the cloak, sodden breeches and shirt, then draped them over a bale of hay. She picked up her own dry things and felt very guilty. She knew Griff had little else to wear, and because of her he would now be miserable even before the day had started.

But breeches could be washed and dried. Witton might have died if she had not gone to him.

Tegen splashed her face in the horse trough and ran into the kitchen, drying herself on the skirt of her shift.

Just at that moment, Griff stumbled out of the barn in his thin undershirt. He peed against the stone wall, then stamped back inside to get dressed. He cursed as he pulled his wet, smelly tunic over his head.

'Tegen! Tegen!' he yelled. 'Them piskies have been atta my things. They done pissed on everything – lookee!'

She ran out, caught Griff by the hand and brought him into the kitchen. 'Never mind, take them off and I'll put them by the fire to dry. Wrap yourself in my cloak for a bit. Here. Mam has been simmering porridge next to the fire all night and it's ready now. I'll put honey and butter on for you. If you're warm on the inside, you'll be warm on the outside too.'

She served him a large bowlful and spread the wet clothes over a couple of stools. They were just beginning to steam nicely when Clesek came in, unwinding his bandages.

'How are you this morning, Da?' Tegen asked, stifling a yawn.

Clesek stepped nearer the light of the wind-eye, stooping so Tegen could look at his burns. Thick dark scabs had already formed across his skin. There was no sign of swelling or yellow pus. While Tegen looked, Clesek jerked his thumb at Griff. 'Hurry up, lad, I need you to get into the village to sell the spare charcoal today. No time for sitting around, you've got a man's work to do!'

Tegen tried to tell him that Griff's clothes were wet, but Clesek was not in a mood for discussion.

'Warm clothes are for babies. Get out there now, boy, before I put the pony's whip across your backside!'

Clesek was a fair man, but he expected to be obeyed straight away. Griff swallowed the rest of his porridge in three huge spoonfuls.

Tegen touched her green shawl, still twisted around her waist. Then she tried to envisage Griff being dry and warm as she draped the sodden cloak around his shoulders. She felt guilty, but she could do nothing more.

Outside, Griff harnessed the pony to the cart and Tegen helped with the loading. The sacks were heavy and damp. That would do the charcoal no good, and the glowering sky threatened more rain before noon. Autumn was getting a grip on the land; the winter waters would be rising over the meadows soon.

'I'll go with him,' Tegen said. 'I can make sure he gets the right price.'

Clesek grunted, pulled on his jerkin and went to his workshop.

Tegen was worried that if Derowen was around, she might recognize Griff's cloak, so she tugged it off him.

'What you'm a-doin'?' Griff moaned. 'Give'tus back, Tegen. Mine.'

She smiled. 'I'm just putting it on right,' she said as she flipped the cloak inside out before wrapping it round him again. Her mother had taught her that would also ward off any unwelcome spells. She squeezed his hand and tapped the pony on the rump with a stick. 'Gee-up,' she said.

As they walked down the slope towards the village, the cart slipped on the fallen leaves. Sliding uncontrollably, the wheels cracked on every stone in the way. Griff held the pony's bridle tightly and chatted gently into the creature's ears. Tegen walked behind, watching the sacks and steadying any that looked as if they might fall.

But she was becoming increasingly worried. It wasn't just the struggle to keep the cart on the track that bothered her. Something was wrong. Someone was looking for her, reaching out to her . . . and it wasn't old Witton. All around, the nearly leafless trees seemed to be crowding in, stretching their twiggy fingers, trying to pluck at her hair and eyes. The gold of autumn was rapidly turning to menacing dankness. Taking a corner of her magic shawl, Tegen traced the pattern of the Watching Woman on to her right palm. She didn't want to scare Griff, so she pretended to be brushing mud off his clothes while she made the sign over him as well. Although the stars rested in Tir na nÓg during the daylight hours, Tegen knew that she would never be alone, for the Goddess was in the land as well as in the sky.

As they entered the village palisade, the press of people made movement with the cart difficult. The path that led to the central marketplace was narrow, winding between clusters of heavily thatched roundhouses. Geese, dogs and small children ran free, causing chaos.

But at last they turned into the muddy square and Tegen's breath caught in her throat. Derowen was standing on a large bale of straw, dressed in her best blue gown, hair plaited with ivy strands and red ochre smeared on her face and hands. She was decked for a festival or a great announcement.

Griff stopped the pony by hauling on its bridle. He looked at his foster-sister with wide eyes. 'Wa's happening? Wa's goin' on? It's summat nasty, in't it?'

Tegen put one hand on Griff's and with the other she gestured him to be silent. They both stood still. Watching.

He was quite right, something sinister was happening. Derowen was smiling as she performed to the excited crowd, although her voice sounded like a knife being scraped on a sharpening stone.

'I tell you, a new druid is here. One wiser and greater than all the rest. His name is Star Dancer. He appeared to *me* in Witton's house. Miraculous it was. He told me I was doing all the right things and, apart from the final spell, which only he knew, I had almost saved Father Witton myself!'

The crowd muttered and nodded their approval. No one

doubted Derowen's skills, although they all feared the spirits she met with to achieve those ends. The old woman drew herself up straight and put her bony hands together, pursing her lips in a look of intense satisfaction.

'So, will Witton live?' Enor, Budok's woman, wanted to know.

'Live? He's practically dancing this morning! It was all I could do to make him stay in bed!'

'So where is this Star Dancer?' asked old Fionn, so bent he always looked as if he was searching for something.

'What's he like?' demanded Gwion, a straw-haired lad who never believed anything anyone said.

'Who is he?' squealed a child Tegen couldn't see. 'Is it me?' The crowd laughed.

A young woman pressed forward, clutching a motionless bundle wrapped in a grey wool shawl. 'Will he cure my baby?' Her voice was full of anguish and fear. Tegen's heart went out to her. But she dared not do anything; in fact some instinct told her to duck down behind the cart.

Griff refused to be pulled down as well. He stood mesmerized by the display. Then to Tegen's horror he began to slowly inch his way forward towards Derowen. 'Come back, stay with me,' she hissed, but he ignored her.

By now, the whole village was present and the wise woman was relishing her power. 'One question at a time. One . . . at . . . a . . . time.' She smiled, showing her very long teeth. 'I'm certain he won't stay around if you all pester him like this. Why, he's only a slip of a lad, and yes, I saw him quite plainly.'

'What does he look like?'

'Is he here?'

'When's he coming back?'

'What's a Star Dancer?'

Just then, Derowen caught sight of Griff staring open-mouthed and wide-eyed right at her. At first she greeted him with her usual sneer, but then her look changed to shock, then horror, finally settling into a broad, satisfied grin. 'Why, look, there he is now! Come here, *dear* child.' She stretched out her bony hands towards him and beckoned.

Griff was panic-stricken. He glanced back but couldn't see Tegen. There was no escape from Derowen. The old woman terrified him. She had often beaten him for being stupid or for getting in her way. Now she wanted him to stand next to her in front of everyone!

The wise woman beckoned again and the crowd pushed the white-faced boy right up to where she stood. He looked around in panic. Tegen leaped forward and managed to grab his hand, but they were wrenched apart. Derowen smiled as the crowd heaved Griff up on to the straw bale beside her. She gripped him by the shoulders and turned him to face the crowd. 'Look!' she proclaimed gleefully. 'I stained the boy's clothes with beetroot juice while he was in Witton's house so that I would know him again. See.' She tugged at Griff's breeches and held up a brownish-purple stain for the crowd to see.

Tegen bit her lip . . . she hadn't been careful enough. The old woman *had* pushed against her with the cooking pot . . . She must have daubed the breeches with some of the broth.

She groaned to herself. He'll get into terrible trouble and it's all my fault as usual. I've got to do something.

'We must take him to Witton's house!' announced Derowen, her hand firmly grasping Griff's arm. 'The Star Dancer must be properly thanked and proclaimed.' She jumped down from the bale of straw and pulled him after her.

Soon the whole crowd had joined in, cheering and dragging the terrified Griff further and further away from Tegen.

'Help!' he squeaked, looking around, his small eyes wide in his flat, pale face.

I won't let him go through this alone! Tegen told herself. She crept from her hiding place and struggled to think quickly. She didn't have time to close her eyes and 'see' what the Goddess might put into her mind. She cast around and searched for Gilda in the crowd, but there was no sign of her cheery face. What could Tegen do by herself to help Griff? She couldn't confess. No one would believe her and if they did . . . if they did . . . who knew what would happen? Tegen's hands shook, and she began to sweat, despite the chill wind.

The noisy crowd had almost pushed and shoved its way out of the marketplace. She could still hear the terrified squeak of Griff's half-broken voice calling her name.

Tegen swallowed hard and forced herself to focus. Griff loved her and needed her. Her father's advice to keep her mouth shut was more easily said than done. She could hear his voice in her head: 'Silver is a funny metal,' he said. 'It is easy to work, but at the same time you have to be firm and shape it the way you want it to be, or the piece you are making will be ruined.' Tegen knew she must take control.

If she followed Griff to Witton's home to try to explain things to him, he would recognize her, echoes of her magic would be everywhere. But instinctively she knew the time wasn't right for him to know yet . . . She rubbed her face where he had struck her at Beltane. The timing had to be right.

Elbowing her way through the crowd, Tegen called out in as high-pitched a squeak as she could manage so the old woman wouldn't recognize her voice from the night before: 'Hey, Mother, stop!'

The crowd halted and fell silent. Derowen looked around suspiciously. 'Who's that?'

'It's me, Tegen, the silver-worker's daughter.' She wriggled forward through the people, then bowed her head. 'Forgive me, Mother Derowen, but it couldn't have been Griff. He was asleep in our barn all last night. I know because I woke up. We had a prowler. I heard footsteps and a door shutting, and I went to have a look. Griff was fast asleep. Just after dawn I heard more noises and I went out again. It was raining very hard but there was enough light to see someone running into the barn. When Griff came in for breakfast his clothes were all wet, but his undershirt was quite dry.'

'Is this true?' Derowen demanded of Griff, digging her claws painfully into the boy's shoulder.

Griff's knees were knocking as he stammered, 'I dunno nothin', Mother Derowen. But . . . but . . . when I went to bed, me clothes was dry, and when I woke up, them piskies had a-peed on them. Look how wet and soppin' I is!'

Derowen held the boy at arm's length and glared at him in disgust. Suddenly, with a rush of fury she shoved him so hard he fell sprawling in the mud. 'How *dare* you imitate a druid? You lying, cheating brat! I should have you stoned to death for this!' and she drew back her lips and hissed.

Everyone in the crowd shrank back in terror. Derowen was beginning a curse! They didn't want to get caught in it.

Tegen ran forward and stood in front of the dazed Griff. 'Forgive him, Mother, he's only a halfhead. Perhaps the real new druid wants to remain unknown a little longer and disguised himself in Griff's clothes. Who knows? I'm certain Griff knows nothing. He was asleep every time I looked. Honestly.'

Derowen spat at Griff. 'I'll be merciful this time, as you're young and a halfwit, but next time you try to deceive me with lies I'll send the piskies to pinch you all the way up the hill to Witton's house, then he can deal with you as he sees fit!' She raised her fist and cuffed him around the head.

Griff's eyes widened and his bottom lip quivered, but remembering he was a man now, he got up from the mud and took a step forward. 'Tegen an' me ain't dun nothin' wrong, not nohow, Mother Derowen. We'm both good 'uns. Blame them piskies not us if there bin any mischief. I'm a-takin' my sister home cos you's full of nasty stuff!'

Tegen looked from one to the other. She couldn't think of what to do or say.

Derowen's eyes were black as iron and her face quite white under the smeared ochre. She knitted her grey eyebrows and pushed her face into Griff's. 'You'll die for that insult, boy. Do you hear me? You'll die and it'll be nasty and painful and it won't be cosy-comfy in your bed with that scrawny foster-sister of yours to look after you. Nor will it be with valour on the battlefield: it'll be in a cold, dark, wet place, and what is more I'll make sure that in your next life you come back as a wild pig for my stewpot!' Then she stepped away, scooped up a lump of mud and threw it at Griff with all the malicious force her strong arm could wield, hitting him in the chest.

'*Ow!*' he squealed.

'*Stop it!*' Tegen screamed, but she was pushed out of the way.

Derowen turned to the crowd. 'Do what you like with him,' she said. 'He's beneath contempt.' Then she strutted away, a smirk on her face. But before Tegen could get to Griff, the villagers had closed in around him.

'Die, liar!' several voices yelled. Some picked up mud and stones and began to pelt him. He cowered and looked around in panic as warm pee dribbled down his legs.

'Leave off!' shouted a bull-necked man who came and stood beside him. No one argued with Budok; he could best any fighter in the village. 'You have no right to condemn the lad. This is a druid matter; he'll be tried properly when Father Witton is well enough. Go home. The show is over.' He turned to Griff and patted him on the shoulder. 'Just walk away, lad. Go with your sister.'

'Halfheads are no sport anyway!' said a tall boy at the back. 'They're just lumps of lard. Let him go.'

The crowd parted, some muttering curses, others support.

Griff ran back to Tegen. 'Let's get home!' she said. She longed to throw a curse at the villagers. But she knew that would only make things worse. In her mind she imagined she was twisting her magic shawl into a ring of safety around both of them. Then she saw herself and Griff dancing around Derowen's dead body in darkness. She knew she was making a real curse, but she didn't care. She hated the old woman, and Derowen's curse had been much worse.

They found their pony munching at a basket of turnips forgotten in the turmoil and they coaxed it away, trailing the rattling cart behind.

Tegen wanted to kick herself. Beetroot juice! She would have to be much, much more wary in future. No one else must suffer for her, especially not Griff.

8. Griff the Blessed

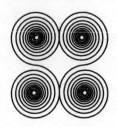

As quickly as they could, Griff and Tegen unloaded the sacks of charcoal at the homes of the two village potters, collected bronze coins, fruit and smoked fish in payment, then turned the pony around to go back home.

As they passed one of the last houses in the village, Gilda rushed out, wiping her hands on a cloth. 'Are you two all right? I heard the row, but I was busy with a birth and I couldn't come.'

Tegen told her briefly what had happened. When she finished she caught Gilda's hand. 'Please, tell me, what is a Star Dancer? You said the stars danced when I was born, but does that make me one? Derowen says I am not. I don't understand what it all means. Why is it so important? Why is everyone so angry?'

Gilda shook her head. 'I am not sure. It is something to do with auguries about a coming evil – no one is certain what it is, but a child born at Imbolg while the stars danced is said to be the one to prevent the terror. So yes, it could be you, but then, it might not be.'

She briefly inspected Griff's bruises. 'Don't take the villagers' bullying to heart. They don't know or care about Star Dancers and druids. They just like a good show. They are so scared of Derowen they'd jump to the moon if she told them to!'

At that moment, a woman's voice called out from inside the house and Gilda turned to go. 'I will come and talk with you soon, Tegen. For now, just get that boy home and clean him up.'

Rain lashed at them as they struggled wearily up the slope.

As they walked, Tegen's exhausted mind raced. Why did Derowen proclaim Griff? she wondered. She must have known it couldn't be him, even with the beetroot juice . . . She cast a glance at her foster-brother, tall, strong, but distinctive with his moon face and flattened head. Even if she didn't see my face, she heard my voice – Griff has his own way of talking. Everyone knows that!

Poor old Griff . . . she thought as she trudged the slippery leaves underfoot, he could never become a druid. They have to learn so much. Perhaps Derowen thinks Griff's been possessed by a benign spirit? I suppose that'd make him one of the 'Blessed Ones', who know the future or can make crops grow. Tegen yawned and longed for her bed. The light was fading fast as the rain became heavier. The cold, wet clinging of her woollen clothes made her sore and miserable.

Ahead, Griff was marching determinedly onwards, his head bowed and his square, solid frame pitched unhappily against the rain.

Tegen leaned on the pony's swaying back as she forced herself onwards. Derowen never does anything unless there's something in it for her. What is she up to? she wondered. Once they were back, Tegen sent Griff to rub the pony down with clean straw and she went inside to warm some water. The house was empty. Outside in the barn, the bellows were wheezing and a small hammer was tapping, which meant Clesek was busy and Nessa was helping him.

A few minutes later, Griff came in, wiping his nose on his sleeve. He was covered in straw that matched his hair. His kind, broad face and slanting eyes looked sad and forlorn. Tegen told him to shut the door and sit by the fire. She made him undress down to his undershirt, then, taking the bowl of warm water and a cloth, she very gently bathed his wounds. When he was clean, she handed him an oatcake smeared in honey. But instead of the usual beam of delight at a treat, Griff looked at her, wide-eyed and scared.

'What happened, Tegen? Why does they thinks I'm somthin' I ain't?'

Tegen shrugged. 'Eat up, the honey's dripping.'

Suddenly Griff clutched at her, squashing the oatcake between his fingers and hers. 'I knows why! Because it's *you*, ain't it? You come into the barn last night. *This* many times.' He held up two honey-oaty fingers. 'You nicked me breeches, din't ya? I've seed yus out dancin' with that green thingy of yourn, making them gooses lay. It takes one of them druids to stare at the stars like you dus. And you've got it, ain't ya? The Gift, I mean? We all saw yus make Clesek better! What ya gonna do, Tegen? I's a-scared!'

Tegen stared into the fire. 'Gilda thinks I am the one they want, but I don't know. Derowen says I was tested and I failed. For the moment, I'm going to do nothing and neither are you.' She turned and looked hard at Griff. She had to make him understand. 'It's life as normal, got it? And you mustn't watch me if I'm doing magic, for the less you know, the safer you'll be.'

'Yes, Tegen,' he said obediently, and at last began to lick the crushed oatcake from his thick fingers. Then he stopped, a large drip of honey caught on his chin. 'Tegen . . . ?'

'Yes?'

'Why does Derowen hate me?'

'Nonsense. Now, lick up that honey and we'll get you clean again,' she said, washing the crushed gooey mess from her own hands.

'She does. I knows things like that sometimes. I knows I'm all stupid. But I knows stuff in *here* . . .' and he struck himself in the middle of the chest. 'But I don't knows how to sez the stuff I knows.'

Tegen looked at her foster-brother. His honest face glowed in the firelight. 'What sort of things do you know?'

Griff shrugged. 'All sorts. I knows me and yus are gonna get marry-ed, and I will always look after yus as long as I live. I seen it. And I'll be kind, like Clesek.'

Tegen went cold. *Marry? Griff?* But they couldn't . . . he was her brother, or as good as. And he was . . . well . . . he was what he was.

'No', she said softly. 'No, Griff, you've got it all wrong.'

She wanted to hug him close and tell him that she would always be there for him but not like *that*. She sighed. He just didn't understand. That was all. He had meant no harm. What he had 'seen' was that they would always love each other as they did now. Maybe even live in the same house? It was easy for a halfhead not to understand.

She was about to ask him more, but he was contentedly humming as he sought out the last vestiges of sweetened oatcake from the cracks between his fingers.

Perhaps Griff really did have a touch of the Gift, even if he didn't always understand what he saw? Tegen's head ached. She wanted to be alone. 'Go and help Clesek with the bellows. He'll be wondering where you are,' she said.

'But I ain't got no clothes,' he whined, snuggling closer to her side, not wanting to leave the fire.

'You must go,' she said. 'You're a man now. You must work like one. You'll be warm in there. Look, I'll come with you. Let's tell Da what happened so he doesn't scold you for not having any breeches on. You show him the coins and barter we got for the charcoal. That'll cheer him up.'

Clesek said nothing when Tegen told the tale, omitting her part in Witton's healing. He pursed his lips and frowned.

Standing on the other side of the smelting oven, Nessa scowled. 'I told you to keep out of that stuff! Dealings with magic and spirits only bring their own trouble in their wake! This proves it. There'll be more to follow, you mark my words!' and she turned to the bucket of water by the door and washed the soot from her face and hands.

Then she turned back. 'But,' she added a little more kindly, 'your father's face is much better today. I am sure you helped as best you could. You always do.' With that she dried herself on her apron and hurried into the house.

'Da, I am so sorry, I forgot to ask how you were.'

'I am doing well,' he said. 'Now, keep out of trouble and do your best to be kind to your mam. She loves you very much. She's only worried for you. Are you all right, Griff?'

Griff nodded and bunched his shoulders together as he put his hands to the bellows. 'I's a man now. Does yus want fast or slow puffin' today?' he asked.

Tegen longed to go to the village to see Gilda, but she was scared of meeting Derowen. On top of that, Nessa was still cursing the midwife's interference. So Tegen stayed at home.

So did Griff. Since the disastrous encounter with Derowen

he never went far on his own if it could be helped, although Clesek wasn't happy. Their food had to be earned. It was almost Samhain, the days were getting shorter and the weather was getting worse. It was now time for Griff to be sleeping by the charcoal fires in the woods. He would have to fend for himself alone up there. Not many of the villagers went up into the lonely Mendip hills. With any luck, no one but the family would know that he was there and if anyone saw smoke they would think it was some of the hill folk.

The day Griff was to leave, he stood forlornly in the courtyard. Tegen wrapped a whole week's worth of bannocks and cheese in a new woollen shirt she had spun and woven for him. He nodded his thanks and hung his head. 'I's gonna be lonely up there on me own,' he said with a sniff. 'Yous ull come and visit me, won't yer, Tegen?'

'Soon as I can,' she smiled and gave him a hug.

Just then Clesek strode across the yard leading a great lolloping mud-coloured hound. As soon as the dog saw Griff he sat down by the boy's side and looked up at him with adoring eyes, his pink tongue hanging out as he panted.

'He's for you,' Clesek said. 'I bought him from the hill people to keep you company. His name is Wolf.'

Griff's eyes opened in delight as he scratched the dog's head and reached into his new shirt for a piece of bannock. The dog ate hungrily, immediately looking up for more. 'Thanks, Clesek. I's-a really good and happy with him! I think he likes me an' all.'

'You'll have someone to talk to,' Clesek said, 'and he'll soon see off anyone from the village who comes snooping around.'

Tegen stroked the wiry hair behind the dog's ears. 'I bet he's even tough enough to see off old Derowen!'

Clesek grunted. 'Don't tempt the spirits, Tegen. Now off you go, Griff. Take Wolf. But make sure he hunts for his own food. If you keep feeding him your bannocks you'll have an empty belly before the fire has burned through.'

'Yeah.' Griff nodded as he slipped the dog the remains of his first day's rations, then the two of them trotted happily away from the house and into the wood.

As Yule approached, most of the village's supply of seed wheat and oats had begun to rot in the storage pits. When the baskets and crocks were broken open, a sticky white stinking fungus covered the blackened grain. There would be hunger before Imbolg and famine before the year's end next Samhain. The perpetual rain swelled the stream and washed down the village street, sometimes swirling in at doorways. The Winter Seas were rising much higher than they usually did. It would not be long before they began to lap at the palisade that surrounded the enclosure.

Witton's little hill was already almost an island.

Tegen longed to do something to help ease the hunger and illness that would come. She was sure she could. She wanted to go and see the midwife – she needed to learn so much more, she had to know what a Star Dancer was, and what it had to do with her – but Nessa and Clesek kept her too busy to go. Sometimes she was sent to see how Griff was getting on in his shelter of sticks and moss by the charcoal fires in the hills. Gleefully she would put fresh bannocks, bean cakes and cheese into her basket and set off.

Unless it was raining, Tegen always stopped on the way at her favourite clearing in the oak trees. There she unwound her green silk shawl from her waist and danced. As Gilda had taught her, she tried to imagine things as they ought to be: the land staying above the Winter Seas, the homes dry and warm, the grain coming golden and sweet-smelling from the storage jars and pits. In her head, she danced to the beat of the little drummer boy and tried to make the pictures in her head become real. But as she danced, she also worried. Was her dancing magic having any effect? Was she doing it right? Should she use charms and spells and goose blood like Derowen?

One afternoon, as the approaching darkness of the mid-winter solstice swallowed the days, Tegen stayed talking with Griff until after dark. She poured out all her worries about the weather and the coming famine. He just munched his food. 'Got any more?' he asked, rummaging in her basket.

Tegen sighed. 'No, Griff, this is what I am trying to tell you, food is going to be short . . .' She wished he would have one of his lucid moments when things were clear to him.

'Listen, it is late. Da and Mam will be worried about me. I must go.'

'Wolf an' me'll walk back a pace with 'ee,' he said. 'Them fires is good for a bit.' As they came to the clearing in the oak wood, Griff stopped and said, 'You orta be a-dancing tonight, girl,' he said. 'Why don't ee?'

Tegen smelled the night air and looked up at the Watching Woman. The brilliant points of light gleamed like a newly polished silver necklace for the night sky. The air and light surged through her and she longed to dance and dance and to make everything come right. She may or may not be the 'Star Dancer', but if she could make geese lay and her Da's face get better, then she must do what she could.

It was a bitterly cold night, but she gave Griff her cloak. 'Don't ever tell Mam, will you?' she said. 'She'd marry me to that spotty potter's boy tomorrow if she found out.'

Griff shook his head, his small eyes earnest in the silvery light. Wolf whined and licked her hand. She scratched him behind the ear and stepped out into the clearing. The bare black arms of the oaks stretched up towards her beloved stars like supplicants in prayer. It was a night for real magic. She looked up at the Watching Woman and tried to focus all her energies into the twinkling lights, willing them to work with her.

Then a question came very clearly into her mind: *What do you want, Tegen?*

She didn't know who asked it, but she knew what the

answer was. Her feet began to make patterns across the frozen ground and she swayed her arms and hips to the beat of the invisible drummer boy. She raised her arms and spread her fingers like the oak trees as she danced her answer: *To find the Star Dancer – whoever it is, may he or she be found so the land may be healed. Please . . .*

She knew she was making a very deep spell. She also knew that death was the punishment for a non-druid to do such things. But she must do what she could.

The wind blew bitterly and clouds scudded across the stars. The night was getting very dark.

At last Tegen stopped dancing and picked up her cloak. 'Time to go, I think,' she said. 'I can see the house from here. You go back to your fires and I'll be all right.'

Griff hugged Tegen. 'Night, girl,' he said. 'Wolf and me luvs yer.' Then he turned and was swallowed by the peaty shadows.

Tegen shivered. Now she had stopped dancing she was getting cold, and her stomach hurt. As she walked, another image came unbidden into her mind. It was Derowen's face staring at her, full of bitterness and hate. Whatever needed to be done to make things come right, the wise woman would try to prevent it.

Back in her crook loft, Tegen lit a small rush light. Its mutton fat spat and guttered in the darkness of the draughty little attic room. In every dancing shadow, Tegen could still see the old witch's face. 'I will go to the village tomorrow, come what may,' she promised herself. 'I have got to find Gilda. She will know what to do. Mam need never know.' Tegen sat on her bed and held her belly. Her stomach cramps were getting worse.

'I don't care if Mam finds out where I've been . . . yes, I do,' she added. ' I will just have to think of an excuse.'

Tegen thought of the beautiful dark-skinned dancer who had put the magic green shawl into her hands. Without her, none of this would have happened. She spread out her beloved silk on her lap. It no longer floated lightly as she danced. It was faded and full of tears and stains and the fine tasselled edge had become matted. She kissed the fabric, still soft and comforting to touch, then twisted it around her waist.

It had been given to her to do good, of that she was sure. Nothing, not even her mother, would make her get rid of it. Tegen closed her eyes and remembered the little drummer boy and the women stamping and dancing on the summer grass. Goodness would come again. She just had to believe it and wait for the right time.

Tegen lay down and snuggled into her warm straw mattress, but she felt uncomfortable. Her belly still ached. Suddenly she realized that her thighs were wet, yet she had felt no need to go to the privy. She touched the dampness with her fingers. Even in the rush light, she could see she had dark smears of blood on her hand.

'Oh help!' she gasped. 'Mam! *Mam!*' she howled. 'Help me! Mam, I'm *bleeding*!'

9. The Naming

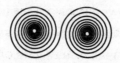

Tegen longed for her mother to cuddle and comfort her as she used to when she was little. But she guessed it wouldn't happen. Over the years, Nessa's fear of the spirits had grown. She blamed them for Clesek's accident, and for her three little babies born still and blue. Her harshness grew with each little funeral.

Tegen was right. There was no reassurance.

As soon as Nessa saw the blood on her daughter's legs, she snatched the rush light from Tegen's hand and wedged it upright between two planks of the table. 'No time for dreaming,' she snapped. 'Get dressed! Put on two smocks, it's cold outside. Don't utter a word, not a sound, I tell you! We must hurry. I will explain on the way!'

'But . . . ?'

'Silence!' Her mother's face looked tense and dark in the guttering shadows. 'Here are your stockings and clogs. Put them on. Don't fuss about the blood, you can wash later. Wear a shawl as well as your cloak, I will meet you downstairs.'

Tegen heard her mother go into the back room and say something to her father. Then she came out again, wrapped in her own thick shawl and carrying a lantern. 'Hurry. Outside. Not a moment to lose!' and she pushed the door open. They were met by a slamming gale of icy cold air.

The lantern cast grotesquely dancing shadow-shapes into the howling blackness of the hilltop. Below, the lane wound down into the valley and through the bare winter trees. 'Shut the door behind you!' Nessa said as she stepped out into the darkness.

Tegen did as she was told. The cold slapped her in the face.

Mother and daughter walked in silence until they reached the bottom of the lane, then they took the right-hand fork, which led towards old Witton's home.

'Pray to the Goddess that he is there,' Nessa muttered, 'or we are in deep trouble! You and your silly magic dancing – if you just minded the business of staying alive and keeping the bellows going and the flour ground, you would probably have been all right. As it is, the Goddess alone knows what spirits are following us right at this moment . . .' She hesitated and looked around as if she expected to see a ghost hovering in the shadows behind her.

Tegen longed to ask what the matter was, but her mother

was so tense, she dared not. Her stomach hurt. All she wanted to do was to lie quietly in bed with a soothing brew of willow-bark tisane. What was worse, the blood was still trickling down her thighs, leaving cold, sticky tracks that stung in the biting wind.

As they picked their hurried way along the narrow lane, stepping over the black tree roots and splashing through ice-cold puddles, her mother began to talk.

'As you know, when a girl becomes a woman, she bleeds every cycle of the moon. It is her offering to the Watching Woman. No, don't say a word. We must go straight to Witton so he can give you your true name, for until that is done, you are at risk from every spirit in the air. For now, in the between-time when you are neither child nor woman, you are vulnerable to any evil presence. You are in worse danger than most girls because the spirits know you for sure, dabbling around in their business as you do. Only your true name can protect you. If you utter a word, the spirits of the air will know your state and be on you in a trice. If you move swiftly and silently, we'll be safe.'

Tegen trudged behind her mother, shivering under her cloak despite all her layers. She wished the wind would lessen. She could smell snow in the air. It was the sort of night when wolves prowled the lower slopes of the hills. Oddly, she was more frightened of fangs ripping into her body than of being possessed by unfriendly spirits. She ignored her mother's lantern. The wildly dancing light made it difficult to see where she was putting her feet. Instead she kept her head down and tried not to slip.

'I don't know what we shall do if Witton is away or too ill to see us,' Nessa continued. 'I suppose we will just have to go and find Derowen; she will know.'

Dread clutched at Tegen's throat at the thought of consulting the wise woman, but she obeyed her mother and said nothing aloud. Witton, please be there, she pleaded silently into the night. I know you are angry with me, but please don't hate me. Please give me my name.

The path dipped down and the icy mud underfoot crunched beneath their clogs. Nessa held the lantern high as she picked her way, using tree roots as steps.

Tegen's heart was excited and miserable at the same time. She was a woman at last. But now she must face whatever fate was upon her – she was no longer a child. Despite her trust in the old druid, she could not shake a sense of dread of what would happen when they got to the roundhouse. What if he recognized her as the 'boy' who came to heal him? Would he be angry and throw her out, unnamed and at the mercy of all that was roaming in the wild air?

Tegen trudged, silently wrapped in her worries. Witton would tell her mother everything. She would be livid. She would beat her for certain. But I did save Witton's life, she reasoned, so perhaps they will both understand. I will beg forgiveness. She glanced around at the deep black of the night. Above her, the bare trees creaked and clattered their branches together in the wind like dry bones. She hurried on behind the scurrying figure of her mother. I only tried to help, she reminded whatever spirits were listening inside her head.

Tonight she was only a young woman coming to the druid for her true name. She wasn't pretending to be anything she wasn't. She comforted herself with the touch of her silk shawl, knotted around her waist.

'Hurry! It is a dying moon tonight,' Nessa called out, fear in her voice. 'You won't be safe until you are at Witton's roundhouse.'

The path was treacherous. Tegen dared not close her eyes to 'see' deep inside herself, to know what she must do. She sensed the night was crowded with things she did not understand: spirits, omens and malice. On top of that, she was too cold and out of breath to be able to think clearly.

Was this bad timing all her fault like everything else? If she had not made a spell in the woods, might the bleeding have come when the spirits of the air were in a better mood or when the moon was stronger? Was she being punished for her audacity?

The fear that grew inside her chest was so tight she could hardly breathe. She began to pant loudly. 'Keep quiet!' her mother snapped.

Tegen could see Nessa's worried frown by the harsh light of the lantern. She stopped and tried to calm her mind and took two or three slow breaths. Perhaps the spirits are trying to enter me already? she wondered. Well, I won't let them! She held her head high and tried to follow her mother with dignity and certainty. The Watching Woman had the stars dance for me when I was born, so I must be here to do something special. I won't die tonight, she told herself.

She began to feel a small glow of certainty: even if her path through life would not be an ordinary one, the Goddess would always care for her.

Suddenly Tegen tripped over a tree root that stretched itself, claw-like, across the way and she landed heavily, crying out in agony as she fell.

Not far ahead, at the mouth of the valley, Witton was sitting on his bed, wide-eyed and awake.

The Star Dancer was coming. He was sure. He could hear his footsteps treading through the woods as clearly as if the Blessed One was in his own home with him. But why now, tonight? The moon was dying and it was two days before Yule; the magic Witton had at his disposal would be at its weakest. In a few days time, yes. Let him come then when the Sun God rose from his winter grave and married the Watching Woman, leaving her with the Child of Spring in her belly . . . the moon would be waxing and there would be strength for magic then – oh yes and *what* magic!

But there must be a reason for the boy coming tonight. Witton pulled himself up on to his feet and twisted a blanket around his shoulders. Painfully he shuffled across the room and poked the hearth-ashes until a flame sprang to life. He added a fresh log. If only Derowen had been there to help prepare things for his guest . . . But it was probably better he was alone; there would be much to talk of that was not right for a non-druid's ears, and he was weary of Derowen's bitter and demanding spirit.

Trying to straighten up, Witton searched in his back room for his amulets and Ogham. Soon his small table was spread with a strange array of twigs and bones, pieces of twisted leather and coloured feathers. Then he took a handful of juniper shavings and rosemary leaves and threw them into the glowing ashy edges of the fire. The incense began to smoulder. He breathed deeply so the smoke would give him clear sight.

If only it had been four, or even three nights hence . . .

Suddenly he heard a short, painful cry.

The Star Dancer was hurt! Witton pulled himself upright and staggered to the doorway. The latch was stiff in his feeble fingers. At last he stood facing the night. The old man braced himself against the wooden jamb, closed his eyes and summoned all the good spirits to his aid. 'Do not fall, child,' he called into the darkness. 'Keep going, I have straightened your path to my door . . .'

There was danger in the air. He could feel it everywhere.

Strange things brushed past his face in the night wind. Things even he did not know the name of.

Things that smelled of hate and unspoken anger.

Things unnatural and unbound – spirits and demons hungry to destroy the good that was struggling alone in the night. It was a powerful good, the best that had come to the valley for many generations.

Witton inhaled the sweet, clarifying fragrance of the herbs smouldering on his hearth. There was only one more thing he could think of that would save the new druid . . . he must call him by his true name! With the mantel of that spell thrown over his shoulders, the boy might get through the tangle of evil spirits crowding his way.

Taking the deepest breath he could, Witton stretched out his right hand into the darkness and called into the wind: 'I name you Star Dancer! I acknowledge you, druid! Come to me!'

Tegen grasped her mother's hand and clambered to her feet. The magic of the old man's spell carried the words into her mind. The moment Tegen heard them she knew there would be no going back. She really *was* the Star Dancer. She had been named. She had been acknowledged. All the druids together could not undo what had just been said. She stood and rubbed her sore ankle, then limped on in silence behind her mother, her heart pounding with excitement. At last, slips of light from Witton's tiny roundhouse came in sight, glowing like eyes in the heavy darkness.

Nessa dropped back. 'You must go alone from here,' she said. 'Even a mother does not know her child's true name. My blessing goes with you. I'll wait for you here . . .' she paused for a moment, 'and remember . . .' she whispered, 'remember, I do love you. I may seem harsh, but I am only frightened for you.' Then she kissed Tegen very quickly on the forehead.

With that, Nessa pulled her shawl around her shoulders and huddled against the trunk of a tree. 'Say nothing until he speaks to you,' she whispered. 'Then you will be safe.'

Tegen was so terrified she did not think she could speak at all. Lowering her head against the biting winds, she forced herself up the slope to the roundhouse at the top where Witton's bent silhouette stood in the fire-lit doorway, waiting for her.

She stopped and steadied her breathing. She wished her ankle did not throb so much. But she had to live with that. At least she could walk. She tried to wipe some of the blood away from her legs with a wad of cold wet grass.

What Witton said cannot be unsaid, she reminded herself silently. The Lady Goddess danced for me. She will not fail me now.

10. Acknowledged

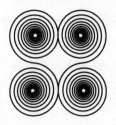

'Come in! Come in, child! Welcome at last! Perhaps you will accept my hospitality tonight? You left too suddenly when you came to heal me and we have so much to talk about. I only wish I had found you earlier. There is so little time left . . .' the old druid wheezed as he stepped back inside, indicating his visitor should follow.

Tegen hesitated by the doorway. What should she do? At last she stepped forward. Too nervous to meet Witton's eyes, she stared at the rush-strewn floor.

She heard Witton's voice, but his words weren't registering. Without thinking, she let her cloak fall back and shook her untidy long black hair loose. Then she stepped into the light.

Witton turned to smile, but the welcome deadened in his eyes as he saw Tegen clearly for the first time. 'No!' he said huskily. 'Not you!' and he staggered, his hand on his chest as he struggled for breath.

Tegen ran forward and caught him under his elbow. 'Easy, Father. Let me help you to sit.'

Witton shrank deep within himself. He sat hunched on his bed, his head sunk between his shoulders. 'How can it be?' he whispered. 'What have I done?' he said. Then he looked at her pleadingly: 'I have named you. I have acknowledged you. There is no undoing!'

He struggled to stand. 'I know what it is; it is the waning moon. That and the death of the Sun God. I was tricked into naming you by evil spirits who brought you here. There must be ways to unsay what has been said. No good can come of magic worked tonight. Let me see, let me see . . .' And he started to shuffle backwards and forwards across the floor, his leather slippers scuffing up the dusty reeds.

Tegen said nothing, but watched; then she moved closer and took his hand. 'Father,' she said quietly, 'I don't mean any harm. I can't help being here.'

Witton glowered at her. His eyes were as strong and alive as they always had been. It was only his body that was failing. 'Why did you do it, eh? Why did you sneak up here to do your witchcraft on me when I was ill? Did you hope to persuade me while I was weak?'

He turned and jabbed a bony finger into Tegen's arm. 'Well, I'm not ill tonight. You can't fool me now. It may be midwinter and a dark moon but my guardian spirits are still with me.'

Tegen raised her hands and let them fall uselessly. What was the point in arguing? 'I only came when you called, Father.'

Witton sank on to his bed and pulled his bag of divining bones from under his pillow. Muttering an incantation, he tossed a few on to the sheepskin covers beside him. He seemed irritated by what he saw.

Suddenly he looked up. 'Take your clothes off.'

'What?' Tegen was aghast. She backed towards the door.

'Your clothes!' Then seeing the anxiety in her face he softened. 'Not everything, you silly child. Just let me see your back.'

With shaking hands, Tegen let her shawl fall on the ground, then fumbled with the circular brooch pins at her shoulders. First one smock then the second slipped down to her waist. Turning away, for she had never before undressed in the presence of even her father or Griff, she clutched the front of her undershift over her small breasts and let the back fall loose.

'Pull your hair out of the way and come over here by the fire so I can see you!' he snapped.

Trembling, Tegen obeyed, clutching at the dragging folds of heavy woollen cloth. What was going to happen? Was he going to whip her with birch rods like they did with thieves? She bit her lip and clenched her fists. She had to be brave.

'Closer!'

Tegen glanced behind her and shuffled backwards until she stood next to the old druid.

He lifted his hand and very gently traced the pattern of small white scars across her back.

The room was silent except for the light crackling of the half-burned log on the fire. Tegen bit her lip and wished her heart did not thump so loudly.

At long last Witton closed his eyes. 'You are the Star Dancer,' he sighed. 'I have always known it was you.'

Tegen pulled her clothes back into place and refastened her brooches. She glowed with excitement. 'Why did you want to see my back?'

'Your parents probably never told you, but I came to bless you as a newborn baby. When I tested you with fire, the sparks rose and burned your back in the pattern of the Watching Woman. I threw bones into your caul. They told me you were born to be a great druid. The signs were all there. I just did not want to see them.'

'But Derowen told me that – she said I failed . . .'

'I didn't tell her the truth. I can't always trust her. Anyway . . . I didn't want to believe it myself,' he replied sadly.

Witton paused and looked across at Tegen with grief in his eyes. 'And . . . and . . . I am sorry for striking you that day . . . I saw you dancing with magic that sparkled like sunlight on frost. We druids had always looked for a boy we could train from birth. But there you were, a girl wielding fully formed spells that many of us old white-robes only dream of . . .' He hung his head. 'I was afraid. Can you forgive a foolish old man?' He eased himself on to a three-legged stool and leaned forward with his head in his hands.

Tegen sat on the ground next to him. Relief washed over her – he did not hate her. She patted his arm. 'It is forgotten, Father.'

He did not look up. He seemed so small, his hair wild, his beard unplaited and his frail arms trembling. 'There will be anger and hatred, maybe even bloodshed, because of this. Why did the Goddess do this, tonight of all nights? My magic is too weak . . . It is the wrong time.'

Tegen closed her eyes for a moment. In her head she could see the stars she loved, sparkling brilliantly. She said out loud, 'The moon and sun may be weak behind the clouds, but the stars are still there. The Watching Woman is still strong. The Goddess has not forgotten us. It is just difficult to see and understand it all at the moment.'

Witton stared into the fire. 'Who taught you to say that?'

Tegen glanced at him. Had she said something wrong? 'No one, Father. I thought I ought to say what I saw as a picture in my head. It has happened before.'

'Like the night you came to heal me?'

'Yes.'

'Ah, you have the Awen, the druid's gift of inspiration.' He closed his eyes and held his head high as if he too was hearing or seeing something deep inside.

His face became more peaceful. 'Perhaps all will be well in the end.'

Tegen said nothing. Witton's words were comforting and terrifying at the same time. This all seemed so big . . . so beyond her . . .

O Lady, help me, she said to herself. What am I getting into? She sat silently and listened to the fire and the low, insistent, bitter moaning of the wind.

'Oh no!' she exclaimed suddenly, jumping up. 'My mother! She is waiting outside. I'd forgotten all about her! She'll be so worried!'

'Why did your mother come, child?' Witton looked up, the firelight catching his bony face.

'Because . . . because . . .' She looked down with embarrassment.

Witton followed Tegen's glance down to her stockinged feet pushed into wooden clogs. Splashes of blood mixed with the clinging mud.

'Because you came for your name,' he sighed. 'Well, now you have it. For better or for worse, it is yours, but my heart sinks for you that you should take such a name on a night when all is so dark. Go home, but be sure to return in the morning. We have much to discuss and my time is short.'

Tegen felt the blood rise to her face. 'Then you will teach me, Father?'

'What little I can in the time we have. I do not understand why things have happened this way. It is partly my own intransigence, I suppose. But what is, must be. Go home and get some sleep.' And with that, Witton staggered to his bed, lay down and pulled his cover of sheepskins over himself. 'Shut the door tightly as you go. And pray for me.'

Nessa was crouched in the dark, at the base of the bare tree. Her teeth were chattering, for snow had started to fall. The night had an eerie glow.

'Mam?' Tegen called out. 'Are you all right?'

Nessa coughed. Tegen pulled off her own cloak and wrapped it around Nessa's head and shoulders. 'Here, have this. I still have a thick shawl and I am warm.' Taking her mother's hand and the lantern, Tegen led the way back towards their home.

When the sun had set that evening, she had been a nameless child. Now, barely a few fingers' depth of a candle later, she and her mother had swapped places. It was now Tegen's task to protect, to move them both urgently homewards. She was the Star Dancer and about to begin the druid's training!

The wind was at their back at first, so they made good

progress, but as the snow thickened they began to slip and slide in the mushy, half-frozen mud.

Nessa slowed. 'I feel tired,' she said. 'You go ahead, I'll catch you up.'

'No.' Tegen grasped her mother's hand firmly. 'We are going home together.' But every step they took forwards seemed to slide them further and further into the mire. 'We must get back, we *will* get back!' she muttered between chattering teeth.

They trod warily in the dark lest they slipped down a swallet, a bottomless hole in the ground where the hungry hill demons swallowed victims to sate their desire for life-blood. Tegen knew these traps appeared in many places. Some said they were always in the same spot; others thought the demons moved them around. Even without the snow, holes like these would not always be visible.

Everything seemed to change shape in the lantern light. Where trees and rocks had stood by daylight, now loomed giant's bones, empty eye sockets and shattered teeth. The meagre light skidded across the white icy softness. Tegen wished she could lie down and sleep as if the snow was a bed of white goose feathers. But she knew that would be death.

Nessa started crying. Tegen tightened her grip on her mother's hand just as the lantern flared up, spluttered and almost went out. The flame recovered, but she guessed there was very little candle left. She felt no emotion. Just cold. It had grown past pain to become a throbbing numbness in her bones. The night was so silent and strange. Had one of the demons swallowed them whole?

'Come on,' Tegen said, pulling herself together. 'Not far now. Just think of our hearth.' She longed to have her cloak back, but her mother needed it more.

'We're getting nowhere!' Nessa gasped, tugging the ice-heavy cloth around her face as a bitter blast of snow stung her eyes. 'It's as if all the air spirits are against us tonight. I shouldn't have brought you out – you were safer at home. This is all my fault!'

Tegen stood still. Was her mother right? The wind had risen, the snowstorm was getting stronger and the icy mud was getting deeper. Perhaps the spirits did not like what had been done that night?

She had to use her power – but she dared not close her eyes and she could scarcely walk, let alone dance. Brave words about the Goddess's care were all very well in the warmth of Witton's home, but out here . . .

Bowing her head against the winds, she struggled to imagine the little drummer. Reaching for her green shawl, she thought of the warmth and colour of the women dancing. She sought a steady rhythm for the boy to play so she and her mother could walk in time to the music. But it would not come.

Just then the wind took malevolent delight in renewing

its strength, gathering energy and fury as it howled and screamed. Suddenly Nessa stumbled and refused to get up.

'Tegen, I can't go on,' she said. 'Leave me here. Really. I am warmer now. Let me have a rest, then I'll follow you home later.'

Tegen lifted the lantern high to try to see a way through the blinding black and white of the blizzard. Then another great gust of wind caught the lantern from her frozen hand. It landed deep in the snow on its side and the light went out.

11. Snow-blind

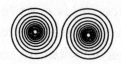

Tegen's ankle throbbed with sharp, pounding pain as fear gripped her throat. She heaved her mother up and put an arm around her. 'Come on, we are almost home.'

Blacking out every thought except the next step, they trudged without direction into the hungry mouth of the lashing winds. Underfoot, ice snapped and shattered as they walked, knife-like shards catching on their clogs and stockings. The two women clasped each other closely.

Slowly an idea formed in Tegen's befuddled brain. 'Mother . . . why did you say I had to be silent on the way to Witton's?'

'What?'

'Why . . . did . . . you . . . say . . . I had . . . to be silent . . . ?'

The winds blasted so hard in their faces they could scarcely hear each other, although they were only a breath apart.

Nessa shouted back into Tegen's ear. 'Because . . . you were vulnerable . . . needed . . . true name . . . to protect you.'

'Think hard . . .' Tegen yelled back. 'Our names protect us . . . so think of *your* true name and what it means . . . think of the warmth . . . of home . . . where we belong!' She didn't dare add, 'It's a magic,' for fear her mother would refuse.

Tegen put the last of her energy into imagining the constellation of the Watching Woman, clothed in light and dancing with joy at the birth of a child who would become the Star Dancer.

A child who was not destined to die in a blizzard.

The warmth of that celebration began to spread a glow of delight. This wasn't her dying day. All would be well – all *must* be well.

She closed her eyes and tried to picture her mother's face. Into her mind came Nessa's thin cheeks, whipped with wild, dark hair by the wind . . . but she was smiling!

Just then a bark and a shout brought them both to a stop. Then a strange rattling noise, then another shout. 'Oi! Oi! Is yous there?'

'Griff!' Tegen yelled in delight. 'Griff, is that really you?'

'S'me! Wolf too!' came a familiar voice. 'Where is ya?'

'Over here!'

Then came the odd rattling sound again and Wolf began to bark madly. 'Come to me noise, Tegen, come to me!'

There was more barking, then a bounding, hairy weight thrust itself at Tegen and Nessa. Puffs of hot dog-breath warmed their hands as Wolf shepherded them onwards. They followed the dog, forcing their aching steps where he led. In the dark they peered around, trying to see their way. At last Griff's strong, square shape staggered to their side. His hand caught Tegen under the arm and tugged her close into a bear hug. 'Could yus hear I? Could yus hear Wolf?' he laughed.

'We could.' Nessa grabbed his hand. 'Thank you, Griff.'

'Yus here too, Nessa? That's good. Now, let's all git us home. It's big cold outta here. Clesek have nice big fire for us, eh?'

Tegen wanted to hug him back, but she was too frozen. 'How are we going to find our way back?' she yelled.

'Yus grab hold o' each other.' Griff caught Tegen's hand. She put her other arm around her mother's waist. 'Good, now, I dun what we dus to Wolf!' he yelled back. 'I tied a string on me neck, so house can tug me back alwus.'

Tegen winced at the thought of what might have happened if he had slipped, tied up like that. She could feel, by the jerking movements of his free arm, that he was reeling himself in – pulling on the cord as it led them all home. All around them Wolf bounced and ran, directing them as if they were lost sheep.

It was not long before the family were all sitting by the fire, steam rising off their hair, their wet clothes a sodden heap by the door.

Clesek, pale and angry, piled rugs and skins around the

backs and feet of his wife and daughter. 'You should have waited till morning, Nessa. It was madness to go out tonight. Tegen would have been safe here. You could have let me come at least. You didn't need to go. If only you weren't so worried about the spirits. They aren't so bad to us. We give them their due . . .'

Nessa sat in silence, rubbing her aching, itching feet and hands. She had done what was right, she knew she had.

Tegen rolled herself in her soft, warm wrappings and smiled at Griff as he prattled proudly, showing them the pot and ladle he had clattered together so they could hear him above the storm. 'This makes a fine big noise!' he announced proudly, bashing it again. 'Yus heard me, right?'

'We heard you – and Wolf.' Tegen smiled and squeezed his hand. 'Thank you for coming out to us.'

Griff grinned back. 'S'good. Yus all warm now?'

Tegen nodded. Her hands and feet hurt, but they were safe and that was what mattered.

Clesek persuaded Nessa to lie back on the skins while he rubbed goose fat on to her toes to warm them up. As fast as he put it on, Wolf was licking it off, but his lick was warm and comforting so Nessa didn't scold him. Instead she scratched her reddened fingers deep into his coat. Colour was returning to her cheeks.

'But how did you *know*, Griff?' Tegen asked, helping herself to the pot of fat as well. 'You couldn't have heard us, or even seen us.'

The lad just shrugged. 'Cos I did. Told you, I *knows* stuff. Wolf wouldn't stop howling. We *both* knowed we had to come.'

'But weren't you right up on the hills with your charcoal fires? When did you start looking?'

'We wasn't long ways,' Griff said. 'Wolf and me was roasting a pigeon in my hut and sudden-like his ears stick up and so did mine. We both jes started runnin'. When we seed snow was horrid, we come here. Then we's got string. Tied it to doorpost. Then off we goes. We did good, hey!'

Clesek patted Griff on the shoulder and roughed his wet hair. 'You did good, Griff. The charcoal will be ruined, but I don't care. You brought Nessa and Tegen back. Wolf and you sleep here by the hearth tonight; we'll go up together in the morning and see if anything can be saved.'

Griff looked blank, as if he didn't understand what Clesek was saying.

Tegen stared at him in amazement. How odd, she thought, a simple invitation to sleep by the fire is beyond him, but knowing we were caught in the storm, and how to rescue us, came naturally. She was feeling sleepy and finding it hard to concentrate, but one tiny thought trickled through her mind: the Awen; Griff has it too – that's why he 'knows' things.

Clesek wrapped a hot cooking stone in an old shawl and gently pushed Tegen up the ladder to her little room in the crook loft. Outside, the wind lessened and the deep stillness of snow enveloped the hillside where the stone cottage stood.

Now it was safe to sleep, Tegen could not do so. Her mind raced. However deep the snow, whatever her parents said, she *had* to be with Witton in the morning.

Things had been left much too late.

The next day was filled with brilliant light blue skies. The sparkling snow lay heavily as silence swathed everything.

Nessa showed Tegen how to make a pad of dried mosses laid within a mole skin to catch her bleeding. 'Bind each end with twine, like this, then tie the ends to a strip of leather around your waist. You change the mosses for fresh ones when these become too wet. Here, put these in your pouch. You will have to learn to collect and dry your own when the snows go.'

'Do women bleed all the time?' Tegen asked, feeling miserable. 'I hate it. My belly aches.'

'No. It is only for a few days every moon's cycle. It is your way of offering your life back to the Goddess. It is called the Little Offering. When each pad is used, you must bury the wet mosses under the oak behind the house. When you carry a child in your belly, you stop bleeding for nine months – sometimes longer. That is a time of the Great Offering – when you are creating, as the Goddess created us. There –' Nessa finished stuffing Tegen's pouch with as much moss as it would hold – 'that will do you for a while. All will pass within a few days – until the next changing of the moon.' Nessa smiled briefly and gave her a fleeting, nervous kiss.

Once more Tegen was a half-child, awkward with her new status as a woman. She was excited at the new horizons of her destiny – but she was terrified too. What would it mean to be the Star Dancer? What was this Awen? What would happen if the wrong thing came out of her mouth at the wrong time? What would Derowen say when she found out? What would her mother say . . . ?

Nessa put her own bag of mosses away and started to scoop a large bowl of porridge for Tegen. On top swam a fine knob of butter and a swirl of brown, waxy honey. Tegen looked at her, amazed at the luxury.

'Thanks – for getting us back,' Nessa smiled. 'It's a long time since I thought of my true name. But you were right. It did help.'

But the moment of warmth melted faster than the butter. 'Busy day today. The cooking pots need scouring and oiling – you can put your old smock on to do that; then I need you to dig turnips out of the clamp and get them unfrozen and chopped up for the stew . . .'

Tegen's heart flipped. This was going to be difficult. She tasted the porridge, then took a deep breath. 'I can't do any of that, Mam. Not today.'

'What?' Nessa turned and scowled, porridge ladle in hand.

'I . . .' She took another spoonful of the porridge and swallowed, plucking up courage she didn't have. 'I am going back to Witton's house. He asked me to come.'

Nessa clicked her tongue and rolled her eyes as she continued serving up for Griff and Clesek. 'He doesn't need you, child. Derowen will look after him. He is very ill. Leave him be.'

Tegen didn't know how to explain without making her mother angry. She wished the Awen would tell her what to say. 'I promised I'd go and see how he is!' she said. 'I'll do the pots tomorrow, I promise.' Then, ignoring Nessa's scolding, she finished her breakfast and grabbed a cheese from the shelf. Tugging on her still-wet cloak, she ran out of the house and slipped down the slope to the track at the bottom. Turning to her right, she wound her way through the white, silent wood and trudged along the hidden banks of the stream. The water seeped icily through her stockings and inside her clogs. Her skin ached with the cold. But at least it was daylight and she had a bowlful of porridge inside her.

It took much longer than she had hoped to get to Witton's cottage, but at last she climbed up the final slope and gingerly knocked on the door. What would the old druid say? Would he have changed his mind? Perhaps it didn't even matter whether Witton acknowledged her this morning or not, for she *was* the Star Dancer. He had named her. There was no turning back. She would find what it was she had to do, whatever happened.

Tegen knocked twice at the roundhouse door before a weak voice called: 'Come.' She lifted the iron latch, pushed the door wide and went in.

12. Beginning

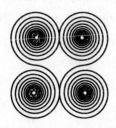

Witton was seated on a stool next to the fire. Beside him a small table was strewn with all sorts of paraphernalia: dried herbs, clay jars stoppered with wooden plugs and sealed with wax, strings of desiccated frogs and fish, small ribbons of different-coloured woven stuff, tall wax candles, a silver bowl, a tiny golden knife and a square metal box no bigger than a child's hand.

He made no sign that he was aware of Tegen's presence. Her heart sank. Had he changed his mind?

She shut the door. Her eyes took a few moments to accustom to the gloom, scarcely lit by the glow from the fire and half a dozen tallow rush lights.

Witton still said nothing, so Tegen shrugged off her wet cloak and spread it to dry over a stool. From her bag she pulled out the small cheese. 'A gift,' she said, holding it out at arm's length, 'from my parents. They greet you.'

The old druid grunted and nodded. She laid the cheese on the table.

'Not there!' Witton snapped, glaring up at her. 'That's for sacred things.' He jerked his thumb in the direction of a shelf piled with bowls and spoons. Red-faced, Tegen hurried to obey and then she came towards the old druid and crouched by his side.

Witton returned his gaze to the flames. 'Look, I don't know how you're going to manage. There's no way a girl can be allowed into my sacred room, so I've brought everything you might need in here. Then you won't offend the Goddess by your presence. You'll have to build your own room when I am gone. One that men can't go into.'

'Now, listen and concentrate hard.' He fixed Tegen with his gaze. 'You must not spill a single word of what I am about to tell you. First, you will need to learn to become a bard, learning the sacred stories and songs. You will also learn how to speak with the inspiration of the Awen and to create your own new words. Next, you will study to be an ovate, skilled in divination, shape-shifting and healing. Lastly, you must study the movements of the stars and the way all things work together in the world. You must also study law and be able to settle disputes. Then you may call yourself a full druid. It normally takes nineteen years to learn these great and sacred arts. You won't even have that many *days* with me. You had better move in here straight away. There's no time for you to go home. I won't live much longer and I will need every moment I have left to instruct you.'

Tegen's mouth fell open. 'But I can't – my mother and father will worry.'

'Oh well!' Witton sneered, poking at the embers with a stick. 'If you want to go back to Mam and Da, then we'll stop right now. I have no time to waste. You go home like a good little girl and play with your pretty things and I'll find an apprentice who deserves the name.'

Tegen's face went hot with embarrassment. She took a deep breath. 'Of course I'll stay, Father. It's just, I'd like to send a message if I may.'

Witton looked up. The girl's weary young face was full of gentleness and concern, but not weakness. The angry lines around his eyes softened. 'Yes. Of course you must. It is natural they should worry, and right you should tell them where you are. When Derowen comes with my food you may send word to your family. But –' he looked around his meagre little room – 'you must make a bed here for yourself. You must not leave my side. If I die and you are not here to breathe in my soul as it leaves my body, someone else will try to take your place. You must be the one to close my eyes.'

Tegen shuddered. The mention of Derowen's imminent arrival was bad enough, but the thought of breathing in the old druid's last breath . . . What would happen when his soul came into hers? Would she *become* him? What would happen when he was reincarnated? Would he take his soul back?

But Witton was still speaking and she had to listen.

'Who knows whether you really have the skills to be a druid or to fulfil your destiny as the Star Dancer? After I'm gone, it will be up to Huval to teach you, although he lives three days' walk away. The nearest druid is Gorgans, although you must be wary of him. He is a White One from Tir na nÓg, a gift from the spirits, but his methods are not the ones I would choose. On the other hand, he is very learned and only lives in the next valley. I am sure he would come if you asked for his help.' Witton leaned across and took Tegen's hand. 'If ever you get the chance, go to the druids on the island of Mona in the land of the Ceangli people. They will teach you.'

Tegen was bursting with questions. She tried to stay still, but she couldn't help fidgeting. She sprang to her feet and started to pace the room. 'But, Father, what *is* a Star Dancer? Gilda has told me a little, but not enough to make sense.'

He hesitated and looked away.

'The Star Dancer has been prophesied for a long time. He, as we once believed you would be, was to be born at Imbolg when a shower of stars danced through the constellation of the Watching Woman: a symbol of a great spirit being born. For many years we have known that an evil and merciless force is coming to the lands of the Winter Seas, one that ordinary magic cannot avert . . .'

Tegen stopped her pacing and clutched a roof support. She looked back at Witton. 'What sort of evil?' she asked quietly.

'We do not know,' he sighed. 'Flood, drought, demon, plague . . . it could be anything. But the child born the night the stars danced was to be our only hope against it.

'We had planned –' he pointed at one bright spark, rising from a shower of smaller embers – 'to find the child and train him as a druid from as soon as he could walk, to teach him in the ways of the old ones. We planned he should understand the language of spirits and trees and birds as easily as the words of his mother, change form at will, know every story and every spell and be able to listen to the wind and see with the eyes of the Watching Woman.

'Although I knew you were the one as soon as I saw you, I did not want to believe it. We were all looking for a boy; we *wanted* a boy.' The old druid closed his eyes and stayed very still.

'But why not a girl?' Tegen clenched her fists and stared down at him. 'What was wrong with me being a girl? There have been women druids before.'

Witton looked up at her and shrugged. 'Men feel . . . We feel sometimes that our dignity has been damaged by having a woman, or even worse a girl, in authority. It is difficult to explain.'

Tegen sat next to him and looked into his face as if the

answers were carved there to be read. 'But if the Goddess has chosen me, how can it be wrong?'

Witton leaned forward and patted her on the hand. 'I know that, my dear, but some of us do not see that which we do not want to see.'

'But the Goddess is female and she protects us all!'

'True, but she is also our very old and very wise mother. It is different, although I don't know how to put it in words. It is possible that this evil may come in the shape of war. For many years, warrior strangers have been coming from beyond the seas in the south. Some say they wish to take our land. They brought the mighty King Caractacos of the Catuvellauni tribe to his knees.' He paused and sighed. 'Although there have been great women warriors, men like to feel that they can protect their wives and children. It is the way we are made. It is not entirely wrong.'

The old druid wheezed and shook his head. 'I think men also fear what cannot be measured. The way women think cannot be calculated or counted in terms of arm lengths or numbers of sword thrusts, and yet their insights can be uncannily right. They often have the Awen very strongly. Most men find this unnerving. We like cold steel we can grip, set patterns we can see, rules and rituals we can follow.

'Now it seems that the Goddess is telling us it is time to change. Maybe it is time to think with our hearts as well as our heads. Do you know the story of Bran the Blessed? He only had a head and no body, and his sister Branwen was all heart. Perhaps it is time to make them into one whole – perhaps it is time for us to work together more closely. You already have the Awen . . . it will help you understand how to teach my brothers to trust you . . . But it will not be easy.'

Witton dared not frighten the child with the truth of just how hard her life as the Star Dancer would be.

Tegen stared into the fire. She did not understand much of what the old druid had said but, to her, the thought of an unknown evil was less daunting than a known one. But she did know that, whatever she had to do, this was a task given to her by the Goddess. With or without the blessing of the druid brethren, she must do her given duty. She was the Star Dancer.

She touched the green shawl around her waist. She could do magic with it, she had proved that, but she decided not to mention it. She didn't think Witton would be comfortable with her using something that hadn't come from his store of holy secrets. If she could learn to do things the druids' way, then they might learn to trust her. She would not let Witton know that without her green silk shawl she was powerless. He might refuse to train her.

Suddenly she realized he was speaking again.

'Now, to practical things. We both know I am dying. The other druids will be here before my bones are cold. They will not like the fact that you are a girl. In fact, I'm not sure they will acknowledge you. You may find your road very rough indeed, child.'

Tegen nodded. 'I am prepared for that.'

'Hmm. Prepared, are you? We'll see. Go and stand by my table and I'll begin with first principles. This house faces east, where the Awen flows from. East is also the home of the spirits of the air. Their offering is incense. You will find that in the silver box – yes, that one. Open it very carefully . . .'

She did as she was told and eased the lid back, releasing a puff of strong-smelling fragrance that caught in the back of her throat and made her cough. She put the box down quickly as she fought to breathe, spluttering the fine contents everywhere.

'Careful! That little box cost a whole fat ox. It will have to last a year at least. You must make an offering of incense to the spirits of the air every morning. They protect this house and therefore the valley. Just put a tiny pinch into the glowing embers at the eastern edge of the fire and open the door to the spirits; they will do the rest.'

Tegen was dying to ask *what* they would do, but it was obvious that Witton was not going to allow time for questions. The old druid was already talking again – about offering a new beeswax candle every morning to the spirits of fire in the South, and fresh spring water in the silver bowl to the spirits in the West. Then he made her repeat after him the words to bless the great stone beside the darkest wall of the roundhouse, to greet the earth spirits of the North.

Then he spoke of herb lore. Some of the uses of the plants Gilda had taught Tegen already: rosemary for clear thought, dog rose for healing the heart, lavender for burns, yarrow for protection, and juniper and pine for purifying. Then heather, holly and oak for luck. But Witton's list was endless: herbs for cursing as well as for blessing.

Scarcely had he finished herbs than he had begun to explain when to use a dried frog and when to use a toad. Ugh! Tegen thought, They both look all dry and twisted. I hope I never have to touch either of them!

Witton mistook the look of panic in her face. 'Don't worry,' he said. 'Derowen knows all of this. You can always ask her if you forget.'

At that Tegen redoubled her efforts to remember everything, for the thought of asking Derowen for help made her blood run cold. 'Doesn't Gilda know too?' she asked shyly.

Witton stopped in his tracks. He fussed with his sacred objects as he spoke, avoiding Tegen's eye. 'Gilda is very wise. But I have not worked with her . . . not for many years. She deals with women's magic. Derowen and I have been . . . *together* more. She knows everything a woman can know without becoming a druid. She has studied magic in depth . . .' Then he added under his breath, 'perhaps too much depth . . .' He tapped a row of deep, straight cuts carved along the edge of his table. 'Now, no time for chatter. Listen and learn,' he snapped.

'Repeat after me, *beith, luis, nion, fearn, saille* . . .'

'What does it mean?'

'They are sacred names of trees, and these cuts are the Ogham marks that represent them. Now *just say it!*' he snarled: '. . . *huath, duir, tinne, coll* . . .'

Tegen was getting thirsty; she looked around for a water pot, but was frightened of the old man's temper. '*Beith, luis, sa* . . .'

'*Nion, fearn, saille* . . .' Witton scowled at Tegen. 'May the spirits preserve me, I have been sent an idiot for an apprentice! Even Griff knows these by heart.'

'Griff?'

'Yes, Griff. *Huath, duir, tinne, coll* . . .'

She swallowed hard and licked her lips. '*Huath, duir* . . .'

'Don't think about it, just say it.' Witton reached behind him and pulled a small drum out from under his stool. 'Try saying it to a rhythm.' He started to tap, and Tegen responded.

'*Muin, gort, ngetal, striaf, ruis* . . .' he went on. It was easier that way, but she was thirsty and she needed to change her mosses. She wriggled, but Witton went on and on, while a whole holly log burned right through to ash.

Tegen's stomach rumbled as Witton described how she must address the spirits of each quarter: East, South, West and North:

Hail and welcome, spirit of the West,
Awen-breather, giver of life,
Flight of eagle,
Wellspring of new hope,
Gift giver of each new day,
Give us gentle winds, we pray.

They chanted. A new log was thrown on to the fire. Tegen didn't dare move, although she felt so uncomfortable – her throat was on fire and her back ached.

'Then Samhain – what is Samhain for?' Witton demanded. He had hardly moved since she had arrived that morning.

Surely he must be thirsty and aching too? she thought.

'*Samhain?*' Witton roared.

'Er . . . It is when the Goddess has grown old. She becomes the dying crone who wraps up the year under a blanket of dead leaves, then frost. The harvest is home and we wait for the long months of cold . . .' Tegen hesitated. 'Samhain is also the meeting between this world and Tir na nÓg, when we . . .'

'Hurry up, child. When what?'

'When we greet our ancestors and give them gifts and thanks. We leave soul cakes and honey wine by our hearths so their spirits know we remember them with love.'

'And your task?'

Tegen shivered despite the heat. 'To walk the shadows

between the worlds of the living and the dead, to ask the spirits to protect and bless the living, to . . .' The thought of going into the dark funeral caves at the head of their valley to speak with the dead was horrible. Sometimes skulls and other bones were washed down in the river. Her mother had told her they were from people who were so evil they had been rejected by the spirits of the Otherworld.

'But why . . . ?' she began.

'You'll find out; you'll understand one day,' was all Witton would say, without letting her finish. 'No time now. Just learn!'

The light was fading before Witton stopped and asked Tegen if she wanted something to eat or drink.

She stood up, ready to fetch the cheese from the shelf, but she felt dizzy and sick. Cramp twisted her stomach. She begged to be excused and went out into the snow to relieve herself and to refill her mole skin. She hurriedly buried the old wad near the North stone, hoping the Goddess would forgive her for not taking everything back to the oak tree behind her own house.

While she was busy doing this she saw Derowen arrive with Witton's evening meal. The wise woman did not see Tegen as she bustled into the cottage, bearing a basket of savoury smells.

Tegen could hear Witton talking in a serious tone of voice, and she thought it wiser to stay out in the snow a little longer. She still did not know how she was going to find the courage to face the other druids, let alone Derowen who seemed to hate her. Inside, Tegen could hear Derowen's raised voice as she clattered Witton's cauldron on to the chain and tripod above the fire.

'Who is it then? Is he someone from the village?' the wise woman demanded.

'From nearby.'

'*Who?*' she snapped. 'Surely not a single child was over-looked? I would have known if another child had been born that night. Gilda would have told me.' Tegen could not understand why Derowen sounded so angry. Surely she should be pleased that the Star Dancer had been found – at least until she knew who it was. But the wise woman sounded upset.

'The Star Dancer is outside. Nature calls to even the chosen ones,' Witton said.

'Pah!' Derowen spat. 'You and I know it is nothing to do with being chosen; it is more to do with who is politically acceptable – or it would have been *him*. If he hadn't been, well, as he is, things would have been very different. The Goddess would have chosen him, for the stars of the Watching Woman danced the night he was born.'

'He was born at *dawn*, and the stars were cloud-covered,' Witton replied sadly. 'We tried to create the perfect druid, you and I. We were presumptuous and we were punished. That is all there is to it.'

'Rubbish, old man. It is politics. You know it and I know

it. If he had been born the most perfect child in the world when the star dance was at its height, our son would still have been passed over. The druids will put in their own favourite every time. Unless this child is something very special, I can see Gorgans in your chair before snow thaw. He is an orator, he has a fine body and can inspire men to follow him. The druid brethren will like that.'

Witton sighed. 'On this occasion, I think you may well be right. I think it is time you met your new druid, the one I am sure you will serve as faithfully as you have served me. The name is given and the acknowledgement is made. What is done cannot be undone . . .' At this he raised his voice and called out: 'Child, it is time you came in. You must be cold out there.'

Shivering, Tegen rubbed her hands in the snow to wash them, and then she pushed the door open.

Derowen screamed and dropped Witton's bowl on the floor, spilling stew and bread across the hard-trodden earth.

13. Rancour

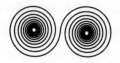

Derowen spat and made the sign against the evil eye.

Tegen brushed it aside. If anyone had the evil eye, it was the old woman, not her. She was tempted to return the insult, but she had to remain calm. Giving insult for insult would only breed rancour.

Tegen bowed her head respectfully. 'Good afternoon, Mother Derowen.'

The old woman turned on Witton, quite red in the face. 'What sort of a jest is this? Surely now is not the time for foolery?'

Witton leaned against one of the house timbers and faced Derowen squarely. 'This is no foolery. This is the one for whom the stars danced thirteen years ago. I knew it and I suspect you knew it too, but we could not bring ourselves to see that the Goddess might have plans other than our own.'

Derowen glared. 'We shall soon see about that! I shall tell the other druids that your last illness has put you out of your mind completely. They will send someone to stop any real damage being done.'

Then she grabbed Tegen by the wrist. 'And as for you, *girl* – it is time you went home. *I* am the one who cares for the druid. I expect you are here to frighten or poison our beloved Father and to hasten his end. Well, it shall not be so.' And with that she started to drag her towards the door.

Tegen flailed her arms around, trying to steady herself, but only succeeded in pulling over the table of sacred objects.

At this Witton rose to his feet, suddenly filled with a strength and steadiness he had not had for many long years. 'Derowen,' he said calmly, 'the Goddess has chosen this one. It is neither my place nor yours to gainsay her. Leave the girl alone and be at peace. Serve her, or not. Do what you will, but she shall stay as the new druid. Tegen is the Star Dancer.'

The silence hung heavily in the room for several moments, and then the old woman shook her hand free of Tegen, pushing her away at the same time.

'So be it!' she spat, and slammed the door behind her.

'I'm . . . I'm sorry about spilling your things,' Tegen

muttered, trying to sweep up the precious incense before it mingled with the remains of Witton's meal.

'It was not you, child. It was Derowen's jealousy. Now, tell me, what will you do to purify these things and to cleanse this place of the bad spirit that has been in here?'

Tegen felt her throat tighten. 'Er . . . pine logs on the fire, oh, and juniper, of course, garlic smeared on the doorposts, and . . . and . . . spring water sprinkled with a bough of ash—'

'Hyssop.'

'Of course, sorry, hyssop . . .' Tegen was guessing and panicking. She had to concentrate. She had to prove she was worthy.

'Good,' said Witton firmly. 'Then do it. You must become a part of the spell yourself so you are purified as well. You must never let ill feeling remain, inside or outside yourself or your house. It only breeds worse things. When you are finished, fetch the cheese your parents sent and we will share it.' And with that the old druid settled back on his bed and closed his eyes.

Tegen's hands shook as she sorted out the sweet-smelling pine logs and put them on the fire, then shaved some flakes of juniper into the glowing embers at the edge. Would she do this right? Who was *she* to be doing such things anyway? An untaught girl with no right to be meddling in the affairs of men who had trained for more than nineteen years to serve the Goddess. She said a prayer of hearth-blessing as she worked:

> *Goddess of the stars of night,*
> *Guide my hands, make fire bright.*
> *Guard all those who by these flames,*
> *Bring to you their sacred names.*

Then she stooped to scoop water out of the pail.

'No,' Witton snapped. '*Fresh* water from the spring on the western side, just above where the stream is spanned by the little bridge. You must never insult the spirits with water drawn beforehand. It is a great discourtesy.'

Tegen muttered her apology and went out into the snow with the little silver bowl in her hand. The wind was bitingly cold and the light had faded to a rich, deep blue, with the snow almost luminous beneath her feet. As she walked she felt afraid. What if the old witch pounced out at her from behind a rock? Hurrying and slipping, struggling to stay upright, Tegen found the stream was still flowing. She thanked the spirits for the gift of water and filled the bowl.

Back in the roundhouse she took a small bundle of hyssop that hung from one of the beams. She dipped the ends of the twigs in the water and sprinkled first herself, then the inside walls. Gritting her teeth against the cold, she ventured back out into the night and cleansed the outside as well. When the ritual was complete, she poured the rest of the water on to the ground on the western side of the cottage, to return what was unused back to the spirits who had given it.

Indigo darkness filled the valley that stretched behind the roundhouse. The night was very quiet. 'Please,' Tegen whispered to any kindly spirits that might be listening, 'may everything be all right.'

When she had finished she went inside, hung the little bundle of twigs to dry and put the silver bowl back on the table. Then she reached for the cheese and found a piece of bread on the shelf as well. She divided everything into two and put Witton's into a bowl. 'Will Derowen fetch the druids tonight?' she asked as she pulled up a stool next to him.

'What weather did you smell in the air, child?'

'More snow.'

'Then no. Not tonight, nor for a night or two more, I fancy. It will be too dangerous for them to travel.'

'I did not get a message to my parents.'

'Oh, they'll know. By now the whole village and all the hill folk will have heard that you are staying here.'

Tegen knew she would have to be content with that for now. Then, as she chewed her food and drank water from the scoop in the pail, she became thoughtful. 'Father, may I ask you something?'

'Is it a big something? I am very tired.'

'Who were you and Derowen talking about? The one whom she thought ought to have been druid in my place?'

Witton sighed. 'Almost fifteen years ago Derowen and I planned that if we had a child then the joining of a druid and a wise woman might produce someone very special. A druid for certain, perhaps even the Star Dancer we were waiting for. But we were presumptuous and things did not work out as we had planned.'

Tegen longed to ask more but dared not, so she pulled a pile of sheepskins in front of the hearth and lay down, covering herself with her cloak. She lay for a long time, staring into the glowing heart of the fire. She did not stir, for she saw and heard things within the flames. Important things she must not miss but did not understand. She twisted her green shawl around her back like a comforting arm and eventually fell asleep.

14. Derowen's Son

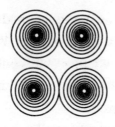

Tegen woke with a start. Where was she? It was still dark, but embers glowed on a hearth by her side.

Someone was moving around with a soft, steady tread. Beyond the fire, an old man's chest wheezed painfully. Ah! She was at Witton's house. She kept her eyes closed and listened to voices whispering. She knew who the visitor was from his peculiar way of speaking. But what was *he* doing here?

Just then a log shifted in the fire, sending sparks out across Tegen's sheepskin covers. Griff leaned across and began to brush the embers away. 'Mussna get ya alight, yu's too important. But dunna fear. I'll be watching ya, jus' like I promised.'

'Griff? Shouldn't you be burning charcoal?' she asked, yawning.

'Get up, Tegen, no time for chatter,' Witton interrupted. 'You have tasks to do.'

Tegen rubbed her eyes and yawned.

'Morning offerings, child, get up!' Witton snapped.

Tegen wondered whether she would be allowed to eat first. 'Is is dawn yet?' she asked, looking around hopefully to see if any food was on the table.

'Just,' the druid replied from his bed. 'We have slept too long. Now move, and see to your duties. We have much to do and say today.'

Tegen pulled on her stockings and clogs and put her cloak around her shoulders. 'We'll talk soon, Griff.' She smiled at him as she picked up the silver bowl for the spring water.

'Concentrate! Incense first,' Witton said, 'then candle, water and lastly bless the stone. Remember: air, fire, water, earth. Think: when you go out of the door you meet the spirits of the East first with the rising sun. The place is called Eostar; it is the point where the sun rises at the spring solstice. Then you move deosil – remember, that means you follow your right hand just as the Sun God does on his journey. You know the prayers and offerings you must make. Hurry, this should all be done before the Sun God shows his whole face to us.'

Tegen took a tiny pinch of the precious incense and

sprinkled it on to the embers at the side of the fire. The perfume was powerful and her head began to reel.

'Open the door, girl,' Witton snapped. 'It's not for you. It's too strong. It's for the spirits.'

Tegen did as she was told and a blast of icy air slapped her in the face. Snow flurried in, hissing angrily as it landed in the fire. 'Now bless the spirits of the air!' Witton commanded. 'Like I taught you. Hurry, I'm freezing in here!'

As if I'm not! thought Tegen as she frantically tried to remember what she had to say. She took a deep breath and began the blessing, but every time she opened her mouth, snow and wind whipped the words away. Perhaps I'm not doing it right? she wondered, but she kept on going. She stepped outside into the bitter morning to greet the other guardian spirits of the white-blanketed valley with their offerings: a candle in a lantern for the South, fresh water for the West and a blessing for the stone of the North.

She ran back inside and sat shivering on a stool by the fire. Griff handed her a beaker of warm mead. She sipped the sweetness and felt her fingers and toes reviving.

'It's nice to see you, Griff, but what are you doing here in such dreadful weather? How on earth did you get through? Does Clesek know you're here?'

'I's a strong man. I gits through snow easy. Father called me,' he said. 'I allus comes when he calls. Allus finds a way.'

Tegen glanced at Witton as he lay under his sheepskins.

★ 150 ★

Everyone called the old man 'Father', out of respect, but there was something in the way Griff said it . . .

Witton raised his head from his pillow. 'Griff is my son, the one I told you about.'

Tegen looked in horror from Griff to Witton and back again. 'So Derowen is his *mother*?' Her mouth dropped open in disbelief.

Griff looked worried and rubbed his runny nose on his sleeve. 'No, her is *not*. I is not *her* boy! I dun-no like her. She's nasty ta me. Nasty ta Tegen too. Can I have anuvver mother? Can I keeps Nessa? Nessa kind.' Griff pushed his bottom lip forward and crossed his arms.

The old druid beckoned Griff to come and sit by him. 'It is true. Derowen is your mother. When you were born she saw you were . . . different. We had been hoping you would be the Star Dancer, the new druid we were all waiting and praying for. Derowen knew you could never learn all that is needed to become a druid. She was sad and disappointed. But it wasn't your fault.'

Griff stared at the floor and kicked at the leg of the bed.

Tegen couldn't tell whether he felt angry or hurt – probably both. She went over to him and gave his shoulder a squeeze. 'I love you,' she whispered. 'So do Nessa and Clesek.'

Witton went on. 'For many years I thought Griff had died at birth. That is what Derowen had always said. One day Gilda came and told me the truth, but she would never say how she knew. I believed her. Gilda is an honest woman, and she knows everything that goes on in the village.

'She also told me I had to open my eyes and see you for what you were, Tegen. She told me you were the Star Dancer when I just couldn't – or wouldn't – see it. But I didn't listen. I was angry. I threw her out and told her never to come back. I accused her of blasphemy.'

Tegen's face flared red. She turned away and stared into the deep shadows of the room. Poor Gilda, she thought. She's suffered so many times because of me. I wish I'd never ever heard of a Star Dancer.

'How did you find out about Griff for certain?' she asked.

'A few moons ago I went to my door and asked the spirits to bring home my son, whoever and wherever he might be. It was Griff who came, with that lumbering great hound behind him.'

Griff nodded. 'That we did.'

'And it was good that we found each other. His love has warmed my heart when I was feeling most alone.'

'I luvs you, old man!' Griff leaned over and hugged him.

Witton lay back and smiled. He laid a frail bony hand on the boy's wide back. 'I love you too, Griff. You are a good son and a blessing to me.'

'But how did Griff come to live with us?' Tegen asked. 'Da always said he found him up by the sacred waterfall.'

'Derowen will say nothing. But Griff is safe and healthy, and that is all I care about. Nessa and Clesek have taught him well – and so have you. He is a fine lad, and he is special; he has the Gift – the Awen.'

Tegen smiled at Griff. 'That is true. You know very important things, don't you? You found me and Mam in the snow. You knew I was the Star Dancer.'

Griff looked at her and a beam spread across his face. 'Luvs you, Tegen,' he said, reaching across to squeeze her hand.

Tegen returned to her stool, muddled with mixed emotions. She was proud of her mother and father for caring for Griff, but furious with Derowen. Who could abandon a baby? Part of her understood that it would have been hard for Derowen to have kept him. People would have said that he was a changeling. If the wise woman could not protect her own child from the jealousy of malign spirits, then who would be safe?

She looked across at the frail old druid, propped up in his bed. 'How did you call Griff this morning? You couldn't possibly have gone out in this weather.'

'He dunna 'aff to.' Griff laughed. 'He jus' calls. I allus knows when he's calling I.' He grinned and wiped his nose on his sleeve once more. 'Bread, Tegen?' he said, offering her a bannock from a basket by his feet.

She was famished and rammed the goodness into her mouth. Her bleeding had almost stopped and her stomach cramps had gone. Today she felt more able to face a day of gruelling lessons. 'Are Mam and Da all right?'

'They's fine. I told un yu's here. Nessa's not happy. Clesek, he tell I ta come and look after yus. They gimme that there bread. I promised I would look after yus and I allus will.' Then he got up and gave her a wet kiss on the cheek, his small eyes crinkling in delight.

Tegen squeezed his hand. 'Thanks, Griff. I'm glad to have at least one real friend. But what about your charcoal?'

Griff shrugged. 'Got other things ta do. Wolf's ta help Clesek now. Tha's good.'

Tegen's heart sank at the thought of her father trying to cope with all his work in this weather. The great mud-coloured dog would be a comfort, but no practical use when it came to burning charcoal.

Witton eased himself to a more upright position. 'I hope Griff will be more than a friend to you over the years,' he said. 'You two have got to get married as soon as possible. It'd be better to wait until the moon is completely full, but I won't last that long and I have to be sure you are hand-fasted before I go.'

Tegen started at him, open-mouthed.

Griff squeezed her hand in his and smiled. He looked so happy.

How can I turn him down without hurting his feelings? she wondered. There's not a kinder person in the whole, wide world, but . . . *marriage*? No!

Witton patted his hand on his bed. 'Come and sit here, child, and let me explain.'

Tegen moved slowly. She had no idea being the Star Dancer would entail *this* . . . Witton couldn't mean it, not marriage to Griff . . . She loved her foster-brother dearly, but he was just that, a brother, not a husband, and he was . . . well, he was a halfhead. There was so much he could never possibly understand. How could she explain that there had been some mistake . . . ? Perhaps the old druid was rambling in his illness? He couldn't be in his right mind . . . he wasn't making sense . . .

Witton's voice was weak and his pale blue eyes were bloodshot and watery. When he reached out and took Tegen's hand he was shaking. 'A druid usually lies with a woman when he is chosen. It symbolizes the marriage union between the Mother Goddess and her people.'

Tegen drew a breath to speak.

'Shh. Say nothing. My every word is vital now. I may not be able to talk much more. Now, it is best if you are wed to Griff because he is my and Derowen's son. When the druids know the truth about his birth it may make it easier for them to accept you. You will find it useful to have a man around, because even though you are the Star Dancer you are forbidden in the sacred room. It will take many years to make your own sacred space and to fill it with everything you need. Until then, Griff will fetch things for you. Don't worry, he will know what to do. My spirit will teach his strong heart what his weak head cannot understand. He already knows how to listen to his Awen. He is a good man.'

'I is that too!' Griff agreed enthusiastically, pounding himself on the chest and nodding his tussock of straw-like hair.

Tegen hung her head and said nothing. She understood what Witton did not want to say: if the other druids saw Witton and Derowen's son here, they might allow her to stay in the roundhouse – as Griff's wife.

She glanced across at Griff and imagined lying in bed next to him. However kind and loving he was, she just couldn't do it. Her stomach tied itself in knots. She had no time now to think about such things. Witton needed her attention every second . . . perhaps if she worked hard and kept his mind on rituals and spells, he might forget about the marriage.

The next two days passed in a stream of learning; Tegen was expected to repeat incantations and rituals until her head spun. She was glad that Witton needed more and more rests.

The third night, as they were preparing for sleep, Witton called Tegen to his bedside. His chest was wheezing and he found it difficult to speak.

'You must stay awake . . . tonight. I know . . . you are tired, but . . . important.'

'What do you want me to do, Father? Are you feeling ill? Do you want me to sit with you?'

'No.' His chest heaved for breath. 'It is more important. You . . . go night fishing for . . . words.'

Tegen grasped his hand. It was hot and sweaty. He had been coughing and vomiting during the afternoon and the stale stench hung around him despite her best attempts to keep him clean.

'Would you like me to wash you, Father?' Tegen asked gently, certain he was not in his right mind. What could he mean by 'night fishing for words'?

The old man shook his head from side to side. 'No!' he snapped. 'No. Go into the dark. Alone. Find words . . . celebrate, celebrate the coming of the new . . . sun.' He stopped and wheezed and coughed and eventually lay his head back. 'I want you to find . . . words for a new song. Star Dancer . . . must be a bard. Find . . . words to teach . . . meanings . . . to people.' He coughed again and seemed to sleep.

Griff came in from peeing in the snow. 'Father all right?' he asked, wiping his hands down his breeches.

'He's not well. He says I have to sit up all night in the dark and make words for a new song, but I don't know how.'

Griff snuggled between his pile of sheepskins by the fire. 'Good idea. I likes songs,' and he sang himself to sleep with a tuneful muttering.

Tegen pulled her sheepskins around herself and sat awake, staring at the fire, until only a few red embers remained. At last she made herself get out of bed and bank up the hot ashes. Starting a fire from scratch was hard work.

If the embers could be kept in, it would make all the difference in the morning.

Suddenly she had it! Bringing living fire out of dead ashes was like the coming of the midwinter sun out of the darkness! The new sun gave the Goddess her spring-child, born like a new flame from the final embers of the fire. That had meaning. That could teach an idea. Tegen was never much of a singer, but she did love the chants and incantations she had learned in the past few days. They had given her a feel for the way the lines of a song ought to run.

In the dark she curled up and let her imagination play until words and rhythms formed within her mind.

By morning, when Witton woke to supervise her morning greeting of the day, Tegen was humming the beginnings of a tune.

> *Greetings, Lady Mother.*
> *You lay awake in bitter night*
> *Aching with the child within,*
> *To bring him to the New Year's light.*
>
> *Greetings, Lady Mother.*
> *From darkest ash and cold was born*
> *A glowing ember of brightest life,*
> *To give to us our Prince of Dawn.*

Witton smiled and coughed. 'It is good. For a beginner. Hmm. Not bad.'

That morning Griff spent a great deal of time alone with Witton in the secret room while Tegen had to remain excluded within the roundhouse. The air stank of the old man's vomit and spittle. She was grateful for the short times she was required to go outside and perform her rites. She longed to catch up on her missing night's sleep, but instead she recited the tree names and incantations Witton had taught her.

For three days the snow had been too deep for Derowen to get through with Witton's meals. Tegen wasn't sorry. She fed the quern with barley from the druid's storage pots and made bannocks from the flour. Then she clawed frozen turnips from the clamp, chopped them into the stewpot and added dried beans, oats and thyme. The room soon filled with the sweet and savoury aroma.

When Witton rested Griff followed Tegen everywhere, grinning cheerfully. He was a dear friend, but she was starting to find his constant attention difficult. The way he longed to hold her hand and hug and kiss her. They had always been close and affectionate, but this . . . this was different.

'Stop it, Griff!' she snapped at last, pushing him away. 'Leave me alone for a bit, will you?' Then, seeing the hurt and disappointment in his forlorn face, she tousled his hair and tried to smile. 'I am just tired.' How could she be nice to him but not encourage him? She did love him . . . but not like *that*.

At last, when her tasks were done, she lay down and closed her eyes. Witton was asleep and she needed to be alone, inside her head at least. Now I understand why Derowen hates Griff so much, she thought. Her son should have been a powerful druid, maybe even the Star Dancer, but his moon face made her feel as if she had failed as a wise woman. She didn't see a little human who could grow to be loving and strong; she only saw an idiot baby. Tegen glanced over to where Griff sat by the fire, busy with his knife and a piece of wood. The old woman has missed the point, she thought. Griff is a good man who has the Awen for sure. Mam and I would be dead if it wasn't for him! Then an awful thought struck her. But . . . but . . . I only hope Witton is wrong about this marriage. What if I refuse? Can I be the Star Dancer without Griff? I can't marry him. I really can't. And she began to cry softly. Please, Lady, don't make me do this. It's not right. It can't be. Please may Griff be wrong, please may Witton be rambling . . .

'Is you all right?' came Griff's kindly voice, and his big hand tugged back the covers a little. 'You's not cryin', is yer?'

'No, I'm fine. Just sniffing. Got a bit of a cold.' Tegen sat up and wiped her nose and eyes on a bit of rag she kept in her sleeve.

'Oh. Cos I wouldna want yus sad.' He grinned. 'I's

carvin' yus a present!' He waved a stick of shaved wood and a knife near her face. 'I's'll not tell what 'tis. S'prise!'

'Thank you,' Tegen muttered, ashamed by his generosity and wishing he wasn't so kind. 'I'll get up in a little while. I'm just tired.' She lay down and pulled the covers back over herself, returning to her thoughts. The image of Derowen drifted into her head: the old woman's long teeth, grey plaits and sour look made Tegen go cold. Now she, the Star Dancer, was at Witton's side instead of her. Derowen was sure to be plotting something . . .

Tegen wished she could walk away. If only she could be back home helping her mother grind the oats and cook porridge for her father. She missed them both so much. Suddenly she had an overwhelming desire to do that and nothing more for the rest of her life. But she could never go back to that. Not only would the truth prevent her, but, for the present at least, she could not even physically get away. Outside, the winds were relentless and although the snow had eased up, the drifts were deep and treacherous. Even stepping outside for the rituals was hard enough. The circular path around the roundhouse had to be shovelled clear each morning.

Then another image came into her mind, the face of the one person she wished she could see more than anyone. It was Gilda. She had believed in Tegen since the moment she was born. The midwife would understand how lonely she felt. She would say something strong and wise that would help.

Tegen slipped out of bed. 'Won't be a moment,' she told Griff, hoping he wouldn't follow her. Outside, the biting cold slapped itself around her in a malicious embrace. Closing her eyes she tried to imagine Gilda: her kindly, wrinkled face like a well-baked loaf, and her deep-set eyes bright and twinkling under an unruly tangle of greying curls.

Tegen's long dark hair whipped her face and her teeth chattered so hard her face hurt. She clutched her green shawl and stamped a few dance steps in the snow, partly to warm her cold feet and partly to summon her friend to her aid.

'I know you can't come to me, or me to you, but please help me, Gilda, somehow,' she told the wind.

The spirits of the wind took her words and tossed them into the sky.

15. Marrying Moon-Face

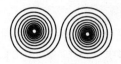

The midwinter solstice came and went with little easing of the weather. The moon waxed, Witton waned and Tegen became more and more apprehensive.

She often slipped out of the roundhouse and closed her eyes. Firstly she thought of Gilda and wished she could come; then she imagined the little drummer boy striking a rhythm to make Witton's heart grow stronger so he could stay alive. But Tegen could not hold the beat in her head. She knew it meant Witton was dying, and it was unkind to keep the old man in this world by magic. His spirit needed to go to the Goddess in the Otherworld of Tir na nÓg, so he could be reborn in a new body.

The snow stopped and village men cleared a path up to Witton's roundhouse so Derowen could resume her visits. When she came she always ignored Tegen and Griff, but worked on the old man with rubbing lotions and tisanes.

Four nights after the Sun God began to regain his strength the wise woman stayed late. Tegen lay in bed as if asleep. She watched from beneath her lashes as Derowen pounded herbs with oils. The steady rhythm of the pestle beating the contents of the mortar made Tegen feel drowsy, but she stayed awake.

At last Derowen stopped, hesitated, looked around furtively. She picked up a rush light and crept into Witton's forbidden room. The horse skin creaked as she pushed it aside. From the gaps around the hide, Tegen could see the weak light dancing with shadows as the wise woman moved around within the sacred space.

Derowen crept furtively back into the main room. Under her shawl she carried a bundle of something dried. From this she broke a small handful, added it to her ingredients and hid the rest in her basket. Then she picked up her pestle and resumed her work. As she worked, a pungent, sickly smell drifted with the wood smoke. She wrapped the oily mess in linen, then wound it around the old man's chest in a poultice. Witton coughed and wheezed, but submitted to her. When she had finished she picked up her cloak and left.

Tegen waited until she was sure the wise woman wasn't coming back, then she crept to Witton's side. 'Father', she whispered urgently. 'Father, I am going to take the dressing from your chest, I . . . I don't think it is good for you.'

Witton stirred in his sleep, flickered his eyes open and looked at Tegen.

'I saw Derowen take something from your sacred room,' she went on, 'and she put it in the poultice.'

'Impossible . . . She wouldn't dare,' he wheezed. 'Go to sleep.'

Tegen ignored him and very gently she unwound the cloth and threw the contents on to the fire. It hissed and spat. Tegen washed the old man clean and went back to her own bed.

But she could not sleep. She lay awake, listening to Witton's chest rattling horribly. Tegen had never heard someone dying before.

I must get up, I must go to him, she thought. But her body wanted to stay in the warm comfort of her bed. No one would blame her if the old man had died in the night without her knowing . . . That's not the way it's got to be, she told herself firmly. I know he stinks and death is coming, but . . . but . . . I have to do it. I have to be there . . . Just because I am afraid doesn't mean I can't do my duty. I have to breathe in his last breath . . . The thought of it made her heart sink. It wasn't just the fear of what would happen when she did it; she felt sick at the thought of the stench.

'Star Dancer,' he whispered, 'are you there?'

'Coming, Father.' Tegen got up and lit a rush light, bound her dark hair back with her green shawl, then scooped some water from the bucket into a bowl. Sitting on the edge of Witton's bed, she tried to help him sit up a little and drink. 'What can I do for you, Father?' she asked.

'Marry . . . Griff . . . now,' he whispered. In the glimmering light she could see a mixture of blood and spittle crusted at the corners of his mouth. His eyes were flickering and could not focus. Each breath was an agony.

Her mouth went dry. 'No!' she screamed inside her head. 'He doesn't mean it! Not really. He can't!' But she knew he did.

'Griff!' she called out in panic. 'Come here *now*!'

Griff threw back the skins that covered him and struggled to his feet. 'Wassit to now?' he moaned. 'I's not let that charcoal go to ash, honest!'

Tegen sighed, wishing that he could have one of his moments of insight. 'Come here. Father is dying.'

Griff stumbled across the dark room. Tegen jumped up from Witton's bed and grasped his wrist. 'Come *here*.' She tugged him across to the bed and placed the old druid's limp, cold fingers on top of her and Griff's joined hands.

She swallowed hard. There was no time to think. There was no way out either. She couldn't deny Witton's dying wish. He was her teacher and one of the few people who believed in her. If she disobeyed, who knew what spirits would be sent from the Otherworld to punish her?

'Father wants us to marry,' she told Griff, 'now.' She put her free hand on the old man's forehead. 'Witton,' she said softly, 'we're both here.'

'Jump the fire,' he said hoarsely.

'What?' Tegen asked, putting her ear as near to Witton's mouth as she could.

'Hold hands . . . jump the fire.' He coughed, then tried to suck more air into his painful lungs. 'Jump . . . together . . . Then you'll . . . be . . . married.'

Tegen grasped Griff's hand and looked at his sleepy confused face. I can't go through with this, she thought. I can't do it. We'll be married for always. But will the old man notice if we don't? His spirit will! Oh help! Goddess, help me, I am scared. I want to go home . . .

Tegen closed her eyes and tried to imagine the coming evil, whatever it was, the impending danger to everyone. It was her duty to follow the path Witton pointed out to her, whatever she felt inside. She owed it to him. She owed it to the Goddess.

Griff was rubbing his eyes and trying to wake up. He looked across at her and smiled his big cheery grin, then he leaned over and gave Witton a hug. The old man coughed.

Marrying Griff might not be so bad, Tegen thought. He won't want to do the things that men do in bed. Inside his head he's only a child after all. He's my best friend. He won't ever let me down.

The idea of having her own hearth and children seemed so remote, perhaps it was better to be tied to a moon-face who was kind and loved her, than to a man with all his wits who would not let her fulfil the destiny the Goddess had chosen for her. A man who might even beat her.

Witton opened his eyes and let his focus flicker from one to the other.

Tegen took a deep breath. 'Will you marry me, Griff?' she asked.

The boy beamed with delight. 'I loves yus. Allus have.'

'Good. Now, hold my hand tightly.' She stood up and pulled Griff beside her. 'We've got to jump over the fire. Tuck up your shirt so it doesn't catch alight and when I say, "now," we both run and jump. Got it?'

'Got it, Tegen,' Griff replied, grasping at the edge of his shirt with his free hand and laughing.

'One, two, three . . .'

'JUMP!' Griff yelled out as he lurched awkwardly forward towards the low glow in the hearth. Tegen felt his fingers twisted around her own as together they launched into the air, cleared the pale flames and landed heavily on the other side.

She brushed a few sparks from her skirt and led Griff to sit on Witton's bed again.

'Good,' Witton said huskily. 'Now . . . sit . . . When I go, Tegen . . . breathe my last breath . . . My spirit . . . into you . . .' He coughed in a spasm that seemed as if it would never end. His chest heaved and bloody spittle ran down his chin. 'When I am dead, close my eyes . . . .' He was silent for a long time, then suddenly he spoke again: 'Sew me into . . . bedding skins . . . put me in . . . grave . . . until druids come . . .' The old man began another coughing fit that caused him to choke until his eyes bulged. He tried to lean forward, shaking violently.

Tegen put her arm around him, then with her free hand took the washing cloth, dipped it into the bowl by the bed and wiped the sweat and mucus from the old druid's face. 'Lie back now and rest,' she coaxed. Gradually the shaking subsided and Tegen realized with horror that Witton was no longer breathing. She put her right hand behind his head and tried to help him lie down on his pillow. His eyes swung wildly around, then he sighed.

Then everything was still and very, very quiet.

'The last breath!' Tegen gasped. She had missed it. She leaned over and breathed in above Witton's mouth, pressing down on his chest to try to catch what little bit of his spirit might still be there. This was terrible. Her first great duty and she had missed it! Did it matter? Would she still be a druid?

But then, she told herself, I was there holding him. I was very close. But how close was close enough to catch a man's spirit? She glanced around at Griff, who was standing in the umber shadows by Witton's feet, his head bowed.

'Gone now?' he asked.

'Gone,' she replied, willing herself to stretch out her hands to close Witton's eyes. He felt warm. Somehow she expected him to sigh and turn over. But she knew he wouldn't.

'Come on, Griff, I'm going to need your help. Father will begin to smell soon so we've got to put him outside. We don't want the wolves to get him, so we'll lay him on his bed-skins and roll him up and sew it all together. Until the thaw brings the other white-robes we won't be able to take him to the caves so he can travel to Tir na nÓg. But this will help to keep him safe.'

'Good,' Griff agreed. 'Safe is good.'

Together they took the sheepskins and laid them end to end on the floor. Then, with Griff at the old man's feet and Tegen at his head, they lifted him down and rolled him into a cocoon. 'I will have to wait for morning,' Tegen said. 'It will be impossible even to thread the needle before there is daylight.'

Griff nodded silently. Tegen wasn't sure whether he understood or not. 'Let's try to get a little more sleep,' she said, pulling her own covers over herself again. 'Sleep tight, Griff.'

'Sleep tight, Tegen,' he replied as he wandered over to his pile of skins. After a few moments of rustling around he lay still. 'Father dun stopped? Like goose for dinner?' he asked in a worried tone.

'Yes.'

Then there was a long silence. 'Then that's all right then. Nuffin hurt him no more.'

'No. Nothing can hurt him any more.'

'You the druid now?'

'I suppose so, but I have to be trained first.'

'Can I help you?'

'Yes. I'm going to need all sorts of help.'

'Gonna miss Father,' he said simply. He let a few tears roll down his cheeks, then he lay down by the fire and slept.

Tegen lay awake until the first silvery light began to seep through the crack under the thatch. Very quietly she got dressed, cast incense into the flames and opened the door. She stood facing the cold, endlessly white morning. 'The druid is dead!' she called out. Then she lit the candle, sheltered the flame with her hand and carried it to the horn lantern hanging under the eaves of the southern side of the cottage. Fetching the silver bowl, she drew fresh water from the spring and gave thanks. As she worked, she told each of the spirits of Witton's death. She wept, the tears making freezing tracks down her face.

Finally she turned to the stone on the northern side. A little wren shivered there. Tegen went inside and found the end of a bannock that Griff had left. She crumbled it and threw it to the bird. As it flew down to feast Tegen blessed both the stone and the bird who had come to announce that a great man had died.

'What am I going to do?' she asked the skies as she leaned against the doorpost. 'I feel so alone . . .' She rubbed snow into her face and combed her long black hair with her fingers. Then she went back inside. From the food shelf she took Witton's knife, dipped it in water and whetted it against the hearthstone. Then from the middle of her scalp she shaved a thick swathe of her hair. It was a sign of mourning usually made by the male head of a family.

Griff watched her impassively. Then he picked up some of the fallen strands and held them to his cheek. 'Pretty. Soft,' he said. 'Yus sorry Father dead?'

'I'm very sorry,' she answered. Taking the strands, she threw half on the fire and laid the other half on Witton's skin coffin.

Then she repeated the shaving on Griff's rough straw-like mop. 'Cold!' he said miserably, tying a shawl over his head so he looked like an old woman.

It took much of the morning to sew Witton's skin-shroud together. By the time the work was finished, Tegen's fingers and palm were bleeding from pushing the awl through the tough hides and drawing the thick iron needle up and down a hundred times.

'I's a-hungry!' Griff announced, looking sorrowful. Tegen realized that she too was famished. Derowen only ever brought enough food for Witton. Never anything for Griff or herself. The old druid had always made them share what little there was, supplemented with bannocks and stew from his own meagre supplies. Would Derowen feed them when she discovered Witton was dead? Somehow Tegen doubted it.

There was only one thing for it; they would have to go begging.

Tegen stood at the roundhouse door and surveyed the landscape. The air felt warmer and smelled earthy. The spring at the bottom of the hill was gushing with fresh vigour. They would have to tell the village the news. The story might be worth oatcakes and cheese.

'Come on, let's find food.' Tegen clutched the old druid's bowl to her chest. Griff wrapped his cloak around himself and followed her as she led the way down the hill.

It was soggy underfoot. Before long, Griff's breeches were soaked and Tegen's stockings were wet. Neither of them cared and they both felt better for being outside. They had been cooped up in the roundhouse for seven nights. Being able to move around and breathe real air made up for the wet and cold.

Slipping and sliding, they entered the main gate of the village.

The cluster of roundhouses looked welcoming, nestled safely within the high fence under the bare trees, but the memory of Griff's stoning was still painful. How would they be received? What lies had Derowen been spreading about their time with Witton? Tegen could smell cooking smoke and baking bread. Her stomach rumbled.

The first hearth inside the village palisade was where Budok, his woman, Enor, and their grown-up children lived. Their roundhouse was well repaired and their geese and pigs were fat. They weren't bad people. The bard within Tegen was already composing how she should tell the tale of Witton's death to make it worth at least one plate of food. She wouldn't mention anything about taking the old man's place. Not yet. She dared not think how she was going to break the news to the druids when they came.

They arrived at the whitewashed roundhouse. Under its conical thatch the hurdle door was shut. Inside they could hear voices chatting and laughing. Griff and Tegen exchanged glances. 'Shall we knock?' she asked. 'What if they say no?'

Griff shrugged, lifted his fist and thumped on the doorpost. 'I's a-hungry. Enor makes good bannocks.'

Budok came to the door, gnawing at a meaty bone in his fist. Tegen took a deep breath. 'I have news,' she began.

When Budok heard of Witton's death, he welcomed them into his home. Enor dished up bacon and parsnips while her man demanded the details be retold again and again. He knew he would be given many a draught of mead on the strength of being the first to know the tale.

He looked at Griff. 'I suppose he gave you his last breath then, lad? Many say you were the old man's son, although Enor says Derowen was too old to have carried you, eh? That's why you came out a moon-face, maybe? Never mind, the Goddess will use whom she will, I dare say.' He raised his mead horn in salute. 'To you, my lad. Goddess bless you, whether it's you that's the new druid or not.'

'Aye,' said Griff, not raising his eyes, 'Father gone. Jus' us now.'

Before Budok could ask any more awkward questions, there were hurried footsteps in the snow outside, the door flew open and strong arms wrapped around Tegen in a loving grasp.

'You poor darling!' Gilda said. 'I heard you calling. I wanted to come but the snow was too deep. These days I am so stiff in my joints, walking is hard for an old woman like me.'

Tegen buried her head into the midwife's warm, plump shoulder and cried.

16. Gilda

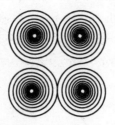

Gilda held Tegen and let her cry. 'You're still a child, even though you're at an age for bleeding,' she said softly.

Griff ran across and joined in the hug with enthusiasm, but Gilda pushed him away firmly. 'I need to talk with Tegen alone,' she said. 'About women's things.' She turned to Budok's wife, a stocky woman, efficient and sensible. 'Enor, will you take Griff to your hearth for today? I need to listen to Tegen here; I suspect this is the first time she has closed an old one's eyes.'

'Of course,' Enor replied. 'I remember my first time well. It is not easy to stare death in the face when you are so young. Griff . . .' she turned to the lad, who was squatting by the fire. 'You'll stay with us?'

'That I will.' He grinned. 'Can I play w'yous dogs? I miss ole Wolf. Big missing.'

'Of course you can; they are in the yard.'

Tegen thanked Enor and let Gilda lead her away to her own small roundhouse on the far side of the village. Once inside, the midwife shut her door against the world.

Gilda coaxed Tegen to the bed of soft white sheepskins spread with brightly coloured blankets, then she sat next to her. Little by little Tegen poured her story into Gilda's lap as the older woman took a comb and untangled the knots in her hair and her heart at the same time. She ran her warm fingers over Tegen's shaved patch.

'I wanted so much to see you. I needed you so many times, but Mam would never let me come. Ever.'

'Nessa finds me . . . difficult.' Gilda smiled. 'Although I have never meant her harm.' She hesitated as she worked at a particularly matted strand. Tegen winced. 'So many hard things for you to bear,' Gilda said at last. 'I always guessed you were the Star Dancer they were looking for. But some men don't like to be told. They have to find out in their own way and their own time. Best to let it be that way.'

'You won't tell anyone, will you?' Tegen choked, her throat so swollen from sobbing she could hardly speak. 'Not yet.'

'You know me, my dear. I never tell anyone anything!' Then she laughed. 'I'm well aware everyone says I'm a gossip who never stops talking, but I never tell anything *important*.' She kissed Tegen on the head. 'The time will come when everyone will need to know, but it won't be tonight. Now, will you let me tuck you in and you can stay here with me for the dark hours? Tomorrow you can go back rested and face what must be.'

'No . . . Thank you, I can't. I have rituals I must perform at nightfall to guard the valley from the night spirits.'

'You had better not stay long then. The light is very short these days.'

Tegen sighed, nestling amongst the skins and wrapped in the pretty weavings. She was longing to be comforted and to still be the child that knew nothing of rituals and druids and spirits.

It was late afternoon before Gilda put her arm around Tegen's back and eased her into a sitting position. 'Child, you must wake up. It would be easy for me to persuade you to stay, to tell you that it doesn't matter. But you were born to this and it *all* matters. People see me as a light-headed chatterbox who never takes anything seriously, but it's all a cover for the secret life I lead. I too make morning and evening offerings. I too listen to the wind and try to see with the eyes of the Watching Woman. I have learned the sacred stories well enough to wear the blue robe of a bard.'

Tegen stared at Gilda in the half-light as if she was seeing her for the first time. 'You?'

The older woman smiled. 'When I was a little older than you are now I was training to be a druid myself. I was apprenticed to a wise man not far from here. But after a while I met Witton and I fell in love with him. I was scarcely halfway through my training when I gave it all up. He asked me to be the woman who lay with him and who would work with him all through his long life.'

'But wasn't that Derowen?' Tegen interrupted, then wished she hadn't when she saw the pain on Gilda's face.

'In the end it was her. I had always believed she was my friend. The night I was to be hand-fasted with Witton she gave me a tisane. She said it would make me always beautiful in his eyes. I wanted that; I wanted that more than anything. I paid her with my silver armbands for that drink, but in the long run I paid much more dearly than that.'

'What happened?' Tegen put her arm around the midwife.

'The "beauty drink" was a sleeping draught. I slept, and Derowen went to Witton's side in my stead. She gave him a tisane too and it confused his mind. He did not know it was not me leaping the fire with him, hand-fasted forever.'

Tegen sat up, furious. 'But surely the druids couldn't hold him to that? How can a marriage by deception be a real one?'

Gilda bowed her head and sighed. 'It was made in the presence of the Goddess. Witton said that an earthly marriage is always a hand-fasting within the spirit world. There was no turning back and Witton was too honourable to break his vows, but he never slept with her after that first night, until . . . until . . .'

'Until Griff was conceived?'

'You know about that?'

'Yes. Witton told me – he had to. He said if I was married to his son, I might be accepted by the druids.'

'Ah yes. I had forgotten. So you are married now. Has he lain with you yet . . . ?'

'No. We have only just leaped the fire.' Tegen hesitated. 'He won't want me, will he? Not . . . not as a woman, I mean? Surely Griff isn't . . . ?'

Gilda smiled and shook her head. 'Griff may be a child in his head, but he is still a healthy man in his body. You must be prepared for whatever happens next. Although do try to make him wait a bit. How many times have you bled?'

'Once.'

'Then it is too early. If you carried a child now it would not be strong. You would not be strong either. See if he will wait another year, but it is a lot to ask of any man. Especially if you are living in the same roundhouse.'

Tegen's stomach lurched. She did not want to think of her dear Griff in any way other than as a brother and a friend. She looked at the pale light struggling in from a small wind-eye under the eaves. 'It is getting dark. I must go. Will you walk back a way with me and tell me more of your story?'

Gilda stood and pulled her cloak down from a peg by the door, then hesitated. 'Would you like me to braid your hair for you before you go? I have a pretty ribbon I would like to give you.'

Tegen nodded, relishing the maternal attention she had always craved but Nessa had never dared to give. 'Thank you.' She stood in front of the midwife, whose skilful fingers twisted backwards and forwards weaving a many-stranded plait.

'So where was I?' Gilda teased a loose lock of hair from behind Tegen's ear. 'Oh, yes. Well, I did not have the courage to go back to my master to continue my training as a druid. He had not wanted me to be with Witton, but I thought our love was more important than anything. So, even though Witton had wed Derowen, I stayed here. Derowen took the title of Wise Woman because she stood at Witton's side. She had wanted it ever since she was your age. But she held that place by deceit. Ill would, and did, come of it.

'I also knew it was my duty to stay here and help guard the village with what little magic I had, until someone else the spirits loved would come and take my place.' With one last deft movement Gilda tied a piece of fine blue silk ribbon around the ends of the many strands that wove themselves into one thick snake flowing down Tegen's back.

The midwife put her hands on Tegen's shoulders and turned her full circle so she could admire her handiwork.

'Well, it seems, thank the Lady, that the right person is here at last. But it really is time to go. Put your cloak on. It is dry.'

Tegen traced the delicate patterns behind her head with delight, then took the cloak and wrapped herself in its warm folds.

Gilda pulled open the door, to be met by icy rain. 'I will walk to Budok's roundhouse with you. Careful, it will be slippery underfoot.'

Tegen followed her out. Dark louring clouds hung low over the hills behind the valley. She looked up into the slopes covered by leafless trees and sought for traces of smoke above her old home. She thought of her father struggling to keep the charcoal burning as well as turning his hand to the silver and lead he loved. Things would be very hard for him now, with both Griff and herself gone. Her heart went out to her mother, who must have been so frightened when she heard the news of the druid's death and even more frightened of what might happen to Tegen.

Gilda followed her gaze. 'They know you are safe. You will see them soon. I have in mind a lad who will be helpful to them. I will send him up when the snow has cleared. And maybe a girl to help your mother too.'

Tegen smiled. 'They would like that.' And she set out across the slush. For a short while they walked in silence along the path that wound its way between roundhouses, pigsties and duck pens. So many thoughts were racing through her mind she didn't know which to focus on first.

But there was one thing she really wanted to know. 'Will you tell me how you knew that Griff was Derowen's son? Witton said it was you who told him.'

Gilda stood still and looked up at the leaden sky, saying nothing as the icy rain poured down her face. At last she sighed. 'A midwife knows when a woman is beginning to swell with a child under her ribs. It is an instinct. Derowen never told me who the father was, but who else could it be? She smirked at me every time I saw her. She wanted me to feel her belly to see how the child lay. I felt a dagger in my heart every time I did so. That child should have been mine . . . he would have been loved and wanted, even though he was a halfhead.' Gilda turned her face away. The rain trickled down her cheeks.

Then the midwife sighed and started walking again, her clogs squelching through the mud in rhythm with Tegen's step. 'Derowen was due to give birth a half-moon after your mother. But the child came at dawn a few hours after the stars had danced. I suspect she tried to make the child come early with herbs. I will never know, but she had the skills to do it.'

They crossed the marketplace where Griff had been stoned. The square was awash.

Tegen was angry. If only I had been able to spend time with you, she thought, we could have helped each other. She took Gilda's arm. 'What happened next?'

'Derowen didn't call for me to come at the time of

the birth. Instead she sent a messenger to fetch me later in the day. When I arrived there was a wicker funeral basket ready woven, with a top tightly stitched into place. She told me the child was a boy but he had died, and she asked me to bury it. I dug a grave, but being a midwife I was intrigued. I wanted to know what had made the baby die. It had seemed healthy enough in the womb . . . Secretly I took the basket into my own house and opened the lid. Inside was a shawl of pale new wool, tenderly wrapped around two fine turnips!'

Tegen bit her lip, trying not to laugh at the picture in her mind. 'So you knew the child was not dead?'

'That's right. I watched Derowen carefully, then two nights later she went out with a bundle in her arms and turned towards the hills. I followed her. She left the baby where the wolves run. I could smell their scent.

'When Derowen had gone, I picked up the child and was wondering what to do. I wanted to dare to take him into my own home, but I knew Derowen would guess what I had done and she would fear and hate me even more, in case I betrayed her secret. Just then I heard your father praying where the water comes from the mouth of the spirit of the hill. He was praying for a boy next time Nessa gave birth.

'It was all too good to be true. I left the precious bundle right in the middle of the path, pinched him so he cried and left the rest to your parents' good hearts.'

Tegen and Gilda had almost reached Budok and Enor's

roundhouse. The snow had slipped from the new thatch; the whitewashed walls and stacks of dried logs under the eaves made the place look solid and safe. Despite the bitter rain, both Gilda and Tegen stopped in the middle of the path. They were not ready to go in yet. There was so much more to say.

Tegen squeezed Gilda's arm. 'So you told Witton?'

'Yes, some years later, when the time was right. But he didn't believe me. Why should he, when Derowen had him where she wanted him?'

'He did believe you.' Tegen smiled. 'He told me so. He acknowledged Griff as his own before he died. He told me you were a good and wise woman.' She hesitated. More unsaid words were burning on the tip of her tongue. But what if she was wrong? Would she do more harm than good to dear Gilda who deserved only blessings and happiness? 'Is this the Awen or my own wishful thinking?' she asked herself.

'He still loved you!' she blurted out loud. 'He didn't say so, but it was there in the way he talked about you. Despite his temper and everything, he never forgot you.'

Gilda blinked and bit her lip, then nodded in the direction of the welcoming door. 'Let's go inside. Enor will have fattened Griff up like a yuletide pig. You had better go in and rescue him. Then you must hurry back. It is time for the next offering.'

Tegen hugged Gilda. 'Thank you,' she said. 'Thank you

for all you did for Griff and for me . . . and thank you for believing in me.'

The midwife stroked Tegen's dark plait. 'That's all right, my honeycomb. Now it's up to you two to believe in yourselves. I will see you soon. You have many things to learn. As soon as I can, I will teach you the sacred stories so you may understand your own tale better, my Star Dancer.' And with that she kissed Tegen on the cheek, turned and stamped through the melting snow, back towards her own home.

17. Taking Witton to Tir na nÓg

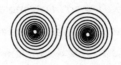

The day after the old man died, Griff and Tegen tried to dig a temporary grave at the bottom of the hill. They dared not leave the body outside just stitched in skins and covered with icy mud. The wolves were hungry and would eat anything. Despite the thaw, the frost had gone deep in the waterlogged meadow and the ground remained too hard for even a shallow hole. They tried to gather stones to pile over the body in a cairn, but the task was endless. High in the inner valley there were large boulders, but these were too heavy to fetch. There was no way Griff and Tegen could carry Witton all the way to the caves by themselves and no one in the village would touch the dead druid for fear of being cursed.

In the end, the body had to be dragged into the little back room.

Griff would not let Tegen help; he insisted on doing the deed alone. 'Yus a girl. Girls not allowed.' He was adamant.

Angry and humiliated, Tegen stood alone in the room, listening to Griff struggling and puffing as he pulled and pushed the awkward burden this way and that. At last there was silence and then Griff came back, smiling. 'I's dun it. Druids cummin' soon. Father put away proper then.'

Tegen didn't doubt that Griff knew the white-robes would be on their way. She sensed he was right.

Two days later the first of the druids arrived. No human messages had been sent; they had come summoned only by the magical instincts they all shared. Within a quarter-moon all that could travel at that time of year were there.

From the moment the first of the white-robes entered the roundhouse, Tegen dreaded performing her sacred morning duties. She was sure she would be in trouble if they saw her do so. One, a tall white-haired man with greedy red eyes, made her particularly uncomfortable. His companions called him 'Gorgans' – the White One.

Tegen remembered Witton's words and she kept well out of his way.

At dawn she awoke to hear the men already muttering and intoning the sacred words. Quietly she clutched at her green shawl and joined in under the muffling sheepskins. She must not fail in her duty just because other druids were present. She hoped that the spirits would forgive her for hiding until her path was clearer.

Tegen wondered whether, without Witton's testimony, she could ever become a druid, let alone the Star Dancer. Half of her was heartbroken at the thought, the other half glad that maybe she would be free to live a normal life after all. Perhaps she could become a wise woman or a midwife? But she remembered Gilda's sorrow at her own life's hope remaining unfulfilled and Tegen knew she would never be at peace with herself if she did not at least try to become what she was born to be.

Derowen turned up early with her cooking pots and took charge of the practicalities. She did not argue with Griff and Tegen's right to be there; indeed, she treated Griff with something approaching civility.

Perhaps she wants to keep in with him in case he becomes the druid, Tegen thought.

But there was little time for wondering. The old witch set her to work sweeping, peeling and emptying the slop buckets. The place was unbearably hot and smelly with so many people, especially at night when the door was closed, but Tegen did not complain. She hoped that if she kept her mouth shut, no one would send her away. She had to stay and perform as many of her sacred duties as she could – at least until things were settled – so she fetched and carried, cooked and mended under Derowen's scornful tongue.

On the third morning Huval, Witton's dearest friend,

took Griff aside and spoke at length with him, asking how his father had died. 'And who was next to Witton when he breathed his last?' he asked.

Griff, who had been eating a bowl of stew, waved a dirty spoon in Tegen's direction. 'Er . . . my woman. She and I bin hand-fasted. She was with Father. She breathed him in.'

Huval shook his head and repeated the question more slowly and loudly, as if Griff couldn't possibly have understood.

Gorgans, who had been hovering just behind Huval's left shoulder, snorted and tossed his long white braids. 'The boy is an idiot. You are wasting your time.'

Griff put down his bowl, got up from his stool and stood tall in front of the druid. 'I's not a iddy-thingy. I knows stuff, I dus. And I is a man. Not a boy!'

Gorgans flared his nostrils. He longed to hit the lad and send him packing with a thick ear, but many believed that he was the old man's son. He also knew that Derowen, who claimed to be the boy's mother, might be helpful to him later and he did not want to anger her . . . *yet*.

Huval ignored Gorgans and laid a friendly hand on Griff's shoulder. 'Yes, you're a man. A good one.' He turned aside and glanced at Tegen chopping salted herring and samphire into a pot. Huval stroked his thick dark beard. To many, the idea of a girl being the one closest to Witton at his death seemed an impossibility – a sacrilege even. But this girl did seem to have something about her. He studied her features. Of course! She was the girl who had danced magic at the Beltane fair. He had wondered about her at the time . . . yet if that was so, why hadn't Witton confided in him?

Seated on a stool by the door, Tegen could hear snippets of the conversation, but kept chopping and said nothing.

'Did you say she's your woman?' Huval asked.

'She is too.' Griff nodded almost as if his head would bounce from his neck.

'You have done well,' Huval replied. Then, turning to a group of men gathered around the fire, he called out, 'Marc and Llew, will you join me? I need to consult with you concerning preparing Witton for his last journey.' Unbidden, Gorgans also joined the committee.

The morning of the funeral was after a full moon. Not the best time for the passing over, but the body was stinking badly, even though the weather was still cold. It was a bright, sunny day and the snow had gone. Everyone from the village was there, but nobody spoke. Four men with an ox skin stretched between two long poles carried the corpse under a white woollen shroud up to the cave at the far end of the valley.

Huval led the way, flanked by Gorgans and Marc. Next came the catafalque, with the other nine druids following behind, richly coloured cloaks flowing over their white robes. Their arms and throats gleamed with silver and golden torques and bands. Polished enamelled brooches glinted at many throats. The men had all shaved the front portion of their scalps as Tegen and Griff had done. The rest of their hair was caked in red clay and worn loose, with amulets and nodding feathers stuck into headbands. They looked like noble and solemn spirits from the Otherworld of Tir na nÓg as they led the procession along the slippery path to the great cave.

Behind them, six or seven young acolytes followed, wearing long white linen tunics over their breeches and shirts. As they walked they rang small bronze handbells and sounded rams' horns to warn the spirits of their coming.

At every stream they crossed Huval threw in a cake made with fruit and honey, as an offering to the water spirits to allow them to approach Tir na nÓg. Each time the procession stopped, Derowen stepped forward so everyone could see her and wailed a piercing shriek that was taken up by all the villagers. The old woman was determined to be seen as chief lay mourner. She was dressed in her best blue dress with her grey hair combed out over her shoulders. She had besmirched her skin with ashes mixed with beaten egg to make a thick black paste that would not fade, however many tears she wept. As the funeral wound along the twisted pathway Tegen could see that under the mask, the old woman's face was alive with pleasure at being almost the centre of so much attention. She was creating a spectacularly convincing performance – and loving every moment of it.

Tegen walked halfway along the procession, with a stony-faced Nessa on one side and Griff on the other. As a silversmith and a maker of holy objects, Clesek was nearer the front, carrying a basket of his best rings and armbands.

The journey took most of the forenoon as the mourners scrambled over rock piles and waded and slipped through slush and icy streams. At last, at the cave mouth, they reached a many-trunked yew tree, ancient and twisted, the black-barked guardian of the underworld. Each mourner bowed to the guardian spirit within the tree, then moved on in silence.

The sudden stillness of the inner cave was a shock. The enveloping echoes and cool darkness soothed the mourners. Even Derowen fell silent. Tegen sensed a peace that was impartial and kind. Once inside, two women stepped forward with clay pots of glowing embers. They offered the fire to the druids, who lit tar-covered torches and handed them to the acolytes. Then the procession moved on, picking its way over slippery boulders and under the hanging stone lintels and daggers of the cave. Footsteps echoed and mingled with the drip and splash of water all around.

At last they came to a wide circular cavern with a pool that stretched from one side to the other. High above arched a wide rocky mouth of red, turquoise and gold, the throat of the earth itself.

The doorway to Tir na nÓg, the Otherworld.

As the chamber filled with mourners they lined up behind the druids along the stony shoreline. No one spoke. Torches flickered, sending eerie stabs of light against the wet walls, making the blackness dance and leap demonically.

Tegen and Griff edged around the back of the motionless crowd until they could see Witton. His corpse was rocking gently on a small wooden raft. His shroud had been removed to show the body released from its sheepskin bindings. His lips were pulled back in his shrunken face and his dark eye sockets stared blindly at the myriad circles of light patterns on the cave roof: the promise of his reincarnation.

The precious symbols of the great druid's life – a small golden knife and his leather pouch of divining bones – were arranged on his chest. Next to his body were a cluster of small clay pots filled with burning charcoal and sprinkled with bitter incense. Four beeswax candles were lit and placed one at each corner of the raft. When all was ready Huval turned to Clesek, who handed him the basket of silver offerings. One by one, armbands, rings and lastly a thick, twisted torque were tossed into the water, each one streaking an arc of light and ending in a splash that echoed loud and harsh.

Then, with a strong shove from the druids' staffs, the raft was launched into the centre of the pool.

Tegen gasped. Golden ripples danced across the black water as Witton's body floated away from them. The pool had seemed mirror-still in the faint glimmer of the torch light, but now, as if the hand of the Goddess herself had reached out for her faithful servant, the current took hold. The raft began to spin, slowly at first, then faster and faster until it was suddenly snatched out of sight behind a rocky outcrop.

The druids chanted:

> *He has gone to the Otherworld*
> *To await his rebirth.*
> *May he tell of our faith*
> *And of our suffering,*
> *that the Goddess may have pity on us.*

Tegen longed to join in with the ritual, but only dared to whisper a prayer to the Goddess for Witton's safe passage. She wished she had an offering to make as well. Then she had an idea. She stooped and picked up a pebble, then unwrapped her beloved green shawl from her waist and pulled out a few precious threads. Deftly she wound the silky strands around the stone and tossed the bundle into the water. It only made a small noise against the sighing and chanting. No one noticed.

At that moment a piercing wail went up from Derowen and was joined by another and yet another voice, until the whole cavern throbbed with sounds that echoed back on themselves again and again, building up into a deafening crescendo. At last it subsided and shivered away into the darkness with a whimper.

Tegen shivered to think of Witton alone in the dark, on his way to Tir na nÓg.

Griff squeezed her hand. 'I know what yus a-thinkin'. Yus a-thinkin' that 'es cold. Well, 'e ain't. 'E ain't there. 'E's dancin' in them there stars wi' the Watchin' Woman.'

Tegen looked at Griff in surprise. He was staring open-mouthed at the spectacle. He looked so . . . so stupid, yet he was so wise. It was almost as if it wasn't him speaking, but a spirit using his body.

She shivered and tugged her cloak more tightly around her shoulders. But it wasn't just Griff's strange gift, nor was it the cold that prickled at her flesh. Something was not right. She glanced around and saw Gorgans standing just behind her left shoulder. He was staring at her. Hard. Even in the darkness his red eyes penetrated as if he was searching her soul for something. Had he seen her offering as Witton was taken away? Had he heard her whispered prayers?

Under her cloak Tegen made the sign to avert the evil eye and clutched at her shawl for comfort.

Just then she caught sight of Clesek and Nessa amongst the departing crowd. She squeezed Griff's hand. 'Thanks. You're right, about Witton being safe. Listen, I need to talk to Mam and Da. I'll see you back at Witton's house – *our* house, I mean.' And she wove her way through the crowd towards her parents.

Catching up at last, she slipped her hands into theirs and together they made their way back into the daylight. They climbed up the southernmost arm of the hills that surrounded their valley. Where the way joined the main track back down to the village Tegen stopped and stood still.

Clesek hugged his daughter. Nessa gritted her teeth and kept her distance.

Tegen took a deep breath. Her parents were not old, but their strength was failing year by year as their hard life took its toll. If she left them now, they would have to work much harder. Even if Gilda sent more help, it wouldn't be the same. She felt guilty for what she was about to say. How was she going to tell them?

She swallowed hard. 'Mam, Da, I'm the new druid. Witton named me and gave me his last breath. I don't know what's going to happen now – with them . . .' she pointed to the retreating group of druids leading the mourners back towards the village. 'But I can't come home. Not to stay.'

Nessa stared at her daughter in disbelief. 'Don't be silly!' she snapped, narrowing her eyes. 'Obviously it's time you were married to a strong man and had children. I will speak to Derowen to see if she has someone in mind for you.'

'It's too late for that,' Tegen said, taking a deep breath. 'I'm already married. To Griff. Witton did the hand-fasting.'

There was a long moment of silence. Clesek and Nessa both stared at their daughter, wide-eyed and open-mouthed.

'*What?*' Clesek breathed at last. He turned and held his daughter at arm's length as if to see her for the first time. 'But you could have married a fine man – you're strong . . . and pretty.' He patted her cheek. 'Why waste yourself on *him*?

Nessa sniffed. 'It's all nonsense. The old man was delirious at the end, saying all sorts of strange things. Nursing him was Derowen's place, not yours!' Nessa put her hand on Tegen's forehead. 'You're hot. You're overtired and you've been sticking your nose where it'll do no good. Time you came home and did your work. And bring Griff with you!'

But Clesek put his hand on his wife's arm. 'Wait a moment, Nessa. There is more to this than we know. Tegen has always been different. Remember how she saved my life?' He put his arm around his daughter again and pulled her close to his side.

Tegen wished she *could* go back home. Everything would be so much simpler . . . and safer.

Nessa clicked her tongue in annoyance. 'I remember how she left the bellows in the fire and almost killed you!'

'She has the Gift. She got it from you, Nessa, although you'll deny it until your dying day.'

'Hush!' Nessa went white and looked over her left shoulder, as if she expected to see a demon waiting to pounce. 'You promised never to mention it!'

Tegen looked wide-eyed from her mother to her father. Now she understood: her Mam had the Gift, but she was too scared to use it . . . why had she never said?

Clesek ignored his woman. 'Don't be upset, Tegen, but old Witton was probably just saying you had the makings of a wise woman; and Griff is a seer of sorts – I'll not deny it. Tell you what, come back home and I'll have words with Derowen about making you her apprentice. How would that be? That tanner's girl is no good, I've heard. Derowen wants rid of her.'

'Da, Mam, I'm sorry, but I can't.' Tegen took each of their hands. 'The Watching Woman danced for me the night I was born. This is what I was meant to do. And Griff is meant to be with me.' She clenched her jaw and tried not to panic at the thought.

Clesek took a deep breath. 'You are too headstrong for your own good. Well, you'll learn.' He kissed her hand and let it go. 'Go and present yourself to the druids and see what they say.'

Nessa turned to him, horrified, but he smiled and put a finger to his lips.

Tegen hugged them both. 'I love you.'

'We love you too,' Clesek said and kissed her on the head. 'Just remember where your real home is.'

Nessa gave Tegen a cool peck on the cheek.

'Goodbye,' Tegen called out as she ran down the path towards the valley. 'And thank you!'

'What was that all about, might I ask?' Nessa turned to her man, hands on hips.

He smiled and put his arm around his wife's thin shoulders. 'She'll be back. Can you imagine she'll be welcomed with open arms by the druids? She'll be sent home with her tail between her legs before nightfall, I promise you.'

Silently Tegen trudged along the valley, heart in mouth, wondering what would happen when she met the druids in the roundhouse. As she walked footsteps shuffled behind her. She knew by the gait it was Griff. She couldn't bring herself to wait for him. She wanted to be with someone who was . . . strong enough to take her side and be a man – someone like her Da.

She had never felt so alone in all her life.

18. Derowen's Testimony

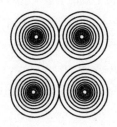

'Wait up gal,' Griff called. 'Tegen . . . I wants to walk wi' yus . . .'

She lowered her head and hated herself as she ignored him and stamped her way through the mud.

He started to run and was soon close enough to link his arm into hers.

She struggled with a mixture of panic and reassurance at his closeness.

Was Gilda right? Would he expect her to lie with him like an ordinary man? What would happen?

At that moment Tegen feared him. What was he? Was he a halfhead who was possessed by some wiser spirit? Or was he dear old Griff who, quite simply, sometimes managed to say and do the right thing?

But, despite her fears, the warmth of Griff next to her and the familiar stickiness of his fingers entwined in hers felt good. Together they followed the path as it plunged its slippery way through the hazel and ash woods down towards Witton's roundhouse.

The place looked like she felt – lonely and forlorn on an isolated little hill. The snows had left the aging thatch black and sodden and there was no smoke seeping between the sagging reeds. The late-afternoon sun shone weak and pale, catching the distant blue-grey range of southern hills in a waning gleam. Everything spoke of coldness and desolation.

They climbed the hill and reached the door. Only a few strides to go. Tegen stopped under the wide eaves and gritted her teeth. She must go inside. She had to face what was coming. Too much had happened to let her just shrug and turn away. She had to at least *try* to discover the meaning of her birth – to unravel her story. This was where she must be until the Goddess told her otherwise.

She pushed the creaking door open. 'Better tidy the place up,' she said aloud, without looking at Griff. 'We'd better make it look as if Witton was cared for.'

He shrugged. 'S'pose,' and followed her inside.

Tegen tied her hair back and laid fresh logs: pine to cleanse the air and juniper twigs as an offering to Witton's spirit. Griff took a besom and began to sweep around the hearth.

Their tasks were far from finished when the druids

returned. Huval came in first. He smiled briefly as he entered. 'Keep at your work, you two. Don't mind us.'

Tegen glowered at him and gritted her teeth. 'We're not servants!' she muttered quietly.

In groups of two and three the rest of the druids gathered at the roundhouse as the light faded. Derowen came too, with a goat, already skinned and gutted, slung across her shoulders. She had washed, plaited her hair and changed her best blue dress for an old grey one. As soon as she arrived she started bustling and organizing. She took a long iron spike and skewered it through the goat's body, then motioned to Griff to set it on hooks above the fire. 'Keep turning it or I'll roast *you* next,' she snapped. Then she squatted by the hearth and began to knead dough for bannocks in a wooden bowl.

Tegen finished stoking the fire, then went out into the biting wind to fetch in more wood.

When she came inside she could hear the talk was about who would succeed Witton. She hovered just by the door and held her breath. Her heart thumped wildly and she began to sweat, but not from the heat of the fire.

This was the inevitable moment she had dreaded . . . .

She glanced around. Griff was busy tending the goat, contentedly chewing on a piece of cheese. He seemed in one of his oblivious moods. Derowen was working at her dough and flipping the hot cakes as they browned on the hearthstones. She would be sure to be listening very hard indeed.

Around the glowing flames the twelve druids were gathered in a great circle. In the heat they had discarded their brightly coloured cloaks so light flickered on their long white woollen robes. The glimmering firelight caught on their amulets of bears' teeth. Tegen shuddered. The ivory fangs gleamed like unsheathed claws waiting to tear her apart.

'More fire!' someone demanded. 'Let us sweat into a trance so we can hear the spirits speak!'

'More fire!' other voices agreed. Tegen struggled forward with the heavy logs and loaded the flames until sparks danced crazily up into the smoky blackness. She glanced upwards and wondered how high she dared build the blaze. The thatch was only the height of three men above them.

The flames were so fierce, poor Griff had to dance forward to turn the goat and then jump back to cool his skin. At last one of the druids wrapped rags around his own hands and dragged the roasting hooks away from the heat so Griff could turn the spit.

Huval handed a leather pouch to Marc. 'Spread the dreaming-incense to give us the Sacred Sight.'

Marc stepped forward, opened the pouch and threw a handful of crushed black seeds into the hot charcoal ashes at the edge of the hearth. They hissed and crackled, and the air became bitter. Tegen's eyes ran and her head swam. The druid's bone and silver amulets clinked as he moved and a sour stench of sweat followed him. 'Tonight,' he boomed, 'we drink to our brother Witton who has gone ahead of us to the Otherworld. We ask his guidance in finding the promised one, the Star Dancer, who is still hidden from us.'

At this Derowen glanced up but said nothing, keeping a steady eye on the baking bread.

Marc swapped the pouch for a heavy ceremonial horn of mead and drank deeply, then he passed it on and stood with his arms folded. Pulling himself to his full height, he eyed his brother druids. 'As the Great One is still on his way here, we must choose a man to succeed Witton from amongst ourselves. This village must not be left unprotected from the malice of those spirits who despise us. Whoever is chosen will be a steward of this house until the True One appears – the one who was born on the night of the stars dancing.'

The men murmured amongst themselves, some agreeing, others arguing. The heat and the stench of the smoke were becoming unbearable. Tegen felt her heart beginning to pound and her mouth was dry. Suddenly, all she wanted in the whole world was to run home and be a silver-worker's daughter for the rest of her life. Being the Star Dancer was too big a task for her. She was only an ordinary girl. She glanced towards the door. Was there any way she could escape without being seen?

The noise of the men's arguments rose to a roar. 'Silence!'

roared Marc, raising his arms above his head. The room fell quiet. 'Who has an apprentice who is ready to become acknowledged? I move that the young man's master must leave his village to his student and come here to step into Witton's shoes and assume his mantle. This way, no village will be left without a druid.'

There were murmurs of assent from some of the men.

Tegen glanced across at Griff, who was getting agitated. She could see he wanted to join in the debate. She put her finger to her lips, warning him to be silent. If the Goddess *really* wanted her to be the Star Dancer, then she would make it happen.

Griff saw Tegen's warning look, but he ignored it. He flushed red and left the goat's corpse to swing in the flames. He strode across the central space and stood facing Marc, feet apart and thumbs in his belt. 'Sirs,' he began, 'I knows I's not very bright, but I knows what I knows, and that is Father, old Witton, chose his app . . . app . . .'

'Apprentice?' Marc offered.

'Yeah. His thingamy what's a-learnin' of him 'ow ta be a-doin' of the druids' things. And that appy-thing is Tegen, that girl over there. I knows cos I knows. I wos 'ere when Father breathed his last bit of air. 'E told Tegen to take 'is last breath.'

'I'm sure you both did your best for Witton,' said Huval kindly, 'but it's just not possible. I don't know how to explain simply for you, but it just can't happen like that.'

Griff hopped from foot to foot and glowered, twisting the hem of his jerkin between his fingers.

'*But I knows what I knows!*' he insisted, his chin raised and glaring Huval right in the eye.

This was awful. Tegen measured the distance between herself and the door. Could she escape?

Suddenly Griff pointed towards Derowen. '*She* knows! My mother. *Tell*, why don't yus?'

At first Derowen said nothing as she refilled the mead horn. Her long grey plaits swayed like old ropes. Her eyes caught no reflection of the fire's warmth, like two black pits that went to the Place of Despair.

Suddenly the wise woman straightened and put down the jug of mead. 'It is true,' she said. 'Witton told me the girl was named and acknowledged as the Star Dancer.' Then she continued with her work as if she had merely mentioned that supper was ready.

There was a moment's silence, then everyone started talking and arguing very loudly. Llew and Gorgans both sprang to their feet at the same time, shouting and waving their fists.

'My friends,' shouted Llew, 'listen . . . .'

'Yes, listen, to *me* . . .' Gorgans raised his right hand and lowered his eyebrows. He looked menacing in the half-light, with his back to the fire, but even he could command only half the room.

Behind him, Marc stood on his stool and raised his staff

in a gesture of authority. 'Silence!' he yelled at the top of his voice, but the men only shouted more loudly to be heard.

'Rubbish! . . . Nonsense!' they yelled.

'Not only is it ridiculous,' scoffed an angry-looking youth with a bristly beard, 'but it is impossible! The boy is a half-head, and the testimony of an old witch woman does not count.'

'Don't jeer too soon, Morgan,' Marc warned, wagging a plump finger at the speaker. 'Remember the old story of Rhiannon: they said she lied . . .'

Tegen bit her lip and shrank against the wall. She glanced across at her enemy. Derowen had taken control of the burning goat and had settled it into the spit holders once more. She was smiling as if she was extremely satisfied. What was she playing at?

Tegen rubbed the stinging smoke and incense out of her eyes. Now was her chance to get out, while they were still arguing. As she picked her way gingerly through the shadows she tripped on a pile of blankets and landed behind an elderly man. He looked at her, walked across to Huval and whispered, jerking his thumb in Tegen's direction.

One by one, the druids stopped shouting and watched as Tegen struggled in the shadows to untangle herself and find her footing.

'Where is the girl? Bring her here,' Huval demanded.

With two bounds, Griff pounced on Tegen and dragged her forward. 'This is her. This is my woman!' he beamed.

She tried to stand straight. The heat, mingled with the sour stench of incense and sweat, made her feel sick.

Huval beckoned her to stand before him. Tegen obeyed, her heart thumping so loudly she was sure everyone in the room could hear it. She risked looking up. He had kind eyes. He stretched out his arms and caught her by the shoulders. He turned her to face the crowd. At last the room fell silent.

'Witton told me once that his apprentice might be someone strange, someone different, someone who might not normally be considered. Maybe he was right. Maybe the Goddess has some scheme, some plan beyond our imaginings.'

Gorgans smirked from under his long moustaches as he looked Tegen up and down in the firelight. She squirmed under his gaze.

'Now, what we will do is this,' Huval continued. 'We will ask the Goddess. We will cast the Ogham and seek the Lady's wisdom. At this time of the year, as the child of spring grows in her womb and the darkest night is past, so may her wisdom grow in us. Hope will be born and tonight must be a part of that. The moon is still swollen and the light of the Spear Warrior can be seen again. Tonight is a good night. So we will test this young woman and see what fate the Goddess has in store for her.' Huval let his hands fall from Tegen's shoulders.

No one moved. Even the logs in the fire ceased to shuffle and fall.

Then Gorgans sprang forward and turned so he caught the attention of everyone present. 'So be it. Huval's words contain good sense. But I move that if the girl is found to be an impostor, then she be sacrificed. We will examine the way she falls and bleeds and read her entrails to see why the Star Dancer has not been found and why Witton named a girl child as his successor. Surely there must be something to learn from these events.'

The men murmured in agreement. Tegen looked at Huval, who obviously had not expected this, then she glanced back at Gorgans. Just the tips of his straight, white teeth showed between the lips of his smile.

Suddenly Griff took her free hand. 'Lady loves yer jes like I dus, Tegen!' he whispered. 'She won' let yes down. I knows what I knows!' And he kissed her on the cheek.

She jerked her face away from him. What a fool he was. Didn't he understand *anything*? If only he had shut up . . . if only she hadn't come back. One by one, the druids were standing and coming to have a closer look at her.

Next to the fire stood Derowen, her chin slightly raised in a look of triumph.

Now Tegen understood. The witch's words had been to trap the druids into testing her, knowing full well the price of failure.

There was no escape.

19. The Casting of the Ogham

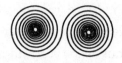

Marc frowned as Huval ordered the wooden staves to be brought forward. 'This isn't right,' he muttered.

'What isn't right?' Huval demanded. 'That we ask the Goddess to speak for herself?'

'It isn't right that the girl should be at risk.'

Huval squeezed Tegen's shoulders gently. 'I am not frightened of the Goddess. None of us should be.'

Tegen kept her head bowed and said nothing. Her heart was pounding. Did she believe in the Goddess enough? More to the point, could the sacred wooden Ogham staves be trusted? Witton had always used bones with red markings to read the mind of the Goddess. But they had gone to Tir na nÓg with him.

Would she really be sacrificed? Would Huval defend her if the others read the Ogham against her?

She glanced around. The men stood in groups watching

her. Gorgans was standing near the door with his arms folded and a long knife in his hand. His red eyes were wide and his pale lips were pulled back in a grimace. He looked like a grotesque death's head. Tegen shuddered.

'Clear the fire circle,' Huval ordered as Morgan passed him a leather satchel. 'Derowen, take those cooking pots away, move the kneading bowl, then find me a birch broom.' She did as she was told and was about to start sweeping when Llew took the besom from her and began the task.

Tegen was intrigued. Why was the druid performing a woman's task? Huval leaned towards her and whispered, 'See, he's making a cleansing circle around the fire, working deosil with the footsteps of the Sun God. That will ensure that whatever happens next will be in the right order, as the day and night follow each other truly.'

Marc followed Llew as he worked, sprinkling water from Witton's silver bowl, chanting softly as he walked.

Once the area was cleansed, Huval opened the satchel and pulled out a yellow linen cloth that he spread on the earthen floor. On to this he gently tipped out twenty-five small wooden rods. Each was a little longer than a man's finger and about the same size, but flat, and along one edge was a neatly cut row of small notches: the Ogham, the words of the Goddess.

'Where is Hew?' Huval asked, looking around. A tall thin man stepped forward. 'Please refill the bowl with fresh water from the spring of the West. Fill it as full as you can . . . And Morgan?'

The young man with the bristly beard stood. 'I am here.'

'Go outside to the rock of the North. Fetch me a pebble, a hagstone with a hole in it if you can find one.' Morgan took a torch and went out.

When everything was brought in, Huval placed the hagstone at the bottom of the bowl and sprinkled a pinch of incense on to the water, then a sprig of rosemary on top. Next he set the bowl on the cloth for all to see, and he began to chant. He used words that Tegen could make no sense of, yet she found she knew them and, despite herself, she could not resist joining in.

Suddenly, and without any spark being brought to the bowl, the incense ignited, sending a brilliant tongue of flame across the water's surface and up the rosemary stem, leaving the air smelling pungent and sweet.

Tegen breathed deeply and felt her head clear.

The flames died. Huval stepped forward and put the wooden Ogham staves into the water.

'The words of the Goddess are in this bowl,' he said. 'The spell is complete. As you all witnessed, the Lady sent the spirits of the South to bring their fire of blessing on our proceedings. Here is also stone for the North, incense for the East, water for the West and rosemary for clearsightedness.' He paused and looked around, making sure that everyone in the room was watching and listening.

Then he breathed over the bowl: 'And here is the Awen for inspiration to know the mind of the Goddess.'

Tegen held her breath. She could feel the intensity of magic in the air; the skin on her neck and arms prickled.

Huval held the bowl high. The creamy silver gleamed with the reflection of red and gold from the leaping flames.

No one moved or spoke.

'Each man, even the halfhead Griff, is to take a stave. Then the women. Yes, both of you – Derowen the wise woman, as well as Tegen. There are more than enough Ogham for us all. There are fifteen of us here present; here are twenty-five symbols. Let the Goddess speak!'

'Let the Goddess speak!' roared the men.

'Let the Goddess speak,' Tegen repeated under her breath.

'If the girl is chosen then she, for some reason best known only to the Lady, is the Star Dancer. If it falls to another of our company, then that person takes Witton's place and the girl will be sacrificed.

'Brothers, are we all agreed?'

'Agreed!' roared the response.

'Griff? Do you understand?'

'Yeah. I gets it. That's good.'

'Derowen?'

Tegen dared to glance at the witch. The old woman was smiling broadly. What could be going through her mind? The chance that she would see Tegen die? Or that her own son might be chosen?

'Agreed,' Derowen replied.

Lastly Huval turned to Tegen. 'And you, child. Do you submit yourself to the will of the Goddess?'

Tegen drew a deep breath. 'I do,' she whispered as her knees threatened to give way.

Huval turned to his right and carried the bowl to each person in turn. 'Close your eyes and choose one stave,' he said as he moved from man to man. Some hesitated, others moved swiftly, as if they dared not think. Others seemed to screw up their closed eyes as if they were trying to scry what was written on the hidden faces of the watery sticks.

Tegen couldn't bear to watch, but couldn't bear not to.

'They are all face down, so you cannot read what they are,' Huval went on, walking slowly around. 'Take the one that calls to you and no other. Hold it high in your right hand as soon as you have taken it. Be assured that if you try to make any spell to change the markings, that stick will immediately turn into a viper in your hand.' He paused as he spoke. Gorgans took a stave and opened his eyes. He stared at Huval without expression.

Tegen went cold.

Huval moved towards Griff, who grinned, closed his eyes and snatched a stick. He waved it in the air in triumph. 'This 'ere's mine!' he chortled.

The druid smiled and kept going. 'When each of us, including the women, has chosen, we will all hold our signs out for everyone to see at the same moment.'

At last Huval came to Tegen. His tall frame towered over her, his shadow enfolding her. She took a deep breath and closed her eyes, resisting the temptation to hold on to her shawl. This must be the Lady's choice. She must not use her gift of seeing. Tegen stretched out her hand above the bowl of water.

Suddenly warmth surged around her fingers. One stave seemed to be almost singing with joy as she brushed it. Just to be sure, she lightly touched others, but nothing happened. They were just cool, wet wood. She moved back to the first stave.

She had to take that one.

Trembling she closed her fingers around the Ogham and prayed. If she was wrong she would soon be dead, but at least the nightmare would be over.

Huval spoke again. 'Now, everyone, open your hands and stretch your arm well in front so all may see the truth.'

With a jingle of bracelets each palm was opened to reveal a piece of wet wood.

Silently, Huval, followed by Marc, walked around the circle and one by one he took the proffered staves and held them high for everyone to see. He called the name of each holder and then the meaning inscribed upon the stone. 'Llew – honesty, Pwyll – messenger, Horth – warrior, Marc – night-seer' . . . and so forth until he came to Gorgans. 'Deception . . .' Gorgans went red, but said nothing, keeping his head held high and his gaze straight ahead of him.

'Griff – insight.' Huval smiled at the lad.

'Derowen . . .' He drew a breath and hesitated. 'Derowen – lies . . .'

The woman flung her stave into the fire, grabbed her cloak and stormed out of the roundhouse. No one stopped her. Llew closed the door against the sudden blast of night air.

Now it was Tegen's turn. Her heart was pounding and her head was shot through with a searing pain. Huval turned to the other druids. 'I ask you all to gather round and witness so there will be no dispute or uncertainty hereafter.' The men shuffled closer as they all tried to see what Tegen held.

She looked up at the towering men. Any moment, she thought as she struggled for breath under the pressure of their presence, I am going to . . . collapse . . .

Huval sensed her terror. He motioned the druids to move back a little and he raised his hands in prayer. Tegen stared at the tattoos on his forearms, intricate mazes, patterns that led Tegen away from here, deep into herself, twisting and turning this way and that, spiralling in until she was falling in an indigo darkness that was threaded with silver lights . . . spinning, spinning so fast . . .

From somewhere a voice called her back. It was Huval, his deep tones like a safe place for her to stand. She shook her head and focused on the reality of the stuffy roundhouse and the heat of the fire.

'Tegen,' Huval intoned, 'are you still willing to accept the verdict of the Goddess?' He hesitated and spoke more gently. 'You know nothing of our ways. If you wish, you may lay your Ogham down unseen. You may go home . . . Nothing more of this will ever be said to you.'

Tegen stared up at him wide-eyed, struggling to remain in the here and now. She longed to fall through the patterns of the mazes again, to see the beautiful lights of the stars dancing . . .

Huval stared right into her eyes. 'If you accept the Goddess's fate for you, there will be no turning back. You will either be the Star Dancer and our new druid, or you will die.'

Tegen's hand shook violently. She forced herself to breathe and gripped her right wrist with her left hand to try to steady it. From the corner of her eye she could see the comforting dark shape of the doorway beckoning her.

But standing between her and the door stood Gorgans. A cruel curve twisted his lips as once more he fingered the blade of his knife.

Suddenly she decided. No more mazes, no more magic, no more stars. This was not her place. She would go.

But to her horror her hands would not open to return the stave, neither could she move. Her legs were rooted to the spot. Vomit burned in her throat. She could not draw a breath.

She swayed violently and struggled to focus on Huval,

trying to draw comfort from him, but his shadowy face was impassive. There was only one answer her lips would let herself give.

'I accept the judgement of the Goddess,' she whispered hoarsely. As she spoke her legs crumpled and she collapsed on to the floor. In the palm of her right hand lay a very ordinary-looking brown piece of wood.

The men all rushed forward to see what was written on it, jostling to be the first to see. 'Stop!' Huval ordered. 'Marc and I will look, then all of you in turn. If anyone so much as touches or breathes on that Ogham before I have spoken, that man will die.'

Murmuring with discontent the druids stepped back a little. Griff moved forwards. 'But she hurt. My Tegen's hurtin' . . . I gotta . . .'

'No,' commanded Huval. 'Wait. She is in the hands of the Goddess.'

Griff twisted his face in torment and tears ran down his grimy face.

'Marc is the wisest in Ogham. He will take and read the marks. Then it will pass to each of you in turn and you will all do the same.'

Tegen lay crumpled and unmoving like a discarded cloak on the ground, her dark hair spread in the dirt.

Marc leaned forward and picked up the stick, then holding it at arm's length he turned it over to show a set of clean, neat cuts in the light from the fire.

20. The Little Sacrifice

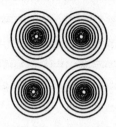

'She has drawn the *Duir*, the oak. The sign of our protection. She is the Star Dancer,' Marc announced.

'That means nothing!' Gorgans spat, striding forwards into the circle of firelight. 'Any of the Ogham can be interpreted with a good meaning – or a bad, come to that,' he added, remembering the reading that had been given to him. 'This was no test. What makes the Awen so special within you, Marc, son of Hwyll, that you can be so certain? What would you have said if *I* had drawn it? Heh? The witch child has cast a spell on your senses!'

A few men nodded and muttered in agreement.

Marc looked down at Tegen, still unconscious on the floor. Griff had managed to wriggle through the crush and was now sitting next to his beloved, her head cradled in his lap, stroking her hair. 'What do you suggest then?' Marc asked. 'She's not in a fit state to answer a challenge of arms and, in case you had forgotten, that is not the druid way.'

Griff pulled a piece of oatcake from his pouch and was trying to push it between Tegen's slack lips. ''Ere, you eats summat, gal, and you's'll feel better soon, eh?'

Morgan pushed himself to Gorgans' side. 'I say we float our Ogham,' he suggested loudly. 'That *is* our way, and has been since our forefathers floated the great stones on to the hills for the sacred circles.'

Marc sighed and looked at Gorgans. 'Will you be satisfied if she passes this test?'

The young man rubbed his chin and stared down at Tegen, lying quite helpless and pale as an owl's wing. Was there a better test, one that would destroy the wretched girl and the half-wit as well? He could not think. He needed time. All eyes were on him, expecting him to speak. Perhaps there would be other ways, other times . . .

'Yes,' he said aloud. 'One more trial and I'll be satisfied.'

Marc nodded. 'Very well, if each of us places our own Ogham stave back into the sacred water, the one that floats belongs to the Star Dancer.'

Gorgans began to worry: But the staves are of wood, they will *all* float. They have to. Unless . . . I can help them do otherwise . . . He bent over and tugged at the underside of his clog. He pulled out a metal stud and slipped it to Morgan. The man nodded and closed his fingers over the cool iron.

In the press of men trying to find their original stave amongst the others Gorgans hurried to make himself conspicuously helpful, finding and handing out the Ogham sticks. He stooped to pick Tegen's up, but Griff pulled back his lips and snarled, 'Don' 'e touch 'm. Yous in't fit, see?'

Gorgans jumped back as if he had been bitten by an adder. 'Stupid halfhead!' He spat on the floor and turned his back.

Griff ignored him but handed Tegen's Ogham to Marc, then accepted a dark green cloak from Pwyll to cover her.

Now that Tegen's *Duir* stave was safely in Marc's hand, Morgan knew the chance was lost. There was no way he could push the iron nail into the wood to weight it down. Cursing, he tossed it away.

Huval clapped his hands. 'Silence!' he called loudly. 'My brother druids, are you all ready?'

Murmuring and shuffling, the men arranged themselves into a circle once again. Marc set the bowl next to the central hearth, where the flames glinted and danced as if rejoicing in their own reflection on the water.

Then Huval called for silence. He raised his arms and addressed the four quarters, turning to each to ask the blessing of the spirits:

> *Hail to the East, Awen, giver of inspiration,*
> *Breathe knowledge of the truth into our minds.*
> *Hail to the South, bringer of the pure fire,*

> *Purger of dross, take away all doubt.*
> *Hail to the West, source of the water of our lives,*
> *Wash away all uncertainty.*
> *Hail to the North, the rock and foundation*
> *Of all that is true . . .*

He paused and looked Gorgans in the eye.

'Speak to us the mind of the Goddess. Show us who is the Chosen One, the Star Dancer for whom we all wait. Allow all our staves to sink, but only that which belongs to the Star Dancer, our new druid of druids, to float. In this manner we may all see and bear witness to the will of the Queen of the Skies.'

Then, grasping his own Ogham stave, Huval stepped forward and laid it carefully into the bowl. For a moment the stick floated, curving the surface of the water under its weight, then slowly one end dipped and pulled the rest of the wood after it.

The druids murmured and looked at each other. Huval was well respected; some had even wondered if he should take the title of Star Dancer himself. Even Gorgans did not dare challenge him too openly. If Huval failed, what chance did any of them have?

Huval took his stave back and held it, leaving the bowl empty except for the trembling gold and silver lights. One by one the druids all followed suit. Some staves sank more quickly than others, but sink they did.

At last it came to Gorgans' turn. He stepped forward. He drew his lips tightly against his teeth and knitted his white eyebrows together. He had always secretly sneered at magic, but his red eyes and white skin proclaimed him as a spirit from the Otherworld and had forced him into the druid's life. He knew he was born to greatness and to gain that power he was willing to try anything.

Hidden in the deeply curved shadows at the side of his robe, the fingers of his left hand performed the pattern of an intricate spell, his thumb tip dancing across his fingers as he tried to summon unseen aid. Then he stretched out his right hand and placed his stave.

Immediately it sank, dark brown and useless at the bottom of the bowl. Gorgans hissed a curse between his teeth as he snatched it back. Then he straightened and glanced at Morgan, who shrugged.

When all the lots were cast Huval looked around. 'Who has Tegen's Ogham?' he asked.

Marc held it high. 'I do,' he said and stepped forward. He stretched out his arm and placed it in the bowl.

For a moment it dipped under the surface . . . then bobbed . . . and rose again and lay at the top, turning slowly in the gentle motion of the water.

Then it sank.

The room was silent.

'Does anyone wish to examine the stave, or to challenge the decision?' Marc asked, his voice sounding strangled.

Huval shook his head and spread his hands wide in despair. 'I don't understand . . .' He looked down at Tegen, still lying motionless on the ground with her faithful Griff still stroking her hair, oblivious to everything else. 'I never meant this to happen,' the druid said quietly. 'I am so sorry, child . . . Griff, I didn't think . . .'

Gorgans pointed to the Ogham lying at the bottom of the bowl. He did not bother to disguise the glee in his voice. 'There!' He laughed, flashing his white teeth. 'The Goddess has spoken through a trial devised by yourselves. The girl dies. I'll do it if you are all too scared.' And he slipped his long knife from its belt-sheath and let the cruel-edged blade catch the firelight.

Suddenly Griff stood up and snatched Tegen's Ogham stave from the bowl. He glowered at the druids. They were mostly taller than him, with strong muscles on long, lean limbs. Many owned grand cloaks of chieftains' bright colours, their necks bore silver torques and their arms and faces were marked with magical tattoos of power. They were nobles, educated and wise.

Griff knew he was flat-faced with no marks of rank and barely enough clothes to keep himself warm, but he refused to be daunted. His father had told him he had the Gift. He *was* a Chosen One. He stood, feet slightly apart, head held high, as he glared at the men standing around him. Then he pointed Tegen's stave at them all, one by one. 'Yus-all don't understand, cos yus-all more stupid than me! I like that!

Ha! Stick thingy don't float when *yus* puts it's in cos it's *hers*, see? Not yurn! When *she* puts it, it'll float. When you lot have a hold, it goes down cos *t'ain't yurn*! T'ain't me the daft one here; it be you druids wot be the gurt fools!'

And he spat to ward off the evil eye.

'I'm not standing for this!' Gorgans roared. He grabbed Griff by the scruff of his tunic and jerked him around. 'I'll whip you and throw you after that witch mother of yours. You both deserve to die!'

Marc caught hold of Gorgans' arm and twisted it backwards, making him loose his hold. Then he turned Griff to face him. 'Look at me, son of Witton.' He stared into the boy's small, slanted eyes. He could sense a spirit of integrity in him that he had rarely seen before. Perhaps it was because he wasn't clever enough to make up a lie? What had the boy's Ogham said? *Insight*.

Marc held out his hand for Tegen's stave, then changed his mind. 'All right, Griff. You take it and put it back in her hand. Then we shall all see what we shall see.'

'What's the point?' Gorgans scowled, crossing his arms and staring down malevolently at the boy. 'It is impossible that *she* could be the Star Dancer. The idiot boy has no place here. He can't possibly understand holy things. Let's just take the girl outside and slit her throat now while she's fainted. Then it'll be over painlessly.'

But no one was listening. Griff took the Ogham and knelt by Tegen's side. Then he placed it reverently within her cold, white palm. 'There yus is,' he said gently. 'That there's yurn, in't it?'

Her eyes did not flicker. Only the slight rise and fall of her chest under the borrowed cloak assured the onlookers she was alive.

The men crowded around, but parted enough to allow Marc to come forward with the silver bowl of sacred water. Then Griff lifted Tegen's hand and opened her fingers so she placed the stave herself.

Scarcely had Griff helped her to let go than the wood began to spin, slowly at first, then faster and faster on the surface until a tiny gleam of light like a minute star appeared in the centre. It glimmered for a few moments. Then the spinning stick slowed until it was simply rocking gently on the disturbed surface of the water.

'The boy is right,' Marc announced. 'The Ogham will only speak about whoever was holding it.'

Huval bent down and took the stick once more from the water, then replaced it. The stave sank like a stone. Again he put it into Tegen's hand and held her limp fingers over the water so she could let it fall. The stave floated and began to spin.

One or two of the other men stepped forward, took Tegen's *Duir* and tried it for themselves. The answer was always the same.

'Put her on the old man's bed,' Huval ordered. 'Make

sure she sleeps undisturbed,' he said to Griff. 'Your woman will have a long day tomorrow.'

Gorgans withdrew to the back of the crowd. There he sat on a stool and scowled, twisting and bending his own stave until it snapped.

When Tegen woke it was just before dawn. She ached all over. She knew she had been afraid but could not remember why. She stretched and tried to turn, but found she could not. There was someone lying next to her. She sat up and rubbed her eyes. In the dim light that seeped from gaps under the thatching, she saw a mop of fair hair and square shoulders. Whoever it was, he was snoring.

Griff! Why was he next to her? Of course, they were married! But what were they doing *here*? For the last few nights their place had been on the floor near the door, where it was coldest. Now they were lying in Witton's bed. The druids would kill her if they caught her there . . .

Then her heart missed a beat. They would kill her . . . She remembered now. That was just what was going to happen!

They had said that was what they were going to do . . . sacrifice her in order to divine why the Star Dancer had not appeared . . .

Her head ached. She tried to think. She had drawn an Ogham. What was it? What had the reading been?

She had no idea, but she guessed that Gorgans would have found a way to contort the decision his way. Her stomach lurched as she peered around in the gloom at all the sleeping shapes huddled around the last remaining embers of the fire.

She had an image in her mind of Gorgans standing over her with his knife drawn, about to slit her throat.

That had not been a dream, she was certain.

So the Ogham must have spoken against her.

Next to the hearth, the badly scorched, forgotten goat carcass hung cold from iron hooks like a prescience of her own imminent fate.

With a sudden and absolute conviction, Tegen knew what to do. She would not accept the judgement. She would honour the spirits and the Goddess one more time, then she would go, as far away as she could. It didn't matter where. Somewhere. Anywhere she could serve the Lady in peace. Perhaps she could find a cave to live in, where she could dance with her magic shawl. She would find a way to protect the people from the great evil that was coming, even if it was from a distance.

Tegen pushed back the sheepskin covers and slid away from Griff's side. Silently she stood and groped around for her clogs and cloak. She could find neither. She couldn't let it matter. She had to flee even if she was barefoot. She was certain that this would be what Gilda would tell her to do – live out her story and be who she was born to be. She was the Star Dancer. It was not her fate to die at the hands of the cruel White One.

But first she must perform her rites one last time and make spells of protection and blessing on the valley. I will do everything properly, she told herself. It might be my last time. Still sleepy, she pinched herself awake. She had to think clearly. The druids could wake at any moment; then her chance of escape would be gone.

East first. Tegen silently ticked her duties off on her fingers. I must put a pinch of incense on the embers of the fire. What else will I need? A candle and light to honour the South. I have to tell the good spirits of the valley that I'm not fleeing because I'm afraid, but because I *have* been chosen. I can't allow myself to die before I've fulfilled all I was born to do.

Then her heart skipped a beat. The sacred bowl and the incense! Where were they? It was too dark to see properly.

She eased the door open, wincing as it creaked. She risked leaving it ajar so she could see what she was doing. The light outside was gaining strength with each beat of her heart. She had to hurry.

Ah, there was the silver box on the table near the bed. Tegen sprinkled a tiny pinch on the last embers of the fire, then grabbed a candle and lit it. At last she spotted the silver bowl and her cloak and clogs. She scooped everything up, but as she turned to go a strong hand shot out and gripped her by the ankle.

'Where do you think you're going?' a deep voice growled. It was Llew. Her movements had woken him.

Tegen felt her heart thumping in her chest. With her free hand she touched her shawl lightly, then spread her fingers towards her assailant. 'It is nothing. Sleep!' she commanded. He loosened his grasp, fell back and began to snore.

Tegen slipped outside.

Trembling, she carefully put the candle down and forced herself to make her prayer to the spirits of the East, begging their forgiveness for having shut the door so the incense did not waft towards them. Then she bowed, picked up the guttering candle and placed it into the little lantern that hung under the thatch to honour the South. Carefully she filled the silver bowl and made her offering to the water spirits of the West.

But when she came to the rock of the North, instead of making the usual prayer, she picked up a sharp stone that lay on the ground and cut the thin skin on the inside of her forearm. The incision was not deep, just enough to make the blood flow a little.

She let a few drops fall on to the rock, red-black against grey in the blue half-light of dawn.

'Good spirits of the earth,' she whispered, 'I was to be sacrificed to the Goddess today. My blood was meant to become one with yours. Dawn is now rising and I must run so that I may serve the Lady in freedom and without fear all the days of my life. Please protect my family and my valley. Please accept my little sacrifice. I will come back and pay my full debt one day, but I know it must not be now. Please forgive me.'

And with that she left the silver bowl on the wet grass and, clutching her cloak around her, she ran.

21. Flight

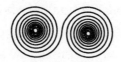

Tegen slipped and slid down the hill. At the bottom she glanced left and right. Her heart pounded and she held her breath, dreading the sound of the door opening behind her. Where could she run to?

She crouched behind a thicket of brambles and thought.

She dared not go back into the valley, yet she had never been beyond it either. High above stood her father's stone house and the little path that led to the caves where Witton had been buried. She might be safe there. The old druid's spirit may not yet have departed to the Otherworld. He might still be lingering . . . he might protect her.

But then, he might not. What if her flight had angered him?

To her right sprawled a forest of oak, hazel and ash, tangled and grim. Ahead spread the shallow waters of the Winter Seas. With the wooden trackway that crossed the marshy waters from her valley to the small humped islands of the south, then ran towards the great Tor and the hills. If she could get on to the track she might be able to flee to safety. It was a dangerous path, just brushwood bundles, planks and hurdles lashed to poles. In this weather it would be treacherous.

Between Tegen and the trackway was a wide meadow. The ground was well churned, with the heavy hoofs of the cattle leaving deep, oily puddles. It was here she had first learned to dance her magic at the Beltane fair two years before.

Now she had to leave the past behind and the track was her best hope. Behind her lay the Mendips, roamed by fearsome bands of hill people. She couldn't go home – how long could she stay without Gorgans and Derowen hunting her down? One of Griff's little charcoal-burning shelters might be safer, but not for long. And what would she eat? She longed to run to Gilda's warmth and love, but how could she hide in the middle of the village?

She took a deep breath and squared her shoulders. 'Today is not my death day. Gilda and Witton both believed I was born to be the Star Dancer, so that is what I shall be.

'Great Goddess,' she prayed, 'show me what I am to do.'

Just then a flock of gulls screamed overhead, flying towards the village. That can't be an omen, Tegen told herself firmly. They are just birds, avoiding bad weather.

With a sigh, she turned to face the trackway. Its rough dark path was clear across the pale ripples of the inland seas, but to reach it she must cross a spur of woodland that stretched down to the water's edge. 'It won't take me long,' she said as she sprang lightly from grassy hillock to grey stone. She was soon standing beneath the first trees, but her way was blocked with tangled briers. Tegen wriggled on her belly in the mud and forced her way through a fox run under the snagging thorns.

As she pulled herself upright and tried to brush the dirt and leaves from her dress she heard the first shout of a man's voice.

For a moment she froze. Then she sank back amongst the undergrowth, crouched low and listened. Now there were many voices – and dogs!

Shouts. Whistles. Barks.

Tegen shifted her feet in the sucking mud, then turned to see how far she still had to run to reach the beginning of her freedom. To her horror she saw that although the trackway stretched across the water to her right, the first stage was submerged. She would have to wade!

The shouts were coming closer. Her pursuers must be halfway across the meadow. Keeping low, she lifted her skirts and began to pick her way between the trees, using the latticed roots as a path. But as she came to the water's edge there were no more trees and the oozing mud was a treacherous soup.

Behind her, the shouts were getting louder. She could hear the dogs yelping with excitement. Was that Griff's voice? She held her breath and listened. No, he would never betray her.

Suddenly she slipped and found herself knee deep in sucking slime. Icy water slurped and gurgled at her feet and legs. But fear gave her strength. She lunged towards a stand of rushes and pulled hard, praying that they would be deep-rooted. Slowly she eased her way forward until she found a firmer footing. She clambered on to a fallen ash tree and lay there exhausted.

Miraculously the leather straps on her clogs had held and they were still on her feet. 'Thank you,' she whispered to the good spirits.

Shivering violently, she wiped splashes of stinking black mud from her face and looked around.

Her heart sank. She had been a fool. What if she did manage to reach the track? She would be plain for everyone to see out there on the water. It would take one of the men hardly any time to fetch her back in a coracle. She should have risked the forest and the hills. At least she could have hidden in one of Griff's huts for a while. His Awen would sense danger – he would keep her hidden.

Now she was too cold to move or care. But to stay still meant death. She rested her head on her arm and closed her eyes as she listened to the men's shouts, and the crash of their boots, getting louder. She didn't know how to go on, yet she had to. She knew that Griff would be heartbroken that she had left him behind, yet there had been no other choice. It was flee or die. At least he was safe – he might even be acknowledged as a Gifted One. She would go back and explain to him one day.

Tegen forced herself to ignore the throbbing cold as she pushed herself down from the tree trunk. Her limbs were stiff and shaking.

She would make for the forest.

Someone yelled her name. They had seen her! Then the first dog, a black shaggy hound, ran panting up beside her, excited by the chase, his warm breath coming in white bursts. Somewhere a man whistled. The dog turned and leaped away. How close were they? She dared not look. Not even a glimpse, or she would despair.

Keeping low, Tegen summoned all of her strength and found a firmer path across higher ground, grassy and thick with reed clumps. She stamped on ahead. She would *not* give up – for Gilda's sake, if nothing else. The old midwife believed in her – she had promised Tegen that she had a purpose. The beautiful dark-faced lady who gave her the magical shawl had said her music was 'starting'. It couldn't be over yet!

From behind came angry splashing and shouting. Her pursuers were caught in the same quagmire that had almost claimed her. This was her chance to leave them behind.

Tegen pushed her straggling hair out of her eyes and gathered her wet cloak and skirt. The ice was thicker here and held as she ran. Perhaps she could make a spell to raise a fog to hide herself? Pausing in a coppice of hazel, she clutched her green silk and closed her eyes.

But her concentration was broken as once again the large black dog bounded gleefully to her side, eyes bright and breath warm.

'Tegen! Tegen! Come back!' That was Huval – she could recognize his voice.

She huddled under her wet cloak and lowered her head as she stamped uphill. The dog danced around her, making her feel dizzy.

Suddenly she realized she had lost her bearings. The hills, the sea and the wood were all one to her. Panic gripped her throat. She tried to run, slipping and sliding in the icy mud. Greedy fingers of jealous witch willows grasped for her hair, brambles clawed at her eyes and twisted roots tripped her feet.

She stopped for a moment and glanced up at the grey hills. She could see a puff of smoke drifting against the heavy sky. 'That's my mother cooking bannocks,' she said. Her stomach twisted and growled. She could not remember the last time she had eaten.

Might a quick and honourable death be preferable to starving and dying slowly?

Suddenly the ice beneath her clogs cracked and gave way. Tegen fell forward with a cry. She lay with her face in the oozing, icy slime and gave up. There was no story. Gilda had been wrong.

Stamping boots and heavy clogs gathered around her. Dogs' noses and strong hands overwhelmed her. Tegen lay limp and allowed herself to be hauled upright. The words of her pursuers meant nothing to her as she was carried back towards Witton's roundhouse. In the distance below she could see men building a bonfire, loading more wood on to its already golden heart. As new branches landed heavily, showers of brilliant sparks rose to do battle with the first large, downy flakes of snow. Tongues of flame leaped into the afternoon sky. *How I wish I could sit by it for just a short while. I could keep going if I was warm,* she thought.

Suddenly she was struck by an awful thought. Perhaps the fire was for *her!* Evil people were sometimes burned alive to prevent their spirits from walking. Tegen felt her throat tightening as if a great hand was throttling her.

Then she heard a voice: a kind, strong woman's voice. *'Go on, Tegen, go forward. All shall be well. You do not need to be afraid.'*

She gasped and stared around at her captors. She could not make sense of their words or faces. Hair and beards, stern eyes and grim expressions draped with sodden cloaks and spattered mud . . .

There was no woman amongst them.

22. Preparations

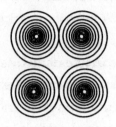

Tegen hung limp in her captor's grip.

'Get her inside!' Marc called out in a stern voice. 'Let her rest for a short while. Make sure she is ready by sundown. Derowen, take her and prepare her. She's filthy! She can't possibly be presented to the Goddess in that condition!'

Tegen did not resist the wise woman's grasp. She was marched up the small hill to Witton's roundhouse and pushed inside. The door closed behind them both. In the firelight, Derowen's bitter, wrinkled face resembled the icy desolation of the water's edge.

'Get your rags off!' she snapped as she tugged at Tegen's torn shift and cloak. Derowen pushed her towards the bed and a cover of sheepskins was tossed in her direction. At last, filthy and empty of hope or fear, Tegen closed her eyes.

She wished that Gilda had been the person to prepare her for her death.

When she woke the light was fading and Derowen was still there. The old woman pointed to a wooden tub, the one she had bathed old Witton in. 'Get yourself clean,' she demanded.

Tegen was too dazed to wonder why she was being made to bathe, but the water was warm and she sunk herself into it gratefully. Even her throbbing feet and fingers felt eased. The sweet smells of pine shavings on the fire and dried lavender flowers in the water made her feel calmer. So, she was being purified. Secretly, Tegen was glad she wasn't going to be sacrificed in her muddy state. She knew the Watching Woman would love her as she was, but it was nice to be clean and ready. She wondered whether the knife would be sharp and quick . . . or whether Gorgans would take his time and enjoy the deed . . . She ducked her head right under the water and tugged leaves and twigs out of the tangles in her hair.

'Up!' Derowen demanded suddenly. 'Enough wallowing! Get dry!' and she flung her a large cloth.

Tegen pulled herself out of the bath and began to get dry, but, as she rubbed, Derowen smeared her skin and hair with crushed garlic. That was for spiritual protection, but from what? If she was going to be disposed of, why should the druids care whether she was protected or not?

Perhaps her spirit was being sent into the darkness of

Tir na nÓg to take a message or to ask something, maybe of Witton? She would need protection for that.

The old woman's long grey plaits swung this way and that as she moved. Under her blue smock her breasts swayed in rhythm. Tegen become mesmerized by a polished golden pin that glinted in the firelight at Derowen's shoulder. Close up, Tegen could see that Derowen had once been handsome, maybe even beautiful; she could envisage her as Witton and Gilda must have once known her: tall, strong and proud. Now she was old and sour. Perhaps she too had hoped to become a druid. But something had destroyed her.

Derowen lifted a white linen smock over Tegen's head. 'Lift up your arms and stop daydreaming!' she snapped. Tegen obeyed. This was a good piece of cloth. Surely they weren't going to let it become bloodstained? Perhaps they were going to give her poison? They obviously had some purpose for her, with all this preparation. It must be a very important message she was taking to the Otherworld.

'Hurry up!' Derowen threw new stockings and clogs on to the floor.

Tegen had scarcely put them on before the old woman opened the door wide. 'Hurry up, they're waiting for you!'

Well, this is it, Tegen thought as she stepped out into the cold grey-blue air. The midwinter afternoon was fading into semi-dark and the tarry smell of torches made her stomach churn, reminding her of just how hungry she was. Exhaustion and fear made her light-headed. The sounds of music and laughter and crackling flames gave the evening a festive feel. *I wonder if my parents and Griff are here?* She looked around. *I'd like to say goodbye to them and to Gilda.*

Just then a cheer went up from the crowd and a horn was blown. Tegen shivered. Her new linen gown was little protection against the biting wind. But she held her head high. She must not show she was afraid. As she reached the bottom of the hill she saw the druids gathered in a sacred circle. Around them stood the villagers, who had left a clear pathway for her. She walked through the silent crowd towards a gap in the druids' circle at the northernmost point. She glanced around, hoping to see a friendly face. But Derowen was not going to let her stop. She pushed Tegen hard.

Six steps to go, now five, now four . . . she breathed deeply, although her chest hurt. Three, two, one. This was it. The circle closed behind her. She stepped forward towards the holy fire at the centre, then turned and faced the North, ruler of the solstice that had just passed.

Pwyll entered the circle and splashed water over her from Witton's silver bowl. It was so cold it hit her like a hundred tiny knifepoints. She gasped. Red-headed Horth took a brand from the bonfire and scorched Tegen's hair around her face. Marc rubbed mud and ashes into the stubbly skin on her scalp where she had shaved in mourning. Then old, lame Timarc breathed into her nose and mouth as Witton had tried to do on his deathbed. His breath stank.

Lastly, Huval stepped forward and drew a knife from his belt. It was a fine bronze blade, with a horn handle and a silver butt on the end. He held it with the edge at Tegen's throat.

She swallowed hard. So, this breath was her last. She had been audacious, expecting to become the Star Dancer – or even a druid. This was her punishment – but it was an honour also. She could at least tell the Watching Woman that she had acted honestly . . . even if she had been wrong.

Just at that moment, out of the corner of her eye, Tegen saw Griff entering the circle, *smiling*. He held out a small baton of wood in the palm of his hand. 'Go on, Tegen. Take it, girl; it's yurn, innit?'

Tegen took the stick, bemused.

'Hold it high,' Huval ordered, 'so we can all see.' Tegen felt faint. They were putting her through this *again*. Why?

Marc came forward with the silver bowl. 'Put it in the water, Tegen.'

She did, and it floated, spinning slowly, then faster until the small light glowed at the centre, making a tiny star.

Tegen drew a breath. 'What's happening?' She looked around for reassurance. Marc's face was impassive in the firelight.

Mutterings and murmurings came from the large crowd that had gathered. Beyond the druids' circle huddled all the villagers, with a few others from the hills and neighbouring settlements. Almost three hundred men, women and children.

Huval raised his hand for silence. In the deepening dark, only the crackle and spit of the fire could be heard. His dark eyes were solemn. 'Is there anyone here who will accuse this girl of being an impostor?' he asked loudly, holding his gleaming knife above her head.

No one spoke.

'Who will deny her right to be proclaimed Star Dancer, Child of the Goddess? Speak now or forever serve her in faithfulness.'

There was a long, heavy silence.

Huval let the knife blade drop away.

Suddenly the druids roared; then the crowd joined in. Tegen reached for the silver bowl and took the Ogham stick. Gripping it in her fist, she looked around wildly. She could not take in what anyone was saying. What did they mean?

Then, to her amazement, she saw the crowd was not angry. Their shouts were cheers. They were all bowing to her – every one . . . even Huval, Marc and . . . *Gorgans?*

'Wise . . . One . . . Wise . . . One . . . !' they chanted.

Tegen spun around, looking for a clue, a friendly face, someone who might tell her what was going on. At last, over the bowed backs in the distant shadows she saw Gilda, standing erect, looking at Tegen as proudly as a mother might.

'Star . . . Dan-cer . . .' The chant had changed.

Gilda waved, then bowed also.

The horn blew again and Gorgans straightened up and walked forward with a small golden-handled knife. The bonfire caught a mean glint in his eye as he pointed the blade at her right cheek. Would he take Huval's challenge and slit her throat, or was she safe now? The cut, when it came, was just below her right eye, the eye of magical sight, and near the ear of mystical hearing. Swiftly, he pricked the sign of the Goddess with the pattern of her nine stars into Tegen's cheek. Then he put the knife into the hand of a fellow druid and took a small wooden bowl. It contained foul-smelling black ashes mixed with rancid fat, which he smeared roughly into the cuts he had made.

Tegen did not wince, but Gorgans seemed to enjoy the pain in her eyes. Then he turned away and Pwyll put a thick, warm cloak around her shoulders and someone else handed her a linen cloth to staunch the blood. Two boys struggled into the circle with Witton's carved oak chair and set it down. Huval motioned to her to sit.

'Wise One, Star Dancer, Druid!' the crowd chanted.

Tegen looked around in disbelief. Wherever she turned, everyone was smiling. She had the emblem of power tattooed into her face. She had been acknowledged before all the people.

This was her feast day, not her dying day!

Griff ran and took her hand. 'Come and eat summat, yu's all-in!' He grinned. He was dressed in a long woollen robe with a blue cloak, new clogs and a mole-skin hat; a handsome young man with much to celebrate. 'I's a Gifted One, I is!' he said proudly, holding up his talisman. 'Yu's Star Dancer – best druid. Good, eh?'

Tegen uncurled her hand from the smooth Ogham stick and dared to look for the first time. There indeed was *Duir*, the pattern of the oak, the sign of the faithful druid, wet and glimmering in the firelight.

'Yes,' she said, 'it's good.'

23. The Peace Offering

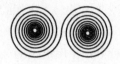

The days that followed passed quickly. Huval stayed in Witton's roundhouse with Tegen and Griff, instructing them both in their work.

'Tegen, you may not go into the back room, where the sacred things are kept; Griff will have to do that for you until you have built your own sanctuary. Griff, do you understand?'

Griff was watching a beetle meandering across the floor. Gently he scooped it up and cradled it. 'Let it go outside,' he said.

Huval sighed. 'If you must. Then will you please come here and concentrate? There is too much to learn in too short a time.'

Griff opened the door and put the beetle on the grass. He stood up, wiped his nose on his sleeve and stared at the view.

'Griff!' Huval snapped. 'Will you *listen*? This is important!'

'Beetle important!' he replied gruffly. 'I dunno about yurn stuff though. Can't make head nor tail of it. Her – Lady Goddess, I means – tells I wot I needs to know when I needs it. S'good 'nough!' Then he came inside, sat down and started to chew on a piece of bread.

'Very well,' Huval muttered. 'Now, when you need something for a spell, get Griff to fetch it.'

'How will I know what I need if you won't let me know what is in there?' Tegen asked, exasperated.

'Look, if Griff intuits as much as everyone says he does, it'll be all right. The Goddess will bless him with knowledge when he needs it. You will start collecting your own talismans and herbs before long, and a couple of men will come from the village to help with the building of your sanctuary.'

Tegen sighed quietly and began to repeat the incantations Huval had been trying to teach her all morning. Her head ached.

The days and nights went by, then at last the moon neared its fullness once again and a few green shoots were beginning to show. It was late one evening when Huval announced he was leaving. 'My own village needs me. I have left my apprentice on his own too long. The moon is waxing, the cold is receding and this is a good time to go. Imbolg will come with the next dark moon. You will be two hands and a foot old on that day. When you have a year for each toe and finger, you will be strong. Meanwhile, Derowen will help you. I know you will be a good mistress to your people. You are honest and caring, whatever some people might say.'

The druid stood and went to his straw mattress by the fire. 'The evil is not here yet. You are the Chosen One. All will be well.' And he lay down to sleep.

After the morning rituals were over Huval shook hands with Griff and bowed low to Tegen. She blushed and bowed as well. 'Good speed, Father. Thank you for your hours of wisdom. I will try to remember all you have taught me.'

'Just do your best, both of you. I will try to visit you soon. Goodbye for now.' Then he turned to go.

Tegen felt empty as she watched Huval's straight back marching down the lane that ran across the meadow towards the forest. Would he come if she needed him? When the druids had been with her, for all their fussing and complaining, she had felt safe and protected. Derowen came with the villagers' gifts of food and mead every day. Huval had helped ensure that Tegen made the right offerings and cast the correct spells for every occasion. Normally this training would take nineteen years to complete, with long periods away with other teachers spent learning the bards' songs, stories and triple truths by rote.

Barely a moon and a half had passed under Huval's care. Now it was all up to her. Maybe Gilda would help when she could, but Tegen knew she would never ask Derowen for help with magic. She had Griff with his strong Awen, but would he really understand what she needed? Once again, she wished she was married to a normal man. But then, perhaps someone who understood with his head might not always understand with his soul, the way Griff did.

Tegen sighed and stepped back inside. She had hoped that despite Witton's warnings everything would be straightforward once she was accepted as the Star Dancer, but she had a feeling that things wouldn't be that easy.

Griff served her a bowl of warm porridge. It was lumpy, but made with love and had a spoonful of thick, melting honey on the top.

He sat down and looked at her with adoring eyes. 'Can we make a baby now they'm all gone?' he said.

Tegen almost dropped her bowl. '*What?*'

'Make a baby, you know!' He grinned and snuggled in close to her. 'Had to wait cos there was so many people around. I didna like a-doin' it with *them* there . . . *yus* knows . . .'

Tegen felt herself going very red. Involuntarily she shifted a little away from Griff. He felt the movement and hung his head. 'Sorry,' he muttered. 'I don't blame yus for not wantin' to make a baby wi' me. I luvs yer, Tegen, and I want to give yus a big cuddle like men dus to women.'

How could she tell him – without hurting his feelings –

that she couldn't face the thought? He was her foster-brother. She would never see him as her hand-fasted man, even though he was.

So Gilda had been right. Tegen put her food down and held his hands. 'Griff, I know I'm your woman and, in a way, I love you very much. But I'm scared. Only a few phases of the moon ago I thought I was going to be sacrificed. Only a moon change before that I bled for the first time, received my name and learned that I have a great task ahead of me.

'It is all a lot to take in. I need to wait a bit. I feel very weak and if I had a baby in my belly now, I'd . . . I don't know what I'd do. I think I'd be even more scared. Do you understand, Griff? I don't know if I'm strong enough to make a healthy child.'

He said nothing, but pulled his hands away and ran into the back room. He let the stiff horse-hide curtain fall across the entrance with a clatter and then there was silence.

Tegen tried to finish her porridge, but it stuck in her throat.

Now she was really alone.

She picked up the silver bowl and went down to the spring above the stream. She scooped up some water and let it flow over her head. The shaved area was growing hair now, fluffy and black like a baby moorhen. She rubbed the water over the patch. 'I wish it was night, so I could see the Watching Woman. Then I might not feel so lost,' she said quietly.

'Do you think that's a proper use of the sacred waters, Mother Tegen?' snapped an irritable voice nearby.

Tegen looked up and rubbed her wet eyes. She hadn't heard footsteps. There was Derowen, scowling as usual, her grey hair scraped back into a severe plait. Under her arm she carried a willow basket. 'I've brought the people's offerings, *Lady*.' She twisted her mouth into a tight knot.

'Thank you,' Tegen said, getting to her feet. 'Shall I take the basket?'

'Then that'll be one more job you've stolen from me, eh?'

'That's not what I meant.' Tegen bowed her head and led the way up the hill.

Inside the roundhouse Derowen slammed the basket down hard, making a small round loaf bounce out and on to the floor. Tegen picked it up. 'How are things in the village?' she enquired.

'We'll see. Good as maybe,' she replied. 'Where's the boy?'

Griff lifted the horse-hide and peered into the room. Derowen took an apple from the basket and offered it to him with a stretching of her mouth that may have been a smile. 'Here, my darling,' she said. 'A sweet thing for you.'

Griff stepped forward. He ignored the apple but slunk to Tegen's side and clutched her hand. He stared at his mother, saying nothing. Tegen was relieved to feel his sticky, sweaty palm again. So she hadn't hurt him too much. They were still friends, at least.

Derowen scowled, then threw the fruit down next to the basket. 'Pah!' she spat. 'She's got you tamed, hasn't she? Well, come to your Mam if she treats you badly. I'll protect you, boy. You are my own son, after all.'

Griff narrowed his eyes and sucked at his lips, but said nothing.

The older woman paused on the threshold, turned and grasped the door latch. 'After thirteen full births and deaths of the moon, the village will see this "Star Dancer" for what she really is. Then you'll be glad to come back to your mother, who's always protected you.'

Derowen scowled at Tegen, snatched up her cloak and left.

Back in her own home, Derowen sat by the fire and stirred a small iron cauldron propped amongst the grey and red ashes at the edge of the fire pit. She sang a nasal chant and smiled a little to herself as she mixed the aromatic-smelling liquor. Then she wound cloths around her hands, picked up the pot and poured the brown tisane into a pottery beaker. The liquid hissed and spat. She added a spoonful of honey and stirred it in well.

A few minutes later she was knocking on Gilda's door. 'It's me, Derowen. Can I come in?'

Gilda rose stiffly from her spinning by the fire and opened the door. 'It's a long time since you have wanted to cross my threshold. What do you want?'

Derowen pushed past her and held out the still-steaming beaker. 'I would like to help you. I've brought you a warming drink for your aches and pains.'

Gilda took the beaker and sniffed at the liquor. She cast a suspicious glance at her old enemy. 'It smells soothing. Can I offer you oatcakes or a skein of wool for your trouble?'

'No trouble . . . call it a peace offering, if you like.' Derowen said. 'Now Witton is dead, I see no need for bad feelings between us – do you?' She smiled, showing her long teeth.

Gilda shook her head, hobbled back to her seat and placed the too-hot drink on the floor. 'Don't trouble yourself about the past. Things happened the way they did for a reason. The Goddess weaves everything to good for those that love her.'

Derowen sniffed in a way that made Gilda look up. Was that derision or just a cold? 'Come nearer the fire and share some warmth.' Gilda pushed a three-legged stool across the hard earth.

Derowen shrugged. 'No time. The girl up in Witton's house runs me ragged. She really doesn't know what she's doing. Tells me to fetch this and do that, never offers to lift a finger to help, of course, watches me carry heavy things around, but it seems her hands are too holy to touch common stuff.'

'Why don't you let me help?'

'You are far too ill. Anyone can see your joints are agony . . . Anyway, Huval told me it was my place. I served Witton so well, they said I and none other was to serve her.'

'I'm not too bad, really. I'll gladly lend a hand. I'm very fond of her – and the boy . . . your son.'

Derowen threw a piercing glance across the flames. 'What makes you call him that?'

There was a long silence. The fire crackled and the wind blew through the thatch. Gilda sighed. 'Do you remember giving me the basket you wove for your stillborn, the morning after the stars danced? I was curious as to why the child died. I wanted to know if it would have made a difference if I had been there to help as I had promised.'

'Well, you weren't, were you?'

'You didn't send for me . . . How was I to know? Well, I opened the basket. It was turnips I buried, not a baby.'

Derowen got up and stormed out, slamming the door behind her.

Gilda picked up the beaker and sniffed the liquor. She could smell dandelion, meadowsweet, yarrow . . . and honey. That was all good. What was Derowen up to? She took a small sip. Then another. She let the warm sweetness bathe her aching limbs. She wanted to drink it all, but underneath the honey there was a taste . . . a very slight taste of bitterness she did not like.

Her aches and pains racked her day and night. Gilda felt ill and tired. She no longer had the strength to fight her old enemy. 'I should have been one of the Wise Ones,' she told the fire. 'I was distracted by love. I was cheated by jealousy.' She raised the beaker in a toast. 'Lady Goddess, I feel in my bones it is almost time for my story to end. The Star Dancer is here, and soon the village won't need me to protect it from Derowen and her evil magic any more.

'I suspect this drink will help me painlessly on my way to Tir na nÓg, so I may rest these weary bones and let my soul be reborn in a new body. But I am well on that road already, without Derowen. I will not drink this. Very soon I will accept her help – but not yet. First I need a little more time.'

And with that she carefully poured the liquid on to the earthen floor.

24. Thirteen Moons

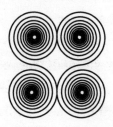

'So, one year. One turning of the nights to day and the days to night. What is Derowen plotting?' Tegen sat down on the bed and put her head in her hands.

Griff came and sat next to her. He tried to cuddle her, but she felt edgy and eased him away. 'Wassa matter? What did she say?'

Tegen took Griff's hand and squeezed it. She knew she was being unfair. He had promised to always look after her 'proper', and he would; she knew it. He wasn't to blame for being a halfhead. 'I think she meant that in one year I may no longer be the Star Dancer. She thinks that some-thing will happen, but I don't know what.'

'So we got one year to do things good?'

'Yes. I suppose so.'

'That's all right, in't it? I mean, we can git stuff done and show Derowen and they men that we's as good as they is. I'm hungry.'

Tegen laughed. 'You're always hungry – but you're usually right as well.'

As the seasons and festivals turned, Tegen and Griff worked hard. They grew healing herbs in Witton's neglected garden. The threatened famine was held at bay. Tegen's spells kept illnesses away and bound the spirits that crept up from the bottomless swallet holes under the earth, where the demons lurked.

Tegen spent long hours watching the birds of omen and learning to listen to the secrets of the winds. Whenever the night was clear she stood outside her roundhouse and stared silently up at the black sky-canopy that carried the dancing silver stars. Most of all she followed the nine shining points of the Watching Woman. *Her* stars, that had danced when she was born.

Now they danced again, but it was a pattern with a sad movement that she did not understand.

Although Tegen was sure the signs were not good, she always felt better after evenings spent this way. She knew that the stars were only an emblem of the Goddess, not the Lady herself, but just watching them strengthened her. She had never forgotten the Lady's words of reassurance before she was acknowledged by the druids and given the blue tattoo on her face.

Without them her spirit would have failed.

'Go on, Tegen, go forward. All shall be well. You do not need to be afraid.'

The Goddess's words still span in her mind like sparks from a fire, and one night she turned them into a dance.

In her movements she became one with the fire's heat: vermilion, scarlet, gold, cadmium and white. Hotter and hotter the colours became as Tegen whirled and twisted, her arms wide. The cool blackness of the sky carried her soul freely amongst the brilliant stars.

At last she stumbled on a tussock and fell laughing with joy on the grass, her green shawl spread around her.

As the year turned, Derowen's threat drew closer, stinging Tegen's mind and threatening to sap her will.

Her main strength came from frequent visits to Gilda. Tegen could see her mentor was not as strong as she had once been. She was no longer plump, and her skin, especially her lips, often had a bluish pallor. If Tegen asked how she was, her old friend always laughed the question aside.

'No time to think about me – I want to talk about more important things.' Then she would pat the bed as a signal for Tegen to curl up next to her and listen to the stories and songs of the bards – wonderful tales of Rhiannon and

Pwyll, Prince of Dyfed and Lleu Llaw Gyffes of the Swift Hand.

One summer's day they were sitting in the patch of land behind Gilda's home, shelling beans and shooing away the geese as they tried to steal the smooth green prizes.

'Remember these tales,' Gilda told Tegen. 'They may be old, but they will teach you to understand your own story. You may have been proclaimed druid, but you still have to walk the whole path to achieve the fullness of that end. You will need to study divination and ritual, healing and shape-shifting. It is a long road you have ahead of you, little Star Dancer.'

Tegen popped a bean pod irritably. 'Why must the training be so long?'

'Being a druid is not just a matter of form and learning words. You have to become wise within your soul. I am trying to teach you all I know about being a bard, so you can sing and understand the tales that instruct us all in the true ways.'

Tegen shook her head and munched on a bean. 'But I can't sing. I have an awful voice.'

'Then tell them or dance them, but sing within your heart. It will help you unravel the meanings. Most people, when they are told a story, hear only the pattern of the comings and goings of the characters. A bard learns how to discover and celebrate the deeper layers within the tale. You must carry those insights in your heart and mind and they will teach you what you need to be the Star Dancer. You will call on them all when your time comes. If you close your eyes and see and sing, you will understand what the stories *mean*. That is your calling and your gift.'

'I'll try,' Tegen said, popping another bean into her mouth.

'You must do more than that, child,' Gilda said, and with difficulty she pulled herself to her feet. Leaning on her stick she hobbled into her roundhouse.

'What do you need, Mother?' Tegen jumped up. 'You aren't well. Let me get it for you.'

'No,' Gilda called back. 'Thank you, but I need to do this.'

Moments later she returned with an old leather bag. She sat on her stool and passed it to Tegen, who opened it and pulled out a neatly folded bundle of light blue cloth. As she shook it open, dried herbs and flowers scattered and crumbled.

It was a dress.

'It's for you. I only wore it once. It is my bard's gown. I abandoned my training to follow Witton. I didn't listen to the stories well enough to understand my own path.'

Tegen stretched across to hold her friend's wrinkled hand. 'But I am glad you were here with me.'

Gilda smiled. 'You have been the best part of my whole tale.'

Tegen took the precious blue dress and stored it with layers of lavender flowers in a wooden box under her bed.

Derowen came every so often with more herbal drinks and honeyed words. Gilda pretended to swallow them both, but secretly threw them all away. She longed to end her painful life, but she had much to teach Tegen first.

Tegen also dreaded Derowen's visits, yet she could think of no way to depose her from the role of wise woman. There was no specific crime of which she could accuse her. It was her job to bring the people's offerings, and it wasn't seemly for Tegen to fetch them herself.

Tegen wanted to earn the old woman's loyalty, so she tried to be kind and willing, but Derowen seemed to hate her with increasing malice. Whenever the old witch was nearby, Tegen's heart sank and she sensed a dark and malevolent cloud gathering around her spirit. In fact, it was so dense it sometimes threatened to block out her inner vision of the Watching Woman's stars, and her divinations became confused.

Tegen dared not succumb to her own feelings of fear and apprehension. She wasn't only worried about her and Griff's future: she knew that everyone's lives depended on her. She was the Star Dancer.

She made herself go on. Her rituals and blessings were given at the right times, the village prospered and the summer harvest was good. When she could, Tegen walked up to her old home in the hills and helped Nessa spin and weave. Her mother's once pretty face became more pinched and she spoke less and less. Tegen could see Clesek's strength was not what it had been. The first white hairs appeared in his dark beard and his blue eyes became paler.

True to her word, Gilda sent helpers from the village, but they were unskilled and did not want to stay up at the lonely stone house overnight.

As autumn came on, Griff often took Wolf and went to help Clesek with the charcoal burning in the woods.

Winter approached. As each household sealed their grain in clay pits or topped their heavy honey jars with a thick layer of wax, Tegen made sure she was there, giving thanks to the Goddess and blessing all the preserves with the strongest spells she knew. She gave talismans of protection to every hearth-holder in the village, whether the people had given her gifts during the year or not. Nothing, *nothing*, must go wrong or have been missed. Yet however hard she and Griff worked and however caring they tried to be, Tegen sensed that the villagers felt nervous of them both.

She was sure that Derowen was slandering them with rumours of dark magic and communion with unlucky spirits. The villagers took their remedies and blessings, left their gifts and scurried away down the lane, often making the sign against the evil eye as they went. Tegen felt sad, but there was nothing more she could do.

Although she worked faithfully with the rituals and spells she had learned, her real magic was worked at night when no one could see. Without saying a word to Griff, she slipped outside and danced with her green shawl for the good spirits and for the Goddess. She closed her eyes so she could see what needed to be done for the sick and needy, imagining each person well and whole, quarrels soothed and the weather kind.

She also learned how to tell the ancient tales with her steps. As she did so, she discovered the inner meanings Gilda had promised.

When Griff came to the roundhouse he sat next to Tegen as she spun wool and retold Gilda's stories. Once or twice he begged Tegen to let him make a child. She was sad. She would have liked to have thanked Griff for all his faithfulness and dedication with the baby he wanted so much, but she could not.

The year had almost turned and all seemed well in the valley. Tegen began to tell herself she had been stupid and that Derowen was just trying to scare her with threats to make her nervous and maybe encourage her to slip up in her duties.

About one phase of the moon before each major festival, Huval came to visit them. He used these times to teach Tegen which blessings and spells would ensure the Goddess's favour and protection. As midwinter approached, Tegen looked forward to his arrival. She had decided to confide in him about Derowen's words of warning. The thirteen moons were almost up and she did not believe that the end of her time as druid could be so close. No great evil had come, and she had not yet performed her role as Star Dancer – of that she was certain.

But the Midwinter Festival was almost upon them, and Huval had not come. The skies were too heavy with clouds for Tegen to watch the moon and stars, but she knew that it would not be long before Imbolg. Then Derowen's plot would ripen.

But when a heavily cloaked and hooded figure arrived at Tegen's roundhouse door in the middle of a downpour of rain, the traveller was in no mood for discussing Tegen's worries.

He had other things on his mind.

25. Proposal

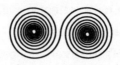

Gorgans tossed his cloak aside. 'Dry this, boy. Then go and find your mother. Huval is busy for the festival. I have come in his place.'

Tegen's heart sank as Griff picked up the heavy woollen robe and spread it out across a couple of stools. She put down her spindle of wool and stood stiffly, waiting for her visitor to bow and present his offerings. He did neither. Instead he sat in an ox-hide chair and put his boots on the edging stones around the hearth.

'Would you like refreshment?' Tegen asked after a few moments of awkward silence. 'Can I offer you mead?'

Gorgans smiled, showing his strong, white teeth.

Tegen felt her heart miss a beat.

'That would be acceptable. Then send the boy away. His mother does wish to see him and I have business to discuss for your ears only.'

'I's a man, not a boy.' Griff scowled, sticking his bottom lip out. 'Wot's my mother want? She don't us-ly want me for nuffin'.'

Gorgans sighed and considered his fingernails. 'I am sure I don't know. Just run along, will you . . . *man*.'

Griff looked nervously at Tegen.

She smiled. 'If Derowen wants you on a night like this, it must be important. Take her some honey. It might sweeten her tongue.'

Griff shrugged, then took a small wax-sealed earthenware jar and pulled on his blue cloak. 'You sure yus'll be all right?' he asked, casting a nervous looks from Tegen to Gorgans.

'She'll be fine,' the White One snapped. 'I am with her. This is simply a matter for two *druids* to discuss, and you are wanted elsewhere. Now GO!' he bellowed, half rising out of his seat.

Tegen longed to call out to Griff to stay, but dared not appear weak in Gorgans' presence. 'I'll be fine, Griff. Go and see what Derowen wants.'

She poured a horn of mead for her visitor but only a small beakerful for herself. Tegen did not want to insult him by allowing him to drink alone, but she needed her head clear for whatever was coming. As she went to sit on the seat facing Gorgans he stretched out an arm and beckoned. 'Bring your stool over here, next to me.'

She would rather have sat next to a sleepy adder than to

this man. Gorgans turned his seat to face her, drained his horn of mead and then, to Tegen's horror, he leaned forward and patted her hand.

'I have a gift for you,' he said, reaching into his waist pouch. She felt cold metal grasp her wrist. It was a silver bangle, one that looked as if it had been made by her own father. Two serpents twined around each other and locked in an endless embrace.

'Thank you,' she said, reddening. 'You are very kind. I am ashamed to say I have no gift for you . . . I had not expected this visit. Is there something else I can do to honour . . . your kindness?'

'Yes, there is.' Gorgans smiled. His heavy, pale moustaches parted and he leaned forward and kissed her on the lips, forcing his wet tongue between her teeth.

Tegen struggled, but his arms were tightly about her, pressing her against him. Her beaker fell and smashed on the floor. Suffocated and horrified, scared and humiliated, she couldn't breathe. Her stool was about to give way under Gorgans' weight. She slid her right hand down and managed to grasp the end of the green silk shawl, tied as always around her waist. She felt its magical warmth spreading through her body. It gave her courage as well as power.

'No!' she commanded, wriggling out from under him on to the floor. 'You must not do this. I am a hand-fasted woman.'

Gorgans seemed quite unperturbed as he pulled away and smiled at her with amusement. 'Hand-fasted you may be, but I bet anything you are still without a child in your belly. He probably doesn't even know what to do with the thing that hangs between his thighs.'

Tegen blushed as she pushed her hair back and replaced her seat firmly on the other side of the fire. She longed to get rid of him, but she knew she should hear him out. Whatever his plan was, she would need to understand it to fight him. She had to keep calm.

'Indeed I do not carry a child, but that is my choice. My first duty is to learn to serve my Lady the Goddess, without a child to worry about. But what my man and I decide and do is no concern of yours.'

'Oh, but it is. I am here as a druid brother – an *unmarried* druid brother. It is my duty to marry, as it is yours.'

'I was hand-fasted with Griff in the presence of all the spirits by Witton himself.'

Gorgans leaned back in his chair and laced his fingers. His red eyes narrowed as he looked Tegen up and down. 'That wasn't a proper marriage. Witton was an old fool who couldn't see what he was looking at. He actually believed in this Star Dancer nonsense, and in his befuddled old age he thought it could be you.'

Furious, Tegen stiffened her neck and bit her lip. Her fingers clutched her silk.

Gorgans quickly changed tack. '*Of course*, I too believe in the Star Dancer, but perhaps not as everyone else sees the role. I have other insights. You were proclaimed, as I myself witnessed, through no fault of your own. You are after all only a woman and not much more than a child at that. You could not help but obey the brother druids.'

Tegen put her hand to where Gorgans himself had made the sacred marks on her face. She said nothing as she stared into the flames, trying to listen to the wisdom of the Goddess speaking in her heart.

Gorgans cleared his throat. 'Forgive me if I was . . . a little presumptuous. It is just that, well, I have watched you more closely than you may have realized over the years and I see a fine young woman with many spiritual and magical gifts well beyond those of her druid brothers.'

Tegen glared at him. The dazed shock of his advances was beginning to clear, although the taste of his spittle still cloyed in her mouth. What was he driving at?

'In short, my dear, I have come to ask you to marry me. With your magic and my gifts of leadership bound together we will lead not only your village, but my own and indeed all the peoples of the Winter Seas. Together we will build a secure peace against the hill people and any other invaders that might come. I have heard the Picts have been seen this far south, and the devilish Romans are coming in greater numbers every year. Someone has to stand between these threats and the people. It is the Goddess's will. *These* are the great terrors of the prophecy.

'Our children will have both our skills combined. The boys will be great warriors and powerful druids; the girls will become beautiful women, wearing the seven colours of chieftain queens. What do you say?' He leaned towards her, his red eyes wide and his taut lips pale as he smiled and held out his left hand.

So he was planning an alliance. Tegen said nothing but stared into the burning logs by her feet. What she wanted more than anything was to go out into the night, wash her mouth out and dance for the Lady under the skies. She couldn't think in here – with him.

'Your marriage is not valid,' Gorgans went on, mistaking her silence for interest in his idea. 'Neither the Goddess, nor the spirits, nor the people you serve will expect you to stay wed to a halfhead. You cannot reach your potential, my dear, not unless you have a *real man* at your side. You cannot even go into Witton's secret chamber, and how can the boy know what is required of him in there?

'It is time you came into your full powers . . .' Gorgans rose from his stool and stood in front of her. He grasped her shoulders and hauled her into his arms. 'Marry me. Now. Tonight.'

She raised her hands. He thought she was embracing him and leaned forward for another kiss, but as he did so she twisted his ears.

Hard.

In agony he sprang back, tripped and fell sprawling, narrowly missing the fire.

'Get out *now*, before I bring the full force of my magic down on you.' With a tug at her silk she released it. Holding it taut between her hands like a narrow shield, she took a step towards Gorgans.

He stood, brushed the dust from his immaculate white woollen robe and reached for his cloak. As he swung it around his shoulders he turned back. 'You are only a child. I will give you until the festival of Imbolg to come to your senses. Meanwhile, I forgive your insult.'

With that he flung back the door and stamped out into the night, leaving the rain lashing in behind him.

Tegen pulled the serpent bracelet from her wrist and threw it after him. 'You can have your gift back as well. If my father had known why he was making it, he would have crumbled the wax to nothing, rather than let it flow with silver!'

And with that she slammed the door, ran over to her bed and cried.

26. Derowen's Plan

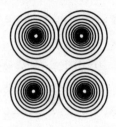

The endless rain made Griff's journey difficult as he struggled down the hill and into the village enclosure. Derowen was waiting for him with hot soup. She took his cloak and spread it to dry. The she patted the soft sheepskin-covered bench, coaxing him to sit next to her.

Griff's love of food and warmth overcame any fears or doubts he might have had. He clasped the bowl and drank. Derowen smiled as she took a bone comb and gently unknotted his hair.

As she worked she talked in a soft voice. 'When you were born, my lamb, I was frightened that Witton might not acknowledge you as his own, or, even worse, he might have ordered you to be put out on the hillside for the wolves. I loved you so much I was scared of that happening, so when you were just two days old I took you into the forest to find one of the hill people to take you in. It was then I saw Clesek up by the waterfall, praying for a son – what could be better? In my arms was a beautiful boy who needed a father. I knew Clesek was a good man, so I interrupted his prayers, gave you to him and asked him to swear never to say how he had come by you.'

Griff slurped his soup, then reached for a honey cake. Derowen pushed the piled wooden platter towards him. She sighed and twisted her hands together as if the memories hurt her, then she glanced at Griff out of the corner of her eye. Was there any point to this? Did the idiot even understand the words she was saying? She continued. 'I knew Nessa too. She was one of my dearest friends. She had just given birth to that girl Tegen. Old Gilda gossips too much, so I knew Nessa had plenty of milk. Leaving you with that family was the best thing I could have done for you, dear little Griff. I am only sorry that Tegen got her claws into you and has been using you for her own ends for so long. It will all be over soon though, trust your mother.'

Griff glanced up from his food and scowled. 'Yus could-a looked arter me if you wan-ned.'

Derowen smiled and tugged at a stubborn knot in his fine hair. 'But that is exactly what I was doing, my dearest. I knew you were safe and well cared for and well away from the scorning eyes of the village people, who wouldn't understand how important you are. People are so shallow; they would have seen you as a halfhead, not as the great druid I know you to be. You needed a safe place to grow to manhood. I did it all *because* I love you . . .'

Griff munched in silence. Then, 'Got any more, Mam?' he asked, his cheeks puffed out with half-eaten food.

Derowen winced as he called her 'Mam', but she put the comb down and rose to get dried fruit from a jar. When she sat again she continued to talk in her soft, sweetened tone. 'Now, my darling, the time has come for you to be proclaimed with your true name. It is *you*, my love, who are the real Star Dancer. The stars were high in the sky when my pains began. It was Gilda refusing to come to the birth, saying she was too tired, that kept you from being born on time. Who knows? If she'd turned up to help, you might not have been born a halfhead at all. It is Gilda's fault that you aren't a full man, my little Star Dancer. Later she schemed with that Tegen girl to keep you away from your true inheritance.'

Griff stopped chewing and looked at Derowen wide-eyed and open-mouthed in horror. 'But I *is* a full man. And a Chosen One. Witton say so. Druids say so. Tegen say so. Gilda and Tegen kind to Griff. Tegen my *woman*.'

Derowen looked taken aback. 'Has she . . . have you . . . is she carrying your child?'

Griff hung his head and looked sulky. ' No.'

'Why?'

He puckered his brow. 'Tegen dusna wanna.'

Derowen leaned back and smiled in a satisfied way.

'Then she is not your woman. Stay here with me and I will find you a better woman, one who does as she is told. Then you can do what you want to prove you are a man. You'd like that, wouldn't you? We'll make Tegen go away, then you can go back to Witton's roundhouse and make it your own. You and your new woman can make lots of babies and I will help you become the Star Dancer as you deserve. Won't that be good?'

Griff stood and looked down at Derowen. She smiled back at him with a hungry look in her shadowy eyes.

'No, I wouldna like that. Not at all. I's going home to Tegen. She looks arter me, an' I looks arter her. We got love. *That's* wot's good.'

Griff tugged the bone comb from his hair and flung it across the room. Then he picked up his cloak and opened the door. Outside, in the rain, Gorgans was striding towards the roundhouse.

Griff pushed straight past him and ran out of the palisade and up the hill.

Gorgans shed his cloak and sat down by the fire. He took a horn of warm mead from Derowen. 'Did you get any-where?'

'No. Did you?'

'No. That little bitch twisted my ears and ordered me to go.' He glared into the firelight and sipped his drink. 'I will get her for that. No one, *no one*, turns me down. I must get rid of her. She will die, I swear it.'

Derowen sat next to him and raised her own drinking horn in solidarity with the vow. 'She has my little boy bewitched. I am certain that Gilda has cast a spell on the girl to make her bold and strong beyond her years. She is a child of that witch's spirit.'

'Then Gilda must die too . . .'

'Oh, she is almost at the gate of Tir na nÓg already. Believe me. But I have made it very slow, partly because she does not deserve a swift death and partly so none will suspect she has been helped to the Otherworld by me. She has friends who are not as insightful as you and me. They do not see how much power she really has.'

'Do not let her live too long. I am summoning the other druids for Sun's Return at Imbolg. That is not long now. She must be dead by then.'

'I have said I will see to it!' Derowen snapped, then regretting her rudeness to her only ally she passed the remains of the honey cakes. 'Will all the druids come?'

'Enough.'

'What about Huval, Pwyll and Marc? How will you keep them away? They are convinced of the girl's calling. She can do no wrong in their eyes,' Derowen said.

'On the contrary,' Gorgans replied. 'We need them most of all. They must see the little witch for what she is. I will send runners with summons soon.'

'Meanwhile –' Gorgans leaned across the fire towards the old woman – 'will you make the spell now?'

'Yes. It is time. Those two upstarts will not listen to reason. They will not step aside for those who deserve power. So they must be got rid of.'

Derowen took her bone carving of the Goddess from around her neck and placed it in a bowl.

'Did you manage to get anything from the boy?'

Derowen picked up her comb and pulled out the tangles of Griff's hair. She placed them next to the figurine.

Gorgans spat next to the hair. 'I kissed the bitch – some of her spit will be in that.'

'Good.' Derowen nodded and took a small, sharp knife from her belt and pierced the pad of her thumb, allowing three drops of blood to fall on the statue, the hair and the spittle. Then, with her forefinger, she stirred the contents of the bowl and chanted through her nose:

> *Spirits of the darkest night,*
> *Bring us power as is our right,*
> *Death to those now in our way,*
> *Bring us victory today!*

Then she paused, her eyes rolled back in their sockets and she hissed between her long teeth:

'*Thumbbar ifrahm-haishesk . . . Towenith-dwire, norprom hadish-camak . . .*'

The fire stopped crackling.

Gorgans could not breathe.

'We swear the deaths of our enemies,' Derowen said, coming to herself again. She picked up the blood and spittle-smeared statuette on its thong and kissed it. Then she passed it to Gorgans.

'We swear,' he echoed, kissing it too. Derowen looped it back around her neck and let the glistening bloody bone slide between her breasts.

The spell was over. Gorgans took a deep breath and sipped his mead. Suddenly a thought occurred to him and he smiled. Derowen's own blood on the statuette was also ensnared within the spell. She too would die!

But he was so consumed by his hate for the old witch, he forgot that his spittle was on it too.

27. Yew

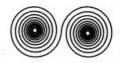

Gilda's aches and cramps grew worse, despite the milder weather that heralded Sun's Return. Her left shoulder and arm were now so painful she could hardly move, and her chest felt as if iron bands had been clamped around it. Tegen often went and sat with her, stroking her hair while she learned as many of the bardic stories and triple truths as she could.

When the old woman slept Tegen draped her green silk shawl across her friend's wheezing chest and tried to picture Gilda standing and laughing in the sunshine. But it did nothing to help.

Just before Imbolg, when the air had definite spring warmth and snowdrops were carpeting the woods in white, Tegen took broth down to Gilda. She let herself in, sat by the bed and felt the old woman's head. It was cool and her skin was pale; her lips and nails had a bluish tinge. 'I will get some fresh water. You must drink. How do you feel?'

Gilda shook her head. 'Don't waste your time on me. You have other people to see and things to do,' she whispered. 'Go to them. I am old now. My story has been told. It is the young who deserve your magic.'

Tegen smiled. 'Giving healing to anyone is never a waste. What is given to you now will come back to us all when you are born again.' She laughed mischievously. 'Perhaps I am hoping for a good child to come to me one day.'

Gilda looked sharp-eyed at Tegen, who shook her head.

'No, I am not with child. Griff will always be more of a brother than a husband to me.'

'You will marry again,' Gilda said shortly and closed her eyes.

Tegen shuddered, remembering Gorgans' unwelcome advances. 'Why do you say that?'

'I can see it. No, not for a while, and . . . things have to happen first. Great things. Terrible things. Who knows? What do you see in the future, child?'

Tegen thought for a few moments. 'I don't know. I have been too busy to try to see things lately. There has been a great deal of illness and several births taking up my time these last few weeks.' She did not want to worry her old friend with all that had really happened.

'Never be too busy to listen and to see what the Lady has to show you!' Gilda said sternly. 'But meanwhile, I smell soup. I believe I could drink some today. I feel a little stronger.' Tegen stood to fetch a beaker for the broth.

'Even at the end it is important to keep listening,' Gilda went on, ' . . . although everything seems so dim and distant these days. I feel as if I am already crossing over.'

Tegen hung her head. Her voice was choked as she spoke. 'Only when the Goddess wills, Mother Gilda.'

'All things are when the Goddess wills, child.'

'Even bad things?' Tegen put the hot beaker on to a table next to her friend.

'Even bad things can have good endings for those who love the Lady. No demon can ever have the last laugh when a soul's intentions are good. Remember that. It is important.'

Just then a pain shot through her chest and Gilda struggled to breathe. As the spasm passed she managed to whisper, 'Please, go to Derowen. Ask her for a tisane to help me. She will know what I need.'

Tegen felt cold at the mention of her enemy's name. 'Do you trust her?'

'This time . . . yes.'

'Do you want me to go now? What gift do I take from you?'

'I can manage. She won't expect payment. We were dear friends once, then we became enemies over . . . something that in the long reach of things didn't really matter. This will be her way of reconciliation. I am happy to accept.'

'Are you sure?'

'Of Derowen?' Gilda reached over the bed covers and grasped Tegen's warm fingers. The old woman's hand was clammy. Such sweatiness did not feel right for someone so cold. 'Derowen may be a bitter woman, but she does understand herbs and she is always right about them. On that you may depend.'

Tegen stroked Gilda's lank hair. 'Is Derowen a bard like you, Mother Gilda?'

'No dear, why do you ask?'

'She wears a blue dress like the one you gave me.'

The old woman lay back on her pillow and closed her eyes. 'She would have liked to have been trained, but she was not chosen when I was. I think that was when her jealousy was born. But that is all over now. I will not challenge her right to wear the blue. What does it matter, after all?'

Still uneasy, Tegen stepped outside into the path that ran by Gilda's home. The muddy track was strewn with straw and ash to make it passable. The way took her between roundhouses and patches of goat-gnawed grass until she came to Derowen's home. If she hadn't been on an errand for Gilda, nothing would have induced her to enter that place.

Griff had tried to tell her what had happened the night he had been sent to see his mother and Gorgans had made his proposal. Tegen could only understand that things had gone badly and Derowen had told lies. Whatever the details were, Griff's anger was enough for Tegen to know she did not want to knock.

But for Gilda's sake she did. The woven hurdle door swung inwards and a malicious face peered out of the smoky gloom.

'Oh. It's you,' Derowen spat. 'Come in.'

Tegen followed. The place was foul with body smells and the stench of blood. The fire burned low in the central hearth, and high on the rafters claw-like bundles of desiccated herbs swung in the smoky heat.

Derowen turned to stir her iron cauldron, settled amongst the glowing embers. She said nothing, but glowered at Tegen, sniffing and wiping her nose on the back of her sleeve.

Tegen's eyes watered and she coughed as the smoke caught the back of her throat. She was terrified, but, she told herself, if she could stand up to Gorgans and win, then she must not let herself be frightened of one old woman. She clutched at the silk shawl around her waist. 'Goddess protect me,' she whispered. But the fear did not go away. This woman was an empty darkness that sucked at Tegen's soul. She wished she could simply turn and go.

'I've come from Mother Gilda,' she managed at last. 'She's very ill and she's asked for a tisane to help her. She says you will know what she needs.' Tegen held the small pot out at arm's length.

Derowen nodded. 'Put it down there – on the stone by

the hearth. You'll need to fetch me some herbs I can't quite reach. Even healers get stiff in their old age, you know.' She pulled back her lips into a grim smile.

The look sent shivers down Tegen's back, but she was determined not to let it show. 'Tell me what you need, Mother.'

Derowen pointed to a row of neatly tied dried leaves hanging at the back of the room. 'That one, in the middle . . . no, the next one, that's it, bring it here, child . . .' Tegen brought the dried bundle of spiky, crumbling leaves and held them out to Derowen. The old woman sniffed and shook her head. 'No, that's awful. All the goodness has gone. You'll have to gather fresh.'

'Where do I look?' Tegen was glad of the chance to go outside.

'Those herbs don't grow at this time of year. You will have to pick some yew instead. Do you know where it grows?'

'I know the sacred tree that guards the cave mouth where the dead go into the Otherworld.'

'That'll do.'

'But it's forbidden to pick it.'

Derowen snorted with derision. 'When you were a *child* you were forbidden, but you are a druid now, in case you had forgotten, and healing is holy work. Now go, before the light fades.'

Tegen hesitated.

'What now?'

'Isn't it poisonous?'

'Not when it's used properly. Do you have a knife on you?'

'Yes.'

'Don't forget to honour the spirit of the tree with a gift when you take from it.' Then the old woman turned her back and Tegen knew it was time to go.

The outside air smelled good. I had better go and tell Gilda I will be a while, she thought. But her friend was asleep, with the soup cold and congealed by her bed. Tegen built up the fire and made sure the door was firmly shut. She glanced at the sky. It would be getting dark well before she could return from the cave mouth. She pulled her cloak tightly around her shoulders and started to walk.

The sun had all but disappeared behind the arm of the hill before Tegen was at Derowen's door bearing a fine branch of almost-black yew leaves. To the east, heavy grey rain clouds were sweeping in, making the evening even darker.

'You took your time,' the old woman grunted. 'What did you leave for the tree?'

'A pebble that caught the light and sparkled.'

'It'll do. Now, I'm far too busy to do everything – you will have to help me for once. Put six twigs with seven leaves each into the pot there by your feet. Add one beaker of spring water and one drop of oil from the jar in the corner, then let it simmer but not boil. Stir it well.'

Tegen knelt down by the fire pit and found a small dusty iron pot. She wiped it clean with the edge of her cloak and sniffed inside. It didn't smell too bad. She chose six twigs with seven short, spiky leaves and dropped them into the pot with the water and the oil. She bit her lip. How do I know I am doing this right? she wondered. I always thought yew was deadly . . . But Gilda said that Derowen must be trusted.

Her hand shook as she poured in the water and stirred the mixture. After a short while the liquid began to bubble and a resinous scent rose in the steam. She pushed some of the embers away with a green stick, so the pot did not boil too fast.

All the while Derowen busied herself in the deep shadows on the other side of the room. Tegen was grateful to be left alone. She shivered as a draught blew in under the door. She felt nervous and worried. Something was wrong, something that made her wish she had never come.

After a while Derowen got up and stood over Tegen. She thrust a pot of honey at her. 'Pour some of that in. It'll take the bitterness away. Then as soon as it's melted, get yourself off to Gilda. She'll need her draught. Make sure she swallows a few of the leaves. Scoop them out and feed them to her if you have to.'

Tegen nodded, poured the liquor into Gilda's pot, then

thanked Derowen and left. It had begun to rain and the path was treacherous. She tried to run, but slipped and almost fell. She steadied herself just in time, saving the precious liquid.

Oh Lady, may this be what Gilda needs. I am worried – this can't be right, Tegen prayed. Once her life had been in Gilda's hands as she struggled newborn into the world; now it was the other way around.

Tegen knocked softly on Gilda's doorpost and went inside. The fire had sunk to a pile of glowing embers. The blast of air from the open door sent the white shadowy ashes swirling up into the thatch. Like ghosts, Tegen thought, and shivered. The place was silent. Was Gilda still alive? Had spirits come from Tir na nÓg to collect her? She pushed a few more dry logs on to the fire and very soon the flames were leaping again, dispelling the empty cold feeling and filling the little room with a golden glow once more.

Tegen sat on the edge of the bed. Gilda was breathing with difficulty. Tegen slipped an arm under the old woman's head to raise it, holding the little pot to her lips. 'Here, this is from Derowen. Drink it. You will feel better.'

'What did she put in it?' Gilda wheezed. Her chest laboured to pull air in, making a hollow rattling sound deep under her ribs.

'Yew. She said you must take some of the leaves as well.'

Gilda managed a smile. 'Yew? Good, it is time. Remember, child, when the world looks as if it is falling apart: all manner of things shall be well.' She took a deep, wheezing breath. 'You must remember the stories. Tell them all through dance, or song, or word . . .' She coughed and pressed her hand under her left breast. 'It doesn't matter how you tell them, but tell them you must . . . You are a bard now. The stories are your pathway.' Then with great effort she pulled her head forward and sipped. One small, black leaf clung to her bottom lip. Tegen pushed it gently inside. 'Leave me now,' the old woman said. 'I need some rest.'

'I'll be back tomorrow,' Tegen promised.

'I know you will, my dear. I know you will.'

Gorgans stepped out of the deep shadows at the back of Derowen's roundhouse.

'She has gone,' Derowen said, her lips drawn into a tight line. 'It is very convenient that the Star Dancer was the one to mix and give the fatal dose. Gilda will be dead very soon. We had better go up to the caves tonight. You have learned your part. Whatever happens, do not forget it. The time has come for the seals to be broken and for the summoning to begin.'

Gorgans let his hood fall back. His long white hair flowed loose and a silver dog-headed torque gleamed red with reflected firelight.

'Good,' he replied. 'My brother druids will begin arriving tomorrow. We must work fast.'

28. The Summoning

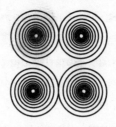

Derowen lit a tallow candle in a horn lantern. Then she and Gorgans stepped out into the night.

The druid carried a large bag over one shoulder and followed the dim, bobbing light as the old witch led the way. The rain had stopped, but the path was slippery as they walked through the woods and up the slope alongside the stream bank. The lantern's faint light flickered and swayed as they walked, the silence broken only by the faint crack of the occasional turned stone and the sound of rushing water.

The way was steep and tortuous. 'How much further?' Gorgans panted.

'Hush!' Derowen ordered as she stamped on. 'We must not be heard.'

Gorgans pulled the bag higher on to his shoulder and trudged onward. The dark of the night was beginning to get to him. He did not like it: too many spirits around for his comfort. He felt vulnerable and, although he would never admit it, afraid. Even though he was a White One, the thought of Tir na nÓg disquieted him. With his free hand he clasped a small statuette of the Goddess that swung around his neck. He did not really honour the Lady, but on nights like this it was better to pay respects.

A small animal scurried across the path and yelped as it reached the shadows. Gorgans stopped, his heart beating painfully against his ribs.

Soon the sounds around them changed. Echoes seemed to close in and Gorgans sensed he was in a narrow, steep-sided place. The wind stopped and the air felt still against his cheek. Derowen halted and set the lantern down. The faint glow lit a cavernous mouth within the hillside and beyond, like a rocky throat ready to swallow the intruders.

They stopped and Derowen held out her hand. 'Fire pot and torch,' she demanded. Gorgans delved into the bag and pulled out both. 'Light it, you fool,' she snapped. Gorgans obeyed. He feared this witch whose evil powers were stronger than he could imagine.

Holding the torch high, Gorgans blinked and shielded his eyes, as fire leaped and the fatty tallow spat. It was dazzling bright after the faintness of the lantern.

Derowen took the flame and turned towards a heavy dark shape on their left. 'Here, this is the sacred yew,' she said in hushed tones.

Gorgans swallowed hard; the many trunks looked like

powerful serpents. The tree's thick black canopy seemed to devour the light.

Derowen swung the torch this way and that. 'Ah, got it!' she said at last and slipped something small into her waist pouch. 'Now, let us enter. Don't forget the bag.'

Gorgans winced. The yew marked the passage from life to death. Beyond this point, in the company of this witch, there would be no protection for him. He would be walking the domain of the spirits. He said nothing as he followed the crone onward, down the throat of the cave, scrambling over the uneven floor and sliding between great boulders. Nervously he looked around, wondering what would happen if the demon guardian of the cave noticed their presence. In this place no one would ever know . . . at least not until the next funeral party came down. He swallowed hard and made himself concentrate.

The way twisted and dipped, until suddenly the echoes of their steps changed. They were in a wide chamber. Derowen held the torch high. The light gleamed on the white and red and green of stalagmites and stalactites that crowded like cadaverous stone faces with long white teeth. Water dripped, sending mournful notes ringing around the cavern. As they trod and slid along the path, a smooth expanse of shiny, rippling blackness opened up to their right.

'What's . . . what's that?' Gorgans stuttered.

'Water, you idiot,' Derowen snapped. 'Grow up! You've

been here before, haven't you? This is where Witton was taken!'

'I've been here, but not . . . not at *night* . . .'

'Night and day makes no difference down here, you fool. Now keep up and try to be quiet . . . oh, and duck – the ceiling is very low.'

Too late. Gorgans cracked his head on the rocks and stifled a cry of pain. Derowen ignored him and walked on into the shadows. Suddenly she moved to the right and Gorgans was quite alone, plunged into absolute darkness.

'Derowen . . . Derowen?' he called. But all he heard was the dancing echo of his own voice. He rushed a few steps forward and slipped into a shallow pool of ice-cold water.

'Help!' he howled.

A light flashed and Derowen came scurrying back. 'What are you doing now, you fool?' Her tall, gaunt figure looked down at him with undisguised contempt.

'I . . . I thought I was drowning,' he whimpered, holding out a hand, begging to be helped up.

She turned on her heel and walked away. This time the glancing light revealed the way ahead. He scrambled to his feet and shuddered as his wet clothes clung to his legs. At last he caught up with Derowen. She was kneeling in the great circular funeral cavern. On the right-hand side the floor gave way to water. Above, the low rocky roof was swirled and carved with twisted shapes. Gorgans felt dizzy. He clutched at his bag.

'Why are we here?' he whispered.

'It's as far as the living can go.' Derowen raised the torch and gestured to a low ledge straight ahead. 'Remember how, at Witton's passing, the water moved and took him under that rock – it is the entrance to the Otherworld, the birth passage of Tir na nÓg.'

She settled back on her haunches and looked up at him. Her face was gaunt and grey in the flickering torch light. 'Now, the plan is this: I will raise the demon that guards the gate to the Otherworld. He will be angry and venomous because we have disturbed him, and very soon he will unleash his anger on the village. When that happens we will tell the people that he was roused by Tegen meddling in magic that is beyond her powers. Then we tell her she must prove her right to the title of Star Dancer by putting the demon back, which of course she won't be able to do because she hasn't been trained in ancient magic.'

Gorgans remembered Tegen holding her shawl like a shield against him. 'I wouldn't be so sure about that . . .' he ventured.

'*Shut up!* I know what I am talking about!' Derowen snapped. 'Then,' she continued, drawing uneasy shapes with water on a dry stone, 'this is the really clever part – the people will stone her for her failure. Neither of us need lift a finger against her. Not even the Goddess can blame us for her death. We will be innocent and free. You can be proclaimed as the Star Dancer and I will be around to help you with my magic.'

Until . . . Derowen thought . . . you are of no more use to me, that is. Then my own *dear* son will take your place. She smiled.

Gorgans looked around nervously. 'But what do we do when the demon comes out and Tegen can't put it back? We don't really want it loose, do we?'

Derowen looked at Gorgans as if he was a halfhead. '*We* put it back, of course. Obviously I can't be seen to take part because I am not a druid, but you and your brother white-robes can see to that. I assume *some* of you can do real magic? Now make yourself useful and hold the torch.'

Gorgans took it and swallowed hard. 'But are you sure she will fail? That green silk of hers is very powerful – she used it to defeat me when I tried to make her my woman.'

The old witch snorted and shook her head. 'Don't be foolish. The shawl didn't defeat you! Your own pathetic stupidity did that. That piece of silk is no more magical than you are. If you are nervous about it, steal it from her. In fact that might be a good idea. If she believes that her power comes from it, she'll lose all her confidence. See to it.' Then she fell silent again and stared straight ahead at the black, swirling water.

Gorgans held the torch high, screwed up his eyes and said nothing. A real unleashed demon was more than he had bargained for. In the broad light of day he had been quite happy about going down into the caves with Derowen to prepare some spells. Things were different now he was alone with the evil old witch, listening to the incessant dripping of the water.

He shivered. 'How long do we have to stay here?'

'Not long, if you shut up,' she snapped. 'Pass me that bag.'

He squatted next to her and put down his burden. Derowen started to unpack. First there came a skull, a short tallow candle, a bowl and the bloodied statue of the Goddess she had worn the day they had taken their oath. She beckoned to Gorgans to bring the torch closer; then she lit the candle and put it inside the skull, so a sickly, smoky light gleamed out from the eye sockets. Next she spat into the bowl and with a flick of her fingers ordered Gorgans to do the same. She dipped the statuette of the Goddess into the slime and stirred it. Next she scooped up a little water from a puddle. In the light of the torch Gorgans could see she was smiling, and the sight made him afraid. He had always known that she worked with the dark arts, but he had never realized just how dangerous she was.

Whose side would she be on in the end? His teeth chattered uncontrollably.

'Silence!' Derowen hissed. Tipping the contents of the bowl on to the rocky floor, she picked up a stone and smashed the image of the Goddess. 'The Lady's protection is hereby destroyed within this place,' she said. Then getting to her feet she stretched herself tall and held her hands out wide to the darkness.

Gorgans shuddered as an icy draught caught him in the back. He held the torch with shaking hands. The guttering flame spat and sent fragmented shadows across the cavern.

Derowen rolled her eyes so only the whites showed. She began to chant:

> Thumbbar timbirrith, ifrahm-haishesk . . .
> Towenith-duffik dwire norprom-norporrim . . .

Her face fell slack and her jowls shook as the ghastly sounds spilled out of her, echoing and re-echoing, building to a cacophony of discordant noises, layer upon layer of horror, sounds that shredded and tore at Gorgans' soul until he could bear it no longer.

He dropped the torch. It went out immediately. At the same moment the candle inside the skull died, plunging the whole chamber into absolute darkness.

But Derowen did not stop. On and on went her song, echoing and jarring.

Then slowly, out of the dark, wound images and shapes: lightless colours of blood and death and fear, eyes and talons, tentacles and wide, swallowing jaws. More and more filled the chamber, each one a manifestation of the horrific sounds issuing from Derowen's mouth.

Suddenly Gorgans was convinced he heard the voice of the demon itself keening a cry of unfillable emptiness.

He sobbed in terror and collapsed shuddering on to the floor, uselessly hiding his head under his cloak. Even there, the dark lights hurt his eyes.

Then there was silence.

And laughter . . .

Not Derowen's. Not Gorgans'.

But a sound of cold mirth that faded slowly away into the stillness of the rocks and the dripping of the water.

Derowen bent down and somehow in the nothing of the blackness she managed to find the torch. She lifted it high and with one word of command it was alight again.

No fire pot.

No flint.

Just magic.

Derowen turned to the shivering druid. 'Pack our things up,' she ordered. 'I want no trace of anything left behind to show we have been here.' While Gorgans was working she scraped the shards of the Goddess figurine together and threw them into the black, swirling water.

'Good riddance!' she spat after it.

Not stopping to look behind him, the druid walked as fast as he could to keep up with the witch as she climbed back up out of the cave. Nothing would keep him in that place one moment longer.

29. Murder

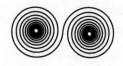

Derowen slept late in the morning. She was woken by Tegen hammering at her doorpost.

'Derowen! Derowen! Come quickly – Mother Gilda is dead.'

The old women assumed a mask of grief and worry and opened the door for Tegen, standing distraught on her threshold.

'When did you find her?'

'Just now. I couldn't come any earlier. I had my rituals to complete and Imbolg to prepare for – several of the brethren have arrived already. Everything has been such a spin, I hardly know which way is up.'

Derowen hitched up her skirts and followed Tegen along the muddy pathway to Gilda's roundhouse. There, her old rival was curled in a crouching position as if her belly had been hurting. She was stiff and pale, her skin and lips were tinged even bluer than usual. Her face lay in a pool of cold vomit.

Derowen examined her, and when she was certain she was dead she scooped ashes from the hearth and rubbed them into her hair. Then she squatted on the stoop outside the door and began to sing a dirge, intoning the keening notes through her nose.

Tegen, feeling uncertain, followed the older woman's example and joined in the eerie song as best she could.

Soon a crowd of villagers had gathered, including Gorgans and two or three other druids who had just arrived. More people came and ashes were passed around, offerings of honey and herbs were brought and left by the dead woman's side. The druids went in and stood around the bed, each intoning their own song to praise Gilda's spirit and to protect her on her way to the Otherworld of Tir na nÓg.

Tegen felt nervous. She had dealt with death before, but this woman had been like a mother to her when Nessa had been so distant in her love. Gilda had taught her everything she needed to discover her calling. Now she was gone, Tegen felt as if part of her soul had been ripped away. She rubbed her ashy hands through her hair and rocked. Pain racked her head as well as her heart. What should she do first?

Just then the kindly face of Huval appeared in the crowd. His tall, warrior-like frame commanded respect; the village people parted to let him through. His chestnut hair, although still thick and wavy, now had streaks of silver. He stepped forward, holding out his strong arms to Tegen.

'Child,' he said, 'come here,' and he pulled her towards him and held her like a father. The smell of his woollen robes mingled with fresh mud and incense made her feel safe and warm. She longed to stay next to him. But her head was spinning with the fact that thirteen moons had now passed since Derowen had given her warning that Tegen's time as druid would end. What was going to happen? She wished she could have time with Huval to talk alone.

Gorgans strode forward, his head held high. Under the broad brim of his hat his eyes gleamed red, and the weak sunlight caught on his golden earrings and his silver dog-headed torque. Despite his glittering finery, he looked gaunt. It was only Derowen's dagger-like presence at his back that made him speak.

It was time to perform all she had taught him.

He bowed respectfully to Tegen and Huval. 'My lord, my lady . . .' He turned to the ash-painted crowd, forlorn now their much-loved Gilda had died.

Gorgans waited for silence, then stretched out his beautifully-shaped arm and swept it around in a grand gesture. '*Dear* friends,' he began, 'people of the Winter Seas, a terrible thing happened today. You . . . *we* . . . have lost a dear friend. True, she will come back to us when the Goddess wills and the time is right, but I am sad to say that I have heard this morning that this good woman died before her time.'

He paused and waited for the implications of what he had said to sink in.

'What are you talking about?' came one voice.

'Someone done 'er in?' called another.

''Oo'd do that?'

Tegen stared at Gorgans, then glanced at Derowen. What was going on?

The wise woman was leaning against the roundhouse wall, her arms folded, white ash well rubbed into her long grey plaits. She narrowed her eyes.

Tegen's heart missed a beat. She stepped away from Huval's sheltering warmth. *She* was the Star Dancer – *she* must deal with whatever was coming. She must not hide under Huval's cloak.

Gorgans swung around and pointed straight at Tegen. 'Last night, your precious would-be druid girl murdered your beloved, good, kind Mother Gilda!'

Whatever she had expected, Tegen was not prepared for this. She bit her lip and glanced around, trying to read the situation. It dawned on her. The yew! Of course . . . Derowen had been looking for a chance to make her fail from the beginning, and Gilda's illness had been the perfect opportunity!

The crowd gasped and stared at Tegen, some in disbelief, some folding their arms and nodding as if they had suspected her all along. The one or two friends she could rely on, like Enor and Budok, could do nothing to help her.

Tegen felt herself go red and then white, hot then cold. She would not be daunted. She lifted her chin defiantly. 'You're talking nonsense!'

Derowen stepped forward to stand next to Gorgans. 'Yesterday that little witch came to me asking for medicine for Gilda. She said the spirits had come to her and told her of a secret drink I must make to heal our dear midwife of her terrible pain. We all believed the Goddess had given much wisdom and Awen to this young woman, our very own Star Dancer, so I did not hesitate to assist her as best I could.'

The crowd murmured; some people began to hiss curses between their teeth. Men and women Tegen had helped . . .

It was Derowen's word against her own. The people were so frightened of the old woman they would always believe what she told them . . . Tegen's confidence began to crumble. She turned to Huval. 'But this isn't true . . . !' she whispered in horror.

He said nothing but put one strong hand on her shoulder. 'Listen,' he said softly, 'you will know what has to be said and done when the time comes. All things work together for good if you love the Goddess.'

Tegen swallowed hard. That was what Gilda had told her.

Derowen was speaking again. The crowd was silent, every eye and ear turned in her direction. 'Tegen insisted on going to the old yew that guards the way through to the

Otherworld. She cut six twigs of seven leaves from there. I argued with her – only as much as it was respectful to do so, of course – but she wouldn't listen. I offered her this pretty stone to give as a gift to the Yew-tree Spirit, but she wouldn't take that either.' She held up the stone that Tegen had left as an offering at the tree.

Tegen longed to spring forward and snatch it back, 'Liar!' she shouted, but she felt Huval's hand tighten on her shoulder.

'Wait!' he whispered.

'I warned the girl that yew was poisonous and not to be used under any circumstances. The Yew Spirit guards the dead; it does not shield the living. But she insisted she had had a vision from the spirits themselves. You know how I brought Old Witton back from almost-death many a time and my herbs have healed you all . . .' The crowd murmured in agreement. 'Well, I knew something was wrong, but I didn't dare argue with the *Star Dancer*. But now . . .' Here she hesitated and pretended to wipe away a tear. 'Now I live with my own regrets that I did nothing to stop her!'

Suddenly Derowen flung herself on to the muddy ground and howled. 'It is *I* who am guilty of my friend's death. I deserve to be stoned for not stopping that witch. I trusted her lying mouth rather than my own long-fought-for wisdom and knowledge . . . She paused and raised herself out of the mud. 'And do you know what is worst of all? I told that girl that if she was to give Gilda an infusion of yew, she must on no account let her swallow any leaves. And when I opened Gilda's mouth just now to give her spirit an offering of honey, I found . . . *this* . . .' and in her outstretched palm lay one, black yew leaf.

Tegen felt sick – how could Derowen twist the truth like this?

Gorgans stepped forward and, taking Derowen's hand, raised her up. He looked around at the crowd and put an arm around her shoulders. 'My brother druids, my fellow people of the Winter Seas, I ask you, is it fair to blame this good woman for obeying the words of one she had been told to honour as the Star Dancer? Is she guilty of Gilda's death? Tell me . . . *is* she guilty?'

'Well, no,' came one voice. 'It was the witch child who told her what to do.'

'Indeed,' called another. 'That girl is no druid. She is a murderess.'

'She must pay!' Soon the shouts were filling the enclosure. The crowd pressed in closer and closer. One or two voices shouted, 'Leave off,' or, 'She wouldn't!' But they were too few. Tegen knew if she ran to a friendly house then the thatch might be set on fire, or the door smashed down to get at her. She was surrounded by hate. Many of the people had picked up mud and stones ready to throw, but while Huval stood next to her they hesitated.

Huval stepped forward, holding up one hand for silence.

'Friends, listen: the rest of my druid brothers will be here soon for Imbolg. Bury your friend Mother Gilda in the cave. Send her spirit to the Otherworld. Once that is done she will find a way to speak. If she has bad words to say about Tegen, then she will make it known. If Tegen is innocent, that will also be made clear. Meanwhile, make offerings of peace and reconciliation to the spirit of the yew tree who guards the gateway for you. I will take this girl into my own custody; my life will be answerable for hers. We will wait for the rest of the brothers to come.'

No one dared to argue with Huval, and the crowd dispersed, muttering and restless. Gorgans and Derowen exchanged glances.

Things were going very well indeed.

Preparing Gilda for the funeral and sewing her into her shroud took all day. Tegen didn't go near, but she couldn't rest either. She sat in her little roundhouse with the door open to the east and watched the rain. At last Huval came and sat with her. For a long time she stared silently into the fire. After a while she began to talk and slowly she told Huval the truth about the yew tisane. She did not mention Gorgans' offer of hand-fasting. She was too embarrassed.

Huval sat, head bowed, warming his large hands and feet by the flames. 'Where is Griff?' he asked at last.

'Out on the hills, burning charcoal for my father.'

'Is he alone?'

'No, he will have his dog, Wolf, with him.'

'Then he is safe. It is best to leave him out of all this.'

Tegen hugged her knees and felt tears stinging her eyes. She rubbed them away. She was fifteen – two hands and a foot old. She had to be as strong as if she was two hands and two feet old; that was when she would come into her full strength. How she wished it was now.

'What is happening?' she asked at last.

Huval sighed. 'Use your sight. What do you see?'

Tegen closed her eyes, then untwined her green silk from around her waist and held it to her cheek. After a few moments she spoke. 'I see great danger, terrible things – things from deep, dark places. Things I have not summoned . . . but . . . which *someone else has*?' She looked at Huval uncertainly.

'Yes,' he said simply, 'that's what I see too. Tomorrow Marc will come, and Pwyll, Llew, Horth and Timarc too, if they can make it. Together we will listen to the Goddess and understand. There is a deep purpose in all of this. Rest assured, little Star Dancer, we will seek that purpose out. Meanwhile it is late. Get some sleep.'

Tegen nodded. 'But first I must do something.'

Huval raised one eyebrow.

'It's a small ritual of my own. I . . . I dance for the Lady every night, whether I can see her stars or not – I know they are always there behind the clouds. It's a bit like I feel tonight, the clouds are thick and heavy round my soul, but I know the Lady is there. As long as she knows the truth it doesn't really matter what anyone else thinks.'

'That is good,' Huval said. 'May I sleep here tonight? It is too late to go and find lodgings in the village.'

'Of course. I would be glad of the company.' Smiling to hide how lonely and scared she felt, Tegen loaded a pile of sheepskins on to Griff's bed for Huval, then picked up her precious green silk on her way towards the door. 'I won't be long. Goodnight.'

Huval lay down and was soon asleep.

At the bottom of the hill, Tegen untied her long dark plaits and unwound her snagged and tear-stained shawl.

High above, the moon was bright but waning. It was not a good night for the magic she had to work, but she had no choice. As Tegen prepared to dance, the moon settled between two billowing clouds. Suddenly its silver light spilled across them, so for a moment it looked as if a great protecting spirit was spreading her two wide, shining wings.

Smiling, Tegen closed her eyes and imagined the little drummer boy beating a new rhythm, strong and earthy. In her mind Tegen saw starlight shining in a very dark place indeed. She kicked off her clogs and began to stamp her feet in the cold wet grass, swinging her shawl high in the night air. She began to dance as she had never danced before.

The water that squelched between her toes was the tears

of the Lady. The fire of the stars was the fire of hope and cleansing. The wind on her cheek was the Goddess's Awen – the breath of truth. At that moment Tegen knew that whatever happened to her body, nothing could harm her soul, for she was a child of the Goddess.

Her body was one with the stone of the earth. She was alive as the earth was alive and that could not be taken from her.

Filled with joy and certainty, Tegen stamped and moved, swaying in the starlight, performing for the Goddess.

She was so engrossed, she did not hear swift footsteps running across the grass. She did not see a flash of moonlight catching on a twisted silver curve. She scarcely felt the blow to the back of her head, or her face sinking into the muddy grass.

She only knew that when she woke, bitterly cold in the early light of dawn, her head was bloody and her precious green silk was gone.

30. The Way to Tir na nÓg

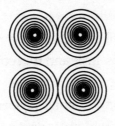

Huval rose at first light for the rituals. It was when he went to fetch spring water that he saw Tegen lying in the grass.

At first he thought she was dead, she was so very cold, but as he stooped to pick her up, she opened her eyes. 'It's gone,' she said.

'What?'

'My shawl,' she replied and closed her eyes again.

'I'm sure we'll find it,' Huval said kindly. He touched the blood on her head. 'You are hurt. What happened?' But Tegen's teeth were chattering so much she could no longer talk. He wrapped her in his cloak and carried her inside. She felt like an injured bird that believes it will never fly again.

He put her on the bed. 'As soon as the rituals are done I will send for a woman to come and help you.'

'Not D-Derowen,' she muttered. 'Please, not her.'

'No. Not Derowen, I promise.' Huval covered her with fleeces, then went to complete his offerings. When he came back inside Tegen was asleep again, but her skin felt very cold. He took one of the hot cooking stones from by the fire, wrapped it in a woollen shawl and put it next to her in the bed. Soon she began to breathe more deeply and colour returned to her face. Huval gave her sips of warm water mixed with honey and rosemary. Satisfied she was recovering, he let her sleep and went out into the morning sunshine to think.

He walked across the semi-flooded fields towards the water's edge until he came to the woods. Tangled hazel and willow twigs were swelling with green and in the fleeting moments of sunlight they glimmered with gold. The air smelled of water, wet wood and damp grass. Ahead lay the expanses of the Winter Seas, a great silver sky-mirror, flat and calm. Everything was still, apart from a heron splashing after prey and a wren bustling in and out of the thickets. Behind him the pale green and purple haze of forest-cloaked hills rose steeply.

The place was beautiful. How could so much evil be working on a day like this? Why did the Goddess let it happen?

Suddenly Huval heard a shout behind him. He turned and saw Marc and Pwyll riding little brown ponies down the steep path from the hills.

Huval shouted back and ran to meet them. Marc mopped his head and greeted his friend with a warm slap on the back. Behind him, Pwyll was unsmiling. 'It is beginning, isn't it, my friend?' he said gravely.

Huval nodded. 'It is. I will walk with you to the Star Dancer's roundhouse and tell you what I know.'

Tegen was up and had put on dry clothes by the time the druids arrived. She had washed the blood from her hair and felt better, but her head still ached. She chewed a piece of willow bark to ease the pain. She greeted her visitors and offered them bread and mead, then sat quietly as they cast the Ogham and talked of divinations and signs. They included her in their discussions, but she hardly spoke as she combed gently at her hair and tried to plait it.

At last Marc turned to her and patted her on the hand. 'What happened last night? Did you slip? Why did you spend all night out there? You are lucky you survived – there was a cold wind.'

'I was hit on the head.' Tegen touched the place and winced.

'Did you see who it was?' Marc asked.

She shook her head. 'I was dancing under the stars. I do it every night for the Goddess.'

'Her shawl was stolen,' Huval added.

Marc smiled. 'Well, if that's all then there is nothing to worry about. You're well, and no real harm has been done.'

Tegen bit her lip. How could she tell them she had lost the source of her magic – that without her shawl she would be useless in the fight against the evil ahead?

Marc smiled. 'This may be the day you were born for, little Star Dancer. Don't be afraid – we are all here to help.'

'Except for Gorgans and some of his friends,' Pwyll mumbled.

Huval snorted. 'He's only in the brotherhood because he is a White One. He has no love and no magic, not like Tegen here.'

'We will combine all our skills and strengths with yours, Star Dancer. Whatever is coming, you are not alone,' said Marc. 'We all trust you.'

'But that's just it.' Tegen could hold it in no longer. 'I *did* give Gilda yew . . . Derowen told me to do it. I didn't want to, but Gilda said I must trust her. I should have known better . . . My dearest friend died at my hand. I am a murderess.'

Huval looked at his friends, then back at Tegen. 'From what you have said, it sounds as if Gilda was dying and wanted help on her way to the Otherworld.'

'She knew what was in the draught, and she still drank it,' added Marc.

'But would she do such a thing? Isn't self-death a sacrilege to life?' Tegen asked.

'Dying can be a painful and lonely process,' Huval explained. 'Many people seek help across the divide at the end. Who knows whether it is really right or wrong? I am certain you were not at fault. Gilda was ready to die.'

Tegen walked to the door and looked outside.

Pwyll quietly recast the wooden staves and stared intently at them.

Tegen swallowed hard and wiped her nose. 'There's something else. I wasn't going to tell you – I didn't want you to know how badly I have let you down – but . . . without my shawl I am not the Star Dancer. I am nothing. My magic was in the silk. It was all I had.'

Pwyll looked up from his Ogham. 'You have not let us down. This pattern tells me there is still hope. All is not lost. You must fight with whatever comes to hand. Remember that. It will be important.'

Marc nodded. 'I agree most heartily. If the Lady chose you to be her Star Dancer, there is nothing you can do about it, with or without this shawl. You must still do what you were born to do. You have a magnificent story in you yet.'

'That's what Gilda used to say,' Tegen sniffed.

'Then she was a very wise woman.' Marc clasped his hands over his round belly and looked pleased.

'Your magic wasn't in a piece of silk,' Huval said. 'It was – and is – *in you*. It might have felt as if you needed the silk, but that is how a child thinks. The Goddess has allowed this theft so you can discover your true strength as a woman and a druid. It is your heart speaking to the Lady's heart and listening to her words that matters. Can you understand that? Now, we must go soon. Wash your face and walk with us. Whatever else happens, we must send Gilda to Tir na nÓg with the dignity she deserves.'

Still unconvinced, Tegen nodded and finished tidying herself while the men walked in the sunshine.

'I don't like it,' said Pwyll. 'The Ogham says that the evil is here, but I am not sure where it is coming from. It is not Tegen's doing, of that I am certain, and although Derowen is wicked, I am not sure even she could raise the tidal wave that is looming.'

'We'll find out soon enough,' Huval replied. 'The important thing is to keep Tegen strong. We have never quite known what the Star Dancer is, or how she will work, but we must be there for her. We must not let the loss of her shawl affect her.'

Inside the dark, gaping cave mouth that led to Tir na nÓg, Gorgans and Derowen stood silently, sheltering from the rain. Behind them were four hill men and a boy: all well armed and grim featured, their skin painted with outlandish symbols.

Gorgans pulled Tegen's green shawl from a pouch at his waist and clicked his fingers. The boy jumped forward with a fire pot in a basket.

'Put it there.' Gorgans pointed to a flat rock. He took the silk and draped it over the embers. Smoke, then flames, licked and devoured the cloth. Soon, only fine ashes remained.

From below in the valley, the drone of a dirge drifted through the rain. Gorgans turned and shielded his eyes against the poor light. 'The funeral procession is coming. Light the torches.' The boy opened a sack and pulled out several thick bundles of dried reeds soaked in goose fat. He dipped one into the fire pot. It spat and hissed and burned with a sour stench.

The flames had barely caught when a group of druids robed in white reached the cave mouth. Behind them, six village men struggled up the stony slope. They were soaked and out of breath from carrying the bier on which Gilda lay. She was sewn into a linen shroud; only her head was free. Her long grey hair was combed loose and woven with late snowdrops and tiny narcissi.

The procession stopped and Gorgans took a torch and held it high. The bearers all lit their own lights from his flame.

'Rest yourselves until everyone else is here,' Gorgans said. The men lowered their burden and squatted amongst the green fronds of ferns and the dry pebbles that lined the entrance. Soon two hundred or so villagers had arrived, including Nessa, Clesek and Griff. Last of all came Marc,

Huval and Pwyll, followed by Tegen, her head shrouded in a white linen veil and her eyes red and puffy with weeping.

'Murderess!' Morgan hissed. Huval glared at him and took his place at the front of the crowd, beckoning to Marc and Tegen to follow him. Pwyll waited until everyone else had gone inside and followed last, his long-bladed knife already drawn in his hand.

As the darkness closed in around them, Gorgans felt the fear of the demon clutch at his throat once more. He swallowed hard and tried to control his breathing. Derowen scowled at him. 'Go home if you can't take it,' she muttered. 'Then live with the fact that I, a mere old woman, am stronger than you will ever be.'

Gorgans slipped his hand under his cloak. His dagger was also ready. As soon as this business was done with, the witch would die. He had no further use for her, and in the confusion and darkness no one would see.

The thought of what they were about to do made him shudder, but he would be strong this time. He knew what was coming. What did he really have to be scared of? After all, when Derowen 'raised the demon' it would only be tricks with sounds and echoes. *Wouldn't it?*

Griff kept pace beside Tegen. He sensed it was not a good time to speak, but he reached out and held her hand. His warmth and unconditional love gave her a lump in her throat. She squeezed his fingers and hoped he knew how much she cared about him.

She kept her back straight as she walked, carefully stepping from boulder to boulder, wondering what great creature had first gnawed its way out through the hillside rock and created this cave. Was it a good being, opening a way through to Tir na nÓg for the dead? Or was it the demon she had often heard stories about – a creature so terrible it had to be restrained with the deepest, oldest, magic of all, known only to a few?

Tegen could feel that all was not well. *Something* was here that she had never met at other funerals. Something lonely and empty and rapacious in its need to devour . . .

She breathed as deeply and steadily as she could. Her free hand longed to curl around the green silk she missed so much. But it was not there. Was Huval right? Was her magic *really* within herself? Even if it wasn't, surely the Goddess wouldn't let her people suffer. She would help, wouldn't she?

The procession turned the final corner and entered the circular funeral chamber.

As it did so, Tegen pushed her fist into her mouth to smother a scream . . .

31. The Spirits Speak

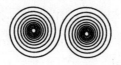

The great cavern was absolutely still. The only sound was the soft tap-tapping of dripping water. The light from the torches glimmered golden on yellow rocks encrusted with layers of milky white crystals. Everything was just as it should be

except

for the fear.

Intense and lonely as death itself.

Cold, empty loss.

As loveless and hollow as the sky on a starless night, as hungry as a swallet on a moor or an unheard scream.

Tegen jumped at the sound of the men behind her beginning their song of mourning. The deep voices set up a drone with the women singing a higher note in a perfect harmonic. The torch lights moved and the shadows flickered.

This sacred place that Tegen had always thought of as

filled with hope – this doorway where good spirits like Witton's could cross to Tir na nÓg – now stood as empty and cold as bones.

Griff squeezed her hand and she felt a little warmth creep back into her fingers. His cheerful voice took the tune and Tegen tried to follow. She breathed deeply and told herself not to be silly as they stood together in the centre of the chamber next to Huval.

The body was set down at the edge of the water. The ivory of Gilda's face, her grey hair, the creamy shroud and the tiny white flowers seemed to radiate a reassuring, gentle light of their own. For a moment Tegen felt better.

Huval stepped forward and lit two beeswax candles by Gilda's head and two by her feet. Marc sprinkled bitter incense on a small pot of smouldering charcoal and nodded to the men, who lifted the bier tenderly for the last time, then laid it on to the waters.

Huval looked sadly at the old midwife, and began to intone:

> *She has gone to the Otherworld*
> *To await her rebirth.*
> *May she tell of our faith*
> *And of our suffering,*
> *That the Goddess may . . .*

. . . The funeral prayer was left hanging in the air as the river swelled, the bier rocked and Gilda's body was tipped into the water. There she bobbed, head up, for a few moments. Then she turned. In the half-light her eyes seemed to be open and her face was streaked with wet hair, black against her white skin.

She was looking right at Tegen.

Tegen shook her head. 'I am so sorry,' she whispered.

The body sank beneath the surface. There were no ripples. Just an eerie flatness.

Then there was a soft rumbling noise and the water suddenly sprang into a million dancing pinpricks of light.

The crowd gasped.

'What's happening?'

'Are the spirits angry?'

Derowen climbed on to on a high rock 'The girl has done this!' she screeched, holding her torch high and pointing down at Tegen. 'Behold! The spirits are speaking.'

The rumbling came again, and this time the ground shook.

'Get out! It's not safe!' voices shouted.

'Wait!' Gorgans commanded, scarcely in control of his own terror. 'It's a sign.' He paused and stared around at the fleeing people. 'A sign of murder – and other things . . .'

Suddenly a terrible screech echoed and re-echoed around the chamber. A draught tossed the flames in the torches and the rumble increased to a thundering from beneath the ground. Above, the roof began to crack and dust and gravel fell.

'Get out!'

'Demons are coming!' someone screamed.

People ran this way and that in blind panic, knocking each other over. Children started crying as parents coaxed them towards the tunnel entrance.

Gorgans nodded to the painted hill men, who drew their knives and blocked all means of escape. 'No one leaves,' he commanded.

'Let the people out!' Huval ordered.

'In good time!' Gorgans replied, his face impassive, his eyes narrow and hard. He was feeling stronger. The so-called demon hadn't reappeared. He could cope with the earth shaking. He had known this before. It was only the sleeping mountain giants stretching. It would pass. But he would use the villagers' fear for all it was worth – just as Derowen had used *his* fears the night before.

Gorgans stood in front of the guards, his arms crossed and his jaw set. 'No one leaves until certain things are known. You all saw the way the corpse's eyes opened and glared at Tegen. It is quite clear that this is a sign that Gilda's spirit has sent to us: this girl is guilty of her murder.'

Tegen's nails dug into her palms. Was this the evil she had to face? Was it *now*? She would not be destroyed by this heartless man. She must be strong, for the people's sake. She shivered.

By her side Griff stood steady, feet apart. His knife was drawn in one hand, and with the other he reached for Tegen. No one would hurt his beloved.

'Yes, we saw those eyes!' voices shouted

'It means nothing!' Huval replied.

Tegen glanced around, but he was too far away to help. She saw her mother weeping. Nessa had always dreaded the spirits hurting her child and now her worst fears were coming true. Tegen could not see her Da, but surely he would help her? She wanted to run to find him, but she stood her ground and held her head high.

'Silence,' Gorgans commanded. 'It is obvious that spirits . . .' he swallowed nervously at the memory, 'maybe even a *demon*, have been let loose by her meddling.'

Right on cue, the ground shook again, only this time the roar of subterranean thunder seemed closer. From above the lake a large rock dislodged itself and fell with a resounding splash. The icy black waters rose and lapped across the rocky floor.

Women held on tight to their terrified children. The guttering torch light showed eyes wide and dark in waxen faces.

Huval, closely followed by Marc, pushed through the crowds until they faced Gorgans. 'Let the little ones out!' Huval demanded, drawing his own knife and holding it to the white druid's chest. 'I don't know what you are playing at, but this is cruel!'

'Not as cruel as murder!' Gorgans replied, coolly pushing the blade aside. 'Nor as cruel as the lies and torture this girl has put you good people through for the last year. It is because of her that you are now trapped in what might well become your tombs . . .' He trembled at his own words, but did not let it show.

'Don't be ridiculous!' Marc snapped, jabbing a finger at him. 'Step aside. You are scarcely more than a novice yourself – what do you know about these things?'

'Enough,' Gorgans replied. 'I witnessed Gilda's murder and I sense that at this very moment the demon is approaching . . .' His voice wavered as he looked around for reassurance from Derowen, but he could not see her.

Trying to appear confident, he clicked his fingers and one of the hill men stepped forward. In each tattooed hand he held a gleaming dagger. The man lowered his head and pulled back his lips in a dangerous snarl as he took his place by Gorgans' side.

Huval pulled away his own weapon and looked Gorgans in the eye. 'Shall we let the Goddess decide?' he asked.

'With your pretty throwing sticks?' he sneered. 'I think not. The time has come for your impostor to be denounced. Things are happening – things that must be clearly understood.'

He swung round and pointed at Tegen, raising his voice so all could hear. 'I accuse this witch child of murder and dabbling in magic she doesn't understand and has no right to. Furthermore, not only has she feigned being a druid, she has also taken the sacred name of Star Dancer upon herself.'

He moved towards her and the shocked crowd fell back. Tegen and Griff stood alone.

'I, Gorgans, Druid of these hills and brother of the Order of the Winter Seas, accuse this woman and demand justice!'

Tegen longed for her lost shawl. She closed her eyes and tried to see the Watching Woman's brilliant stars, but there was only darkness. Her heart pounded.

Griff put his arms around her and looked at the crowd with fury. 'You shuttit, mister, and let her go – all of yus! She ain't done nothing to you lot 'cept nice stuff!' Then, throwing back his head he howled, 'Lady Goddess! Is you listenin'? This tin't fair. Come and do summat!'

Shaking with terror, Tegen tried to speak. 'Good people!' she called out with a bigger voice than she knew she had.

Immediately there was silence. Everyone turned to her. She stepped a little away from Griff so she stood alone on the high ground in the centre of the chamber. She made herself as tall as she could, chin held high and eyes levelled at Gorgans.

She took a deep breath. 'If I have done wrong, I will face the consequences. But you must let the people go. You must not make them suffer for anything that I might have done.'

Mutterings of agreement showed Gorgans he would have to compromise. 'Just the children then, and some women to guide them out. The rest of you must stay as witnesses.' He could not allow an exodus; there must be enough people left to stone the girl before anyone could change their mind about her guilt.

Within moments the children had been bustled away.

Tegen felt as if her heart would break out of her chest with fear. Cold sweat was trickling down her neck. She had to do something . . . dare she believe she still had her magic?

She closed her eyes. *If only I could see the stars and dance for the Lady one more time,* she said to herself, *then I might be able to see what I need to do.*

All around, the darkness and the weight of the hills above were crushing her spirit. *This would be a terrible place to die,* she thought, *here, with no night sky to cover me and no stars to bless me.*

Standing tall, Tegen took a deep breath and said aloud, 'Why must so many people stay? If I have done wrong, it is a matter for you druids to judge.'

'They stay so everyone can witness . . .' Gorgans' words were cut short by the graunching and grinding of rocks. The cavern shook.

He took a deep breath and steadied his voice: '. . . witness that the demon has been released by *your* meddling.' He turned and raised his arms to the watching villagers as they backed away. He shook his jingling armbands. The sound of gold gave him confidence. Gorgans turned slowly on his heel and stared at each person present. 'She has destroyed the balance in the spirit world. There is no protection here.

The Goddess has left this place. The evil that was prophesied is now amongst us . . . and its name is *Tegen!*'

At that moment he caught sight of Derowen. She was crouched a little away from the rest of the crowd, looking like a large boulder in the guttering lights. Gorgans suddenly remembered how she had crushed the statuette of the Goddess in this very place . . . *and that it had his own spittle on it.*

Something unseen gripped relentlessly at his throat.

He had sometimes wondered whether he really believed in spirits and demons.

Now he knew.

. . . And they were a part of him.

Derowen leaned back on her heels, her eyes rolled and she began the terrible ululations she had sung the day before. Once more the sounds swelled and ached through the cave. The villagers wailed in answering terror. Within moments, shattering sounds began to build layer upon layer of discord, sharp and piercing. As the agonizing noise increased, so did the panic.

A torch was dropped, a woman's skirt caught fire and in her desperation to put the flame out she ran to the water's edge, slipped and fell in. She screamed as the icy water dragged her down and twisted her away in the swift, hidden currents. Huval sprang forward to try to pull her out, but he too lost his footing on the treacherous rocks.

Marc held out his staff. Huval grasped it and struggled

back to safety. Sodden and shivering, he looked back for the woman, but there was no sign of her.

'*One more murder!*' Gorgans shrieked.

In frenzied terror the villagers tried to escape once more, but were driven back by the hill men's knives. Screaming, pushing and shoving, bodies slipped and fell.

Still Derowen sang and screeched.

'Let them *go!*' Tegen shouted.

But no one could hear.

There was silence.

Then it came.

First, a foul stench of stale air and rotting flesh.

Next, the eyes. Colours that had never known light.

The tentacle-fingers that groped and sought their way into the people's souls.

The moment held and held.

Then, with an ear-shattering crack that seemed to wrench the whole cavern apart, the last of the torches went out.

32. Star Dance

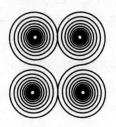

'Do something, *druid girl*,' sneered Derowen's voice from out of the darkness.

Instinctively Tegen's hands groped once more for her silk shawl, even though she knew it was no longer around her waist. 'I . . . cannot,' she whispered.

That one word echoed around the chamber: '. . . *cannot . . . can . . . not . . .*'

Gorgans tried to speak, but the terror within him was too great.

Derowen went on. '*Cannot* or *will* not?'

'Cannot. I have no power,' Tegen replied clearly, 'and I am guilty of Gilda's death.'

Derowen laughed and clicked her fingers, summoning a magical fire to every torch in the chamber.

The people gasped and huddled together even more closely than before.

'Then let us see what *real* workers of magic can do, shall we?' Derowen challenged. 'Brother druids, please send this demon back and make us all safe again.'

In the light, Gorgans found himself forced to his feet. He tried to raise his head and hands, but his torque and armbands pinned him down. He tugged at them and flung them away. They landed, ringing bell-like, on to the rocks.

Trembling, he tried again, beginning the invocation of the spirits:

> *Spirits of air, rain, fire . . . and . . . l-land,*
> *S-still these . . . these rocks . . . a-at . . .*

But he could go no further. His limbs started twitching and he fell at Derowen's feet, jibbering uncontrollably.

'Get up, you idiot!' She kicked him.

Marc, Huval and Pwyll led the other druids forward as they intoned:

> *Spirits of air, rain, fire and land,*
> *Still these rocks, at our command!*
> *Cease your grinding! Peace, be still!*
> *Hold your anger at our will.*

The cracking and screaming of grinding rock was deafening; the place shook with a fearsome shudder. Everyone was thrown to the ground, but the magicked torches stayed alight.

'*Do it, you fools!*' snapped Derowen.

The druids scrambled to their feet, but once more they were tossed aside.

Derowen swore and held up her scrawny arms. 'Enough!' she roared. 'Go back. I command you by the blood I sacrificed. Demon, I command you by the power I took when I banished the Goddess from this place. I command you by the power I bought with my own soul . . .'

Three heartbeats of silence followed. Then with a small, scarcely discernible sigh, Derowen fell to the ground and did not move again. Her body lay grey and empty on the rocky floor.

In the silence that followed, the druids looked at each other in disbelief and the villagers huddled against the rear wall of the chamber. No one spoke.

'Do summat!' Griff whispered to Tegen. 'You can do it, girl. I knows what I knows and I knows yus is the Star Dancer. It *is* yus, girl; I allus knowed it.'

'What can I do?' she whispered. She could feel the demon's cold tentacles clutching her heart as its icy voice whispered: '*You have no power, murderess. Do not compound your sin . . .*'

How could she fight that?

At that moment the earth shook again, and with a roar the waters rose in a thundering wave that swirled around the chamber, tossing the bones of the long dead amongst the living. The vortex of icy water crashed against the walls. People screamed and shoved as they tried to reach the high ground in the centre, or to escape along the tunnel.

'Get OUT!' Huval yelled above the tumult. 'Everybody, get OUT!'

Those who could not run were swept off their feet and tossed helplessly in the raging black whirlpool. Only two torches remained alight.

Without hesitating, Griff waded into the maelstrom and grabbed at flailing hands, pulling terrified men and women back to where others could help them to higher ground.

Tegen knew that, shawl or no shawl, she had to act.

There was no one else.

She bowed her head and closed her eyes. Then it came to her why Gilda had been allowed one last glance in her direction before she was taken: it was to remind her to open her own eyes towards the Goddess so she would see what needed to be done. What had Gilda said?

'Remember, child, when the world looks as if it is falling apart: all manner of things shall be well.'

First, Tegen realized, she must block out the terror and prevent it from reaching her. Huval was right. She didn't need her shawl. She had to hold on to hope. Hope was her story and her dance.

Just then she saw Gorgans' discarded golden armbands

glinting on the wet rock near her feet. She picked them up and slipped them around her ankles. Then, closing her eyes, she began to move, letting them jingle and make a music of their own – louder, clearer and more powerful than the raging water and grinding rocks.

She threw back her head and counted the stars of the Watching Woman in her mind. They were all there and in their correct positions. They shone bright and calm. As Gilda had promised, all would be well.

All she had to do was to dance . . . to tell the story of hope. She breathed deeply and the Awen surged through her. Tegen danced. With her arms and fingers spread wide she called the waters, and with steady rhythmic footsteps she stilled the rocks. She opened her mouth and half cried, half sang:

> *Be still, be still,*
> *Make your rage to cease!*
> *Water and rocks,*
> *Now be at peace.*
> *Demon, I cast you*
> *Far below,*
> *In the name of the Lady*
> *Whose power you know.*

33. Home

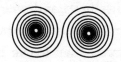

There was one final shudder, and then a whimper as the defeated demon slipped back into oblivion. The waters lessened and retreated.

The sound of sobbing echoed around the darkness. Two faint remaining torches showed the wet rocky ground was full of treacherous pools and littered with old bones and new bodies.

Tegen's head was swimming. Her legs shook and she leaned over and was sick. Huval ran forward and caught her as she fell. Then he helped her towards Clesek's waiting arms.

'Get her out into the air,' he said. 'Take one torch and we will keep the other.'

Clesek nodded and guided his trembling daughter through the debris of bones and boulders.

'Those who are injured, go with Clesek,' Huval called

out. 'Those who are still strong, stay with me. We will look for survivors.'

The search did not take long.

Clesek and Nessa half carried Tegen out of the cave and back up the hill to her childhood home. Between them they made a straw mattress by the central hearth and laid their child in the exact spot where she had been born. With tears in her eyes, Nessa dressed her in dry clothes and tenderly combed her long dark hair.

'I wish it hadn't been you,' she sniffed, 'but I always knew it was.'

Tegen reached up and hugged her mother. 'Where is Griff?' she whispered.

'He is with Huval and the others. They are bringing people out.'

'Griff is a good man,' Tegen said, then snuggled like an infant next to her mother and slept.

Late that afternoon, Huval and the remaining druids made their way up to the silversmith's house. Hearing voices outside, Tegen got up.

'Get back to bed!' Nessa ordered. 'I will send them away.'

'We must let them in. Griff will be with them!' She lifted the latch.

As the door opened the druid visitors knelt silently on the muddy ground outside.

'Star Dancer, we have come to beg forgiveness for ever doubting you,' said Horth humbly. 'I . . . I did wonder sometimes . . .' He looked up at her, his face pale and remorseful under his red beard.

Tegen shook her head and stepped back. 'Please get up and come inside. I doubted as well. Can you forgive *me*? I didn't believe the truth. People died because I hesitated.' She turned and walked back to her fireside bed, where she sat, clutching her knees under her chin. The warm light of the fire played on her dark hair. She looked gaunt, and much older.

The druids followed her into the room, but remained standing.

Nessa slammed the door and put her hands on her hips, glowering at the visitors. Her dark eyes were menacing, her thin face tight with fury. 'You've said your piece, now go away! What more do you want? She's not much more than a child. She's done what was necessary. She needs to come home now.'

Huval ignored her and sat next to Tegen. He looked solemn and weary. His eyes and face were grey, even in the golden light of the fire.

Tegen didn't look away from the flames. 'It's Griff, isn't it?'

Huval sighed. 'We found him washed up just outside the cave. He died the bravest man of us all.' Huval put his arm gently around her shoulders.

Tegen ignored him as she poked a stick into the fire, making a shower of red sparks fly into the roof. 'Griff loved the smell of fires,' she said. 'He was a good charcoal burner. He was a brave man. Only most people didn't realize it. They couldn't look beyond what they saw on his face or the way he talked.'

Behind, in the darkness, Nessa was weeping. Clesek wrapped his strong arms around her and spoke softly, and then he let his own tears fall.

Tegen felt her eyes stinging too, but she wanted to be alone before she mourned. 'And Gorgans . . . Derowen?'

'Both dead.'

Tegen shivered. She pitied the mothers who would bear them next.

'So, it's all over?' she managed to ask at last. 'I have danced the Star Dance? I am free?'

Huval hesitated.

'Tegen, we have come to ask you . . . to ask you if . . .' He glanced towards Nessa and Clesek, then at his nine companions standing silent in the flickering light of the stone house.

'We want to ask you if you will come with us. Be our sister druid. Come and complete your training. Will you be our Star Dancer forever?'

Tegen jammed her stick hard into the yellow heart of the fire.

The flames crackled and spat.

'I've told you, she has done enough!' Nessa sprang forward and hovered, angry but uncertain, next to her child. She clenched and unclenched her thin fists. 'Leave her alone. Please.'

Clesek stroked his cheek where the scars had healed well. 'It may not be up to us, or even to her,' he said gently as he took his woman's hand and pulled her back towards his side. 'The Goddess may have more work for Tegen to do.'

'Damn the Goddess!' Nessa pushed him away and clutched Tegen in a fierce embrace. She scowled up at the men. 'If the Goddess was the Mother of us all, as you druids say, then she of all people would understand. I love my daughter. I want her back! I loved Griff too, but he has gone. This is the child of my body and I have never been allowed to have her, not since the day Witton came and saw the signs. Oh yes, I knew what he was up to with the fire and the bones. It has never been safe for me to show her love! *Never!*' And Nessa burst into uncontrollable sobs.

Tegen was silent and rocked her mother. At last she turned her head to Huval. 'I will give you my answer in the morning,' she said quietly.

34. Morning

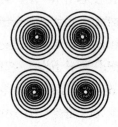

B efore dawn, the straw bed by the fire was empty.

The sun was warm on Tegen's raven hair as she trod the winding stony path up to the hills above her home. She had climbed past Griff's charcoal-burning huts scattered through the woods. At each one she passed she had left a twig of hazel in offering to his spirit. She was certain he was still there. He would never leave his fires unattended. Now, at the top of the hills, she had left the woodlands behind. Ahead, open moorland stretched to the north and east. At her back, the Winter Seas glinted in the light, making sky-mirrors for the morning.

A bundle bounced on her shoulders as she walked: a spare cloak wrapped around her white druid's robe, a pair of stockings, a cheese and some bannocks. The sky was clear and bright, and all around ankle-deep heather was showing early signs of new growth.

She clutched Griff's stout staff. It was sticky, like his hands. It made her feel as if he was still with her, chatting as they walked, laughing and demanding honey cakes.

But she was not at peace. A whirlpool of certainties and doubts jostled inside her head. She talked out loud, although there was none to hear her except a flock of wild goats and a solitary, circling sparrowhawk. 'How can I accept the druids' offer?' she said. 'Most of the villagers have never trusted me. Although Derowen has gone, there will always be rumours. The druids themselves might turn against me if things go wrong again.' Then, with a lump in her already aching throat, she shouted to the winds, 'And my beloved Griff won't be there either!'

She wiped her face on her sleeve, then pulled herself up straight and took a deep breath. 'I will *not* let anything get in my way,' she said out loud. She kicked a stone and watched it roll to the side of the track. 'It's time to continue my training. It's what Gilda and Griff would have wanted. I have got to find my own path for myself. Witton believed in me too. He said I had to find a place called Mona. I will go there.'

Tegen paused for a moment and turned to stare back towards the slopes and valley she had left. She was too far away for wisps of smoke to tempt her back again. 'I know

I'm hurting Mam and Da by leaving, but what else can I do? If I stay, they'll want me to marry and settle down . . .'

She turned and marched along the track once more. Gilda would have said: '"A bard's duty is to learn and to understand the great stories that point the way forward" . . .' She hesitated. 'But . . . how can I learn those until my *own* story is clear? I have to get away, to be free.'

Ahead, the land was dry. No more Winter Seas, just heath, and beyond that more forest. There would be settlements ahead for sure. She would find work to earn her keep and somewhere to sleep.

'When I get to Mona, I will master the bardic stories. Then I will follow the path of an ovate and be a seer and a healer. Witton said I must study law to become a proper druid. Then I'll understand how all things link together in the world. I'll learn to change shape at will and how to cross between the living and the dead.'

She shivered with dread and excitement. That was her story. She must dance *all* of it if she was to become what she was born to be.

Now the evil had come, and gone, she was still the Star Dancer. Her story hadn't finished yet.

As she moved, Gorgans' golden armbands jangled at her ankles. She liked the sound; it made her want to dance. He had offered her silver; in the end, he had given her gold. The air was good – Imbolg had come. The Goddess was walking beside her, over the hills and through the valleys, bringing greenness and hope to the land.

Tegen felt happy at last.

Just then, a sharp bark behind her smashed all her joy in an instant.

Heart pounding, she flattened herself in the heather and lay still. 'Please, *please*, don't let them get me,' she whispered into the earth. She swallowed hard and remembered the last time she had tried to flee. 'What if they force me to come back again?'

The bark sounded more closely this time. She buried her head in the wiry tangle of stalks and held her breath. Suddenly a hot pink tongue licked across her face and warm breath comforted her.

Tegen rolled over and pulled the muddy-brown animal into her arms.

'Wolf!' she laughed. 'You old rogue! Are you lonely without Griff? So am I. Do you want to come with me?' The dog wagged his tail furiously as Tegen jumped up from the damp heather and retrieved her bundle.

Then the two of them set off northeast together, and the blue of Gilda's dress matched the colour of the sky.

A selected list of titles available from Macmillan Children's Books

The prices shown below are correct at the time of going to press. However, Macmillan Publishers reserves the right to show new retail prices on covers, which may differ from those previously advertised.

Lian Hearn

| Across the Nightingale Floor | 978-0-330-41528-6 | £6.99 |

Peter Dickinson

| The Lion Tamer's Daughter | 978-0-330-37164-3 | £5.99 |

Julie Bertagna

| Exodus | 978-0-330-39908-1 | £5.99 |

All Pan Macmillan titles can be ordered from our website, www.panmacmillan.com, or from your local bookshop and are also available by post from:

Bookpost, PO Box 29, Douglas, Isle of Man IM99 1BQ
Credit cards accepted. For details:
Telephone: 01624 677237
Fax: 01624 670923
Email: bookshop@enterprise.net
www.bookpost.co.uk

Free postage and packing in the United Kingdom